D1032724

FAMILY SKELETONS

FAMILY SKELETONS

Henrietta Garnett

ALFRED A. KNOPF

NEW YORK

1987

THIS IS A BORZOI BOOK
PUBLISHED BY ALFRED A. KNOPF, INC.

Library of Congress Cataloging-in-Publication Data

Garnett, Henrietta, [date]
Family Skeletons.

I. Title.
PR6057.A678F3   1987   823'.914   86-46228
ISBN 0-394-55929-0

Manufactured in the United States of America
FIRST AMERICAN EDITION

For Jacques Foisy

with love

· CONTENTS ·

FAMILY SKELETONS

MALABAY

The two young men walked down the street in silence. They paid no attention to the traffic. They had just been to see a performance of *The Cherry Orchard*. They were reviewing it in their minds' eyes. Both the young men were twenty-eight and of roughly the same height. They had known each other for the better part of their lives.

Tara puffed on a cigarette. Gerald kept a look-out for a passing taxi. They had booked a table for dinner at their favourite hotel.

A taxi drew up beside them.

"You know," said Tara, "it wasn't really a very good production, was it? Definitely not first-rate. But there was one absolutely brilliant thing about it."

"I couldn't agree more," said Gerald.

They both leaned back.

"No. The general effect was annoying," said Gerald.

He gazed through the window at the crowds scurrying to and fro. The engine of the taxi was noisier than the hubbub from the street.

"Annoying," he said, "because it was so self- conscious. Why put it in modern dress? It makes nonsense of the text when you consider the question of the luggage. But you're right. Hardly anyone ever gets that right. I've only seen it done like that once before, and that was in Russia."

"I've never seen it done like that before. I've always longed to. But they always mess it up. It gives me the giggles. It spoils the whole of the rest of the play."

"I know."

"I suppose we are talking about the same thing?" said Tara.

They burst out laughing.

Tara fished a coin out of his pocket.

"Heads or tails?"

He spun it high into the air. It hit the roof of the cab and landed on the floor and got jammed in a crack by the door.

The cabby turned his neck.

"Watch it!" he said.

"He's lost a penny," said Gerald.

The cabby snorted.

"Blast the penny!" said Tara. "It was the silence."

"Exactly!"

The cabby pulled up in front of the hotel. The penny dropped into the gutter. Tara stooped to pick it up. Gerald paid off the taxi.

The head waiter was pleased to see them. Tara was one of his favourites. He led them to their usual table.

"Quite like old times," he said.

Tara smiled.

"Been away, sir?" he said to Gerald.

Gerald nodded.

The hotel was well-established and its restaurant still enjoyed a good reputation. It had once possessed a certain grandeur. Traces lingered. But the grandeur was somewhat decayed. The hotel continued to thrive, like some women, on illusion rather than fact.

"I can recommend the turbot," said the waiter.

He hovered while they scanned the menu.

They asked for whitebait to begin with.

"With lots and lots of fried parsley, please," said Tara.

Gerald chose the turbot. Tara asked for stewed pigeon. The waiter smiled and left.

There were certain similarities, a complicity between the young men, as much a result of their shared education and the duration of their friendship as of anything else.

Tara was beautiful. He was not just good looking, but beautiful. He was dark and thin. His eyes were almost black and they were intensely alive. When he laughed, he threw back his head and showed all his very white teeth and the tip of his pink tongue which curled upwards. His hair was curly and it was often ruffled. He ran his fingers through it frequently when trying to make himself understood.

Gerald's good looks were not quite so obvious. His eyes were very sharp. His clothes were more expensive. His gestures were less demonstrative.

"Yes," said Tara. "The silence was the thing. There they are, sitting on this bench rabbiting on about humanity and horizons. It's such a glorious play. But when that old uncle, that Gayev, starts going on about Nature and Life and Death and stuff, I dread it."

"I know."

"Because they will go and put in some ridiculous old fiddle. And it's too much. I just get the giggles. And the play is so brilliant. When they fuck it up, I generally walk out."

"But you know Tchekhov's stage directions?"

"He describes the sound, doesn't he?"

"No; not exactly. He says: 'Suddenly a distant sound is heard, coming as if out of the sky, like the sound of a string snapping, slowly and sadly dying away.' Like the sound. Not the sound of a string snapping. But *like* the sound."

"So why do they always go and bung in some old G string?"

"God knows. I know it off by heart. It's quite sufficient, the sound of the audience listening, rustling. They always do, in expectation. The sound of the actors listening. That is quite enough sound in itself. There is no such thing as silence."

The waiter arrived with two plates heaped with crispy whitebait and an extra plate of fried parsley.

"How perfectly delicious it looks," said Tara.

The waiter beamed.

"No, I couldn't agree with you more about the violin," said Gerald. "It's just extraneous."

"The parsley is perfection," said Tara. "It feels like eating sand ought to, but doesn't. How's your book getting along?"

"Not too well. I keep going. But I'm suffering somewhat from the blank page malady at the moment."

"That sounds grim."

"Yes, it is. It's frightful, but I stick at it. Stick in front of my bloody typewriter and don't budge. It's the only way."

"What, even if the words don't come?"

"Well, they're not going to come if I go off gallivanting, are they? And then, with any luck, I get a spurt and rattle on."

"Writers' lives must be agony."

"Telling me. But then, there are compensations. I'm addicted to words and life's not worth living if I can't put them down."

They continued to eat the whitebait. Tara had ordered a bottle of Sancerre to go with them. They drank the wine appreciatively.

"I thought that Anya, you know the niece, was quite a dish," said Tara. "She reminded me of my young cousin, Catherine. Don't know why. Question of age, I expect."

"Seventeen, isn't she, Anya?"

"Yes."

"You know I'm off to Rome tomorrow?"

"You do gad about an awful lot."

"Speak for yourself. At least I work. You just gad. I find writing in hotels less distracting, more convenient. They have an entertaining aspect which sometimes amuses me when the blank-page malady strikes."

"At least you can afford it."

The waiter took away their empty plates.

"I can only afford it," said Gerald, "because of the money I earn. I don't have an inheritance like yours."

"No," said Tara. "I'm not badly off. But I'm an anarchist at heart."

The turbot and the stewed pigeon arrived. The wine waiter uncorked a bottle of Bâtard-Montrachet for Gerald and a bottle of Chambertin for Tara. They sipped, nodded, and the wine waiter filled their glasses.

"Do you ever see anything of Stella, these days?" Gerald asked.

Tara did not reply immediately. He drank his wine.

Gerald kept quiet.

"No," said Tara at length. "I haven't seen her for some time, now. What went and put her into your head?"

"I don't know." Gerald put down his knife and fork and looked at his friend. "No. I don't know why I thought of her. Out of the blue, you might say. Except you seem, I don't know."

"Seem what?"

"Are you in love by any chance?"

Tara ate some pigeon.

"You're going to Rome," he said, "tomorrow. I'm going over to Malabay."

"You spend an awful lot of time there."

"I always have."

"Yes. I've never been."

"I expect you'll get asked, one of these days."

They refused pudding and asked for cheese.

"Talking about seeing people," said Tara, "have you seen my aunt Poppy since you've been here?"

"Yes. I had tea with her yesterday. We had a lovely time. I took her out to the soda fountain. I think she quite enjoyed it."

"I'm having lunch with her tomorrow, at her flat."

They had finished their cheese.

The waiter brought them coffee.

"Cognac?" he asked.

"Not for me," said Gerald. "I've still got some work to do. How about you, Tara?"

"Why not? No, on second thoughts, I won't."

He lit a cigarette. So did Gerald.

"It's on me," said Gerald when the bill arrived.

"Come off it," said Tara. "Let's go Dutch. Just because you've turned into a bestseller, you don't have to swank."

Gerald laughed.

"It's the tax man," he said. "Now I'm so rich, I have to keep him quiet."

"I don't bother with taxes," said Tara. "I just chuck those awful manillas straight into the waste-paper basket where they belong."

"You're a funny kind of anarchist," said Gerald.

"Anarchists are funny."

Gerald paid.

"I'll write to you from Rome," he said as they left the hotel. "Where shall I send the letter to?"

"Malabay."

"All right. Malabay it is."

They parted at the foot of the steps and went their separate ways.

Catherine woke to find her body drenched in sweat. She lay naked between rough linen sheets. The sheets were damp. She ran her fingers over her thin chest and explored the pools of perspiration which had collected between her small breasts. Her hands travelled further down her body, over her flat belly, and crossed the shallows of her pelvis, the hollows of her thighs between her legs. The tangle of her bush was wet with sweat.

The pale light of early morning came through the blue curtains. Small drops of light rain borne by the western wind had driven in through the open window and were scattered on the floorboards under the sill. The curtains stirred gently.

She enjoyed the feeling of her hands on her body. It was not a fully developed, voluptuous pleasure. It was a tentative, delicate, enquiring sensation.

She parted her lips and smiled. Then she stretched like a cat, arched her back, threw back the sheet and got out of bed. She walked to the window and drew back the curtains.

She leaned out of the window. It opened directly on to the walled garden. The garden had been planned many years ago with formal paths edged with box which led between beds now run wild with convolvulus entangling the old rose trees. Pear trees were espaliered against the walls. In the middle of the rough, unkempt lawn was a fish pond bordered by mint and forget-me-nots, surfaced with the leaves of water lilies. Beyond the garden door was an orchard planted with damsons, mirabelles and apple trees. The orchard ended in a ha-ha and through the open window Catherine could see, between the trees, the lake.

It was early summer. The dew was heavy and glittered on every twig and leaf and blade of grass. The rain, so fine that it seemed to be suspended in the misty air, shone like the frail skein of a cobweb. The air was so moist, the leaves and grass so wet, the fish pond and the lake so scheming with reflections, that the division between land and sky seemed nebulous, amorphous and indistinct.

It was a view which Catherine loved. She had woken to it every morning of her life. She had never been anywhere else. She had spent the whole of her short life here, at Malabay. She had no point of comparison.

Birds were singing. Catherine left the window and went into the bathroom. The bathroom was large and had not been designed for its present use. The bath itself was enormous. It was made of copper.

The water was tepid. The plumbing at Malabay was antiquated. Catherine did not linger long. She dried herself vigorously, like a pony being rubbed down, before getting dressed.

She dressed quickly and carelessly, forgetting a button, neglecting a hook. Her cousin, Tara, was coming to Malabay that day. She could not remember a time when Tara had not been the most important person in her life.

No one else in the house was awake. Catherine went silently down the elm staircase, avoiding the treads which squeaked. She crossed the large, panelled hall and went along a dusty passage. The flaking distemper, coloured with Reckitt's blue, fell in a fine powder where her arm brushed against the wall. She passed the gun room and a curious alcove in a little hall full of old walking sticks and gumboots. There was a great pitted table where her uncle Pake settled the household accounts when his whim or bank balance suited him. The table was strewn with bills rammed on to meat skewers, a ball of string, an outdated copy of Wisden's Almanack, a pair of secateurs and a large black telephone. It was the only one in the house and it was seldom used.

She went into the kitchen. It was a large, airy room with an uneven floor of old flagstones. Against one wall was an immense kitchen range with enough room between it and the wall to dry out the peat cuttings which fuelled it. The kitchen smelled of the sweetness of peat, of baking, of toast, cooking and scouring. Catherine filled the kettle and put it on to boil. Then she opened the door, let the cat in, and stepped out into the yard. She looked up at the elder tree which grew against the wall.

The elder tree was nearly in flower. The clusters of its white, unformed buds, tightly furled, reached up towards the sky. Everything was still fresh with the dew, as she had seen it earlier from her bedroom window. But now the sun had filtered through the clouds and the rain had stopped. The elder tree, the cobblestones of the kitchen yard, the dandelion that grew between the stones quivered in the light. She put her hands on her hips and again felt their thin, delicate bird-like curves. She leaned against the wall. She could not stop shaking.

Through the upstairs windows, she heard the sounds of bathwater running, the plug of a lavatory pulled, her uncle's steps on the stairs. She heard the pantry door open behind her and the sounds of Nan making breakfast. These were the sounds of everyday life. Catherine had never noticed them so consciously before.

Catherine and her uncle Pake sat down to breakfast in the dining room. Nan ate hers, as she always did, in the solitude of the kitchen. The dining room was well lit by a pair of French windows which looked out on to the rough paddock and, through the avenue of double beeches, one could glimpse the lake.

There was never any conversation at breakfast until after the arrival of the post. Pake was in his late sixties. He was emaciated, his nose aquiline, his lips thin. He was dressed in ancient tweeds, impeccably cut and much darned, the colour of the weather. He spread the butter thin on a piece of Melba toast and examined it with care before crunching it with his false teeth. He took a sip of coffee and then glanced at Catherine.

"I hear the bicycle of Mick-the-Post," he said.

He said this every morning when Mick-the-Post skidded to a halt on the cobbles in the kitchen yard.

Catherine licked the honey from her fingers. She got up and went to fetch the post. There was seldom any for her.

Pake watched her leave the room. He sighed. She reminded him too much for his comfort of her mother, his dead sister Nellie.

Catherine came back and stood beside him with a couple of manilla envelopes in one hand. In her other, she held an envelope of thick, white paper.

"What is it?" he said.

"It's from Tara," she said. "It's for you."

"Why shouldn't he write to me?"

"But he's coming to stay today."

She gave him the letter.

She sat down in her place and pouted. Unlike Pake, she had curly and voluptuous lips.

Pake looked at her with a glance of mild reproof.

"I keep no track of time," he said. "Tara's comings and goings are beyond me. But my correspondence isn't any of your business. Finish up your toast and honey, my dear. Will you pour me out another cup of coffee?"

She poured out the coffee. She watched him read her cousin's letter. He did not touch the coffee. She watched him come to the end of the letter and then turn over the page and read it again extremely slowly, paying it the utmost of his intelligence. She sat in silence. She longed to know what was in the letter. She could not bring herself to ask.

After he had finished reading Tara's letter for the second time, Pake folded it deliberately and put it into his waistcoat pocket where he kept his pen-knife, his watch and a small magnifying glass. He looked at Catherine.

"Are you in love with Tara?" he asked.

His tone was mild and one of interest.

Catherine was shocked by this unexpected question.

"What's that got to do with you?"

"Everything in the world."

Catherine burst into tears.

"I am your guardian, my dear, whether we like it or not."

Pake waited. He pulled the magnifying glass out of his waistcoat pocket and peered at a crystal of salt which he had spilled on the table-cloth during breakfast.

Catherine blew her nose.

"Damn and blast you!" she said. "Yes, of course I'm in love with Tara. You know that perfectly well. I've always been in love with him. How dare you ask me something so wretchedly obvious?"

"I simply need your confirmation," said Pake. "But what is your definition of being in love?"

Catherine swallowed some coffee.

"I don't think I've got one," she said. "It's just what I feel. I don't think it's got a definition. Do you?"

He smiled at her.

"It may have, for all I know," he said. "But I've never been able to define it to my satisfaction. No."

"Didn't you try when you were married to aunt Poppy?"

"Defined like mad. But not to her satisfaction, either. The marriage was not a great success, you know."

"But didn't you love her? Haven't you ever been in love?"

Pake lit a cheroot. This was out of the ordinary. Generally, he waited until eleven o'clock when he lit up alone in his study.

"Yes," he said. "I was once in love. But not with Poppy. A pity. A great pity, in many ways. She's a remarkable woman."

"But then why did you marry her, if you didn't love her?"

"Oh, I loved her all right."

"But you just said you weren't in love with her. I don't understand."

"Poppy is very lovable. It's not the same thing. But all this is ancient history. By the way, what time is Tara's train?"

"Six thirty-seven. In time for dinner. I suppose he'll have to walk. He always does, unless he can cadge a lift. I can't meet him with the horses. Suibne cast a shoe. The blacksmith won't be round till seven."

"I'll meet him myself," said Pake.

"But you've never done that in your life!" said Catherine.

"And I daresay I never shall again."

He got up from the table to leave the room. He was half way to the door when he turned and went back to Catherine. He rumpled her dark hair.

"We'll meet at dinner, then," he said. "I suppose you'll occupy yourself as usual?"

Pake never ate lunch. He considered it a waste of time. Catherine ate hers with Nan in the kitchen.

"Oh, good heavens, yes!" she said. "I've got a thousand things to do. Tara's coming and I've got his room to get ready."

"Well, why don't you pick him a jarful of woodruff? But don't neglect your Herodotus."

She laughed.

"No. I like the crocodiles. I've got into rather a tangle with it, though. Can I put it on to your study desk, to go over it for me?"

"We can look at it together tomorrow," said Pake.

He left the room.

Catherine stayed where she was. She lingered over her coffee. It had grown cold. She stared into the cup and gazed at her distorted, murky reflection. She was puzzled. Pake had been so odd. And then Tara had left her no message. She did not understand. She got up. She began to clear the table. She was in a rage. She dropped her coffee cup. It broke. She picked up the pieces. She ran into the kitchen.

"Nan?"

The old woman stirred in her chair.

"Nan!"

"Why, whatever's come over you, my pet?"

"I don't know."

Nan held out her arms. Catherine sat on her knee. The old woman swayed. The chair creaked. Catherine cried.

"Whatever is it?"

"I told you, I don't know."

"This won't do."

"I know it won't."

"And Tara's coming and all."

"I know. Look, I'm sorry, but I just want to be alone. Do you mind if for once I don't do any housework? I want, I just want . . ."

"What is it you want?"

"I wish to Christ I knew."

"You grow more like your mother every living day. Go along, then. Mr Pake's not himself either."

"What makes you say that?"

"Just your voices. And him smoking before breakfast is finished. And straight into the gun room, and not his study either where he should be by the rights of things. You're all of a tremble."

They held each other tight.

"You go down to your books, ducks. We won't say a word. Least said."

Catherine managed a smile. She tried to jump up. The old woman would not let her go. Catherine buried her nose against Nan and was half-comforted, half-sickened by the smell: the smell of Nan's armpits; her sweat; the carbolic soap in her grey hair. She wrenched herself away.

"Be off then, down to the boatshed with your books," said Nan.

Catherine ran. She ran out of the house, through the neglected garden, the orchard, and downhill across the meadow beyond the ha-ha. She did not stop until she reached the boatshed.

The boathouse had been built before the turn of the century. It was much in need of repair. Half of it still housed boats. An old rowing tub lay on its side. A fibreglass trimaran was upside down, its three grey hulls supported by wooden poles. Catherine gloated over it. This was Tara's work. She had helped him to make it, boiling up glue, sanding the fibreglass. But the design and most of the work was his. He had promised her that they would christen it and take it out on the lake on this visit.

She did not stay there long. She went through the door to the other half of the boathouse. It had been made as a tea pavilion for

Catherine's great aunts. Here, they had bickered away the afternoons and munched sandwiches and whiskey cake. She knew them by sight from old photographs. She imagined their conversations. But the sandwiches were finished, the whiskey cake all gone and the scandal dead. She hungered for something else.

She had chosen the tea pavilion as her own private place so long ago that she could no longer remember why. She had, in fact, been discovered weeping there after a solitary game of hide and seek with no one to hunt and no one to find her. No one had missed her until long after her bedtime, and then it was Nan who had picked her up and carried her off, howling, back to the house.

Catherine went to the deal table. A jamjar of wild jonquils stood on it. Most of the rest of the surface was littered with exercise books. Beside the table was a bookshelf filled mainly with Pake and Nellie's old school books, a selection of Victorian literature, and several anthologies of verse. The library at Malabay was extensive, but no new books ever came to the house. Catherine had read nothing published during the last fifty years.

She sat down at the table. She propped her chin on her fists. Which should she do first? Tackle her Herodotus or turn to her own writing? Her own writing gave her infinitely more pleasure, but it had never occurred to her to show it to anyone. She looked out at the lake and then glanced down. Her eyes alighted on the page of a book she had been reading the day before.

"Two forces which are contradictory, feeling and reason, guide the lives of men and people . . . Herodotus still wears the yoke of the old faith; he has the childlike curiosity of a traveller amazed at everything he sees, and except with a few timid interpretations, he believes in all the stories of the Muse. Between Herodotus and Thucydides Greece attained man's estate. The son of Oloros, animated with a freer spirit . . . uses his reason among the men and the events of the past. He avoids dealing with mythological impossibilities, and notices only the great facts . . ."

Catherine closed the book and gazed once more at the lake. She shrugged her shoulders and grinned slyly, imagining herself to be wearing, like Herodotus, the yoke of the old faith. But she did not like the word 'yoke'. There was an old yoke by the cow-byre at Malabay. It was wooden and heavy, with metal chains to suspend the pails of milk. She would not wear a yoke. She would wear a mantle woven of invisible thread which would catch the light and lend her a gleam of extra perception. She would be able to see to write.

Pushing aside the *History of Greece and of the Greek People*, she opened a scarlet exercise book, took up her pen and wrote in curly letters: 'The Two Swans — a Fable'.

She was excited by the idea of a fable. She would write it and give it to Tara for his birthday present. His birthday was later on in the summer. He always spent it at Malabay.

'There once lived two wild swans who made their home on the banks of a large lake. The two swans were very beautiful. They dipped their sinuous long necks into the water to spear fish. They spent many hours gliding over the surface of the lake.

'The lake was large and on it were several tiny islands, mere specks of land. The swans were content in their solitude and lived sad and proud, as is the nature of all swans.

'Then one day, something out of Nature happened.'

She stopped. She would go on with it the next day. She turned to Herodotus. She still had the woodruff to pick for Tara's room.

Catherine was still busy with the horses after the blacksmith had left when she heard the old Daimler coming back from the station. She was stooping, holding Suibne's hoof between her knees, giving it a good polish with linseed oil. The smell of linseed, the straw, the leather tack that hung from hooks on the old stable walls, the smell of horse, was pungent. The light which came into the stable through the open door was blocked. She looked up. Tara stood watching her. He leaned against the door jamb. She could not see his face. It was against the light.

"You're late," she said. "Did you miss the connection?"

"No. Pake drove back the long way round. We stopped at Beakus's Stump. How are you?"

He came forward into the stable. Catherine let go of Suibne's hoof.

"Fine. And you?"

"All the better for seeing you."

He kissed her and then held her in his arms.

He patted Suibne's mane and looked critically at Eorann, half-Arab, half-Welsh mountain, a pinto mare who was Catherine's favourite mount.

"Eorann looks rather thin," he said.

"She is a bit. I've been giving her fenugreek powdered into her feed. I read that's what Pashas give to their harems to make them fat. Doesn't seem to work, though. Yes, I've finished. Help me take them down to the paddock?"

"You might as well try giving her Turkish Delight. She's probably just got worms."

They led the horses down the beech avenue where the light fell dappled through the leaves and then turned them into the rough pasture which led down to the lake. Suibne, who had disliked being cold shod earlier on, shook himself and pranced off into a far corner of the meadow. Eorann stood by the gate, allowing herself to be stroked by the cousins.

"Why Beakus's Stump?" asked Catherine.

Beakus's Stump was an old cairn marked by stones on top of a hillock. It was avoided by the local people and sometimes visited by strangers who said it was the death barrow of ancient kings.

"We wanted to talk. I don't really know why he chose the Stump."

"What about? Tara, why did you write to him without leaving a message to me? I know it's none of my business, what you said, but I did feel most fearfully left out."

"Actually, it is very much your business," said Tara.

"What do you mean?"

"I wrote to Pake asking permission for you to marry me."

"I thought people only did that in books."

"Did what?"

"Wrote letters asking for permission."

"No. I had to write to him because you're still under age and Pake's quite entitled to prevent it. I didn't want a row. Will you then, Catherine?"

"Marry you?"

She stared at the sky, the lake, the lady's smock growing in the meadow, at the horses now together cropping the grass. She reached out a hand.

Tara held her by the arm.

"Will you?"

She looked up at him.

"Yes. Yes, I will."

Nan had prepared an especially good dinner that night. She always did when Tara arrived. But when Catherine went into the kitchen to help her as usual, it was clear that the old woman was put out. She banged a saucepan unnecessarily loudly as she drained potatoes in a colander in the sink.

"So I suppose you think I'll be congratulating the pair of you?" she said.

She did not turn round to look at Catherine.

"How did you know?"

"Pake had me talking in the gun room. So it's wedding bells, is it, now?"

"Come on, Nan. What's the matter? Aren't you pleased?"

Nan faced Catherine. The rims of her eyes were red. There was a sternness in her look which Catherine had not seen before.

"You're green, Catherine," she said. "You're too young. You're as unfledged as an egg. Talk about child-brides. It's not right, Catherine. It isn't right at all."

"But I love him," said Catherine.

"I dare say you do. But that's not what makes the world go round."

She put the colander on the draining board.

"Well," she said. "I'll just have to wish you well, but don't think I'm not against it. What's all the hurry for? It's unnatural. Why don't you wait a while?"

Catherine did not listen.

"No, we won't wait," she said. "We're going to get married at once."

Nan sniffed.

"Dinner will be late," she said. "Take that lettuce and shake it in the yard, there's a good girl."

She sounded angry.

Catherine swung the lettuce round and round in its wire basket. She watched the drops of water splash down on the cobbles of the courtyard.

Dinner was curiously uneasy. They ate their way through green soup, salmon trout and Bakewell tart. Very little was said and nothing of any importance. Catherine was puzzled and disappointed. She watched Pake fiddle with a bone in his fish. When the Bakewell tart was brought on, she looked across the table to Tara in despair. She was on the verge of tears.

He smiled at her.

"I think we ought to crack open a bottle of champagne," he said. "I ransacked the cellar, Pake. I've brought up a bottle of the best. I put it to cool. Why don't we ask Nan to join us and drink to the future?"

He got up with a light grace and left the room.

Pake put down his spoon. He had finished his slice of tart. He ran his fingers through his thinning hair.

"In books," said Catherine, "children get blessings when they marry. Have I got yours?"

"You know I'm very fond of Tara," said Pake. "I want you to be happy."

"But aren't you?"

"I'm not a happy man," he said. "No, I wouldn't say that I was a happy man."

"Nothing is like what they say."

"You're very young. Yes, I know it's one of the most annoying things to be told. If I seem abstracted, it's because I'm reminded of other times, other people's happiness. Yes; it's selfish. But old men are. Do you know these lines?

"'For even daughters of the swan can share
    Something of every paddler's heritage . . .'"

Pake was given to reciting. Catherine could not bear it when he did. It embarrassed her. He went on:

"'And had that colour upon cheek or hair,
    And thereupon my heart is driven wild . . .'"

She wished he would stop, but he went on. She scraped the cream off her plate and would not look at him.

"'She stands before me as a living child.'"

He stopped.

She was relieved when the door opened and Tara came in, pushing Nan in front of him. Nan was half protesting and trying to hide her laughter. She had been cajoled out of her grumpiness by Tara. Nan had always said he could twist anyone round his little finger. He carried the champagne in his hand.

Pake crossed the room and went over to the sideboard. He took out four of the best glasses and opened the bottle.

Tara turned to Catherine and gave her a wink of sheer complicity. She stood up. They all watched the spiral of compressed air escape from the bottle. Pake filled the glasses.

"Here's to the pair of you," he said.

"God be with you," said Nan.

There was an odd croak in her voice.

They clinked glasses. They drank.

Nan swayed like a bolster pegged out to be aired in the wind. Tara drew up a chair for her. They all sat down at the table.

"So when is the happy day?" Nan asked.

Catherine looked at Tara.

"At once. Why not your birthday, Catherine? That's in three weeks' time."

She smiled.

No one spoke.

Pake refilled the glasses.

"You'd do best to get married in the church," said Nan. "God would do you no harm."

"Oh God!" said Tara.

"No," said Catherine. "I'd like to get married in the church. I know you don't care two hoots for God. But I do. Perhaps it's the only difference between us."

"Not exactly," said Tara.

She laughed.

"No, but you know what I mean," she said. "After all, if you don't care and I do, then why not let it be in church?"

Tara took a swig of champagne. Then he lit a cigarette.

"I suppose there's a certain logic in what you say," he said. "All right. Let it be the church. But my God, I wouldn't do that for anyone else!"

"I should hope not!" said Catherine.

Pake smiled.

Nan stood up.

"Oh, do sing us something," said Tara. "It's such a waste of your voice not to."

She bridled in the doorway.

She began to hum.

"'. . . did you ever hear, I wrote my love a letter
And although he cannot read, sure I thought 'twas all the better . . .'"

She broke off, laughing. They laughed with her, for they knew she had Mick-the-Post in mind. She left the room with the door open behind her. Tara finished the verse.

"'. . . that postman so conceited,
No answer will he bring me, so long as I have waited
But maybe there mayn't be one, for the reason that I've stated
That my love can neither read nor write, but loves me faithfully.'"
Pake stood up.

"Catherine and I will do the washing up," said Tara. "Nan seems to have got distracted, for once."

"Yes."

He crossed the room.

"It's early," he said. "But I'm tired."

"Goodnight, Pake," said Catherine.

He went through the open door.

They looked after him.

"Come on," said Tara.

He washed and she dried. She put a blue plate back in the rack.

"Was it sudden?" she asked. "Your idea to marry me?"

"No. It just seemed obvious."

"But what about all those women? That awful woman with a bottom you said was melonious?"

"That was Joyce."

"I dare say. But her name was Stella. And she wasn't awful."

He dried his hands on a tea towel.

"Now you're just being silly," he said.

He walked over to her and put his arms round her.

"Of course I've had lots of lovers. Hundreds and hundreds of them. I'm ten years older than you are. When you were a little girl of ten, I was twenty. I've had more lovers than you've had hot dinners. And instead of being a jealous little goose, you might just as well thank your lucky stars."

"But I thought you always loved me," she said.

"Yes, I did. But don't be daft. You were just a child. Are you complaining that I'm not a child molester? Some of my friends would call it just plain baby-snatching as it is."

"What lucky stars ought I be thanking, then?"

Tara laughed.

He gripped her round her shoulders and they went upstairs into her bedroom. For the first time, it seemed to Catherine that her bedroom was ill-furnished, bare and draughty. The curtains were not drawn. Outside, it was raining. He led her to her bed. The bed was single and made of brass. The sheets were old and darned. The quilt was patchwork, a country design ages old of fox and geese. There were no pillows, but a bolster. Catherine always flung this out of bed on to the floor as soon as she got in between the sheets, for she lay flat as a board every night.

She shivered.

Tara caressed her. She felt his hands travel over her body. Very gently, as though she were a wild creature, he undressed her and threw her clothes in a heap on to the floor.

"Your clothes," he said.

He buried his face in her hair.

"Your ridiculous, ridiculous clothes."

He made love to her very tenderly.

Afterwards, they lay in the tangle of bedclothes.

"I never knew," said Catherine. "I never dreamed."

"How could you, darling?"

She fell asleep at once in his arms.

Once, she woke during the night, frightened by the half-forgotten image of a dream already scudding out of her head. She had been transformed into a hare and was being pursued by dogs. The dogs were not far behind her and she could smell their dreadful hot breath. Her soul was still her own, but the dogs were hunting her. When she woke, she found that Tara was kissing her and stroking the nape of her neck.

"What is it, Catherine? You twitch in your sleep like a frightened animal."

"I was an animal in my sleep and I was frightened."

She kissed him.

They made love again and fell asleep in one another's arms.

It was a beautiful morning. The smells of early summer came in through the window. It was late.

"Why did you say my clothes are ridiculous?" asked Catherine.

She stood naked in the bathroom, waiting for the bath to fill.

"You're terribly thin," he said.

"What's that got to do with it?"

"Your clothes are absurd," he said. "After we're married, I'll take you to Paris and buy you some proper clothes. Silk. Real clothes. Very sexy ones."

"Paris?"

"Why not? After we're married, sweet cousin Kate, we can do anything we like."

"But we'll live here, won't we?"

"Is that what you want?"

"I don't know," she said. "I can't imagine living anywhere else."

"We can live here if you like. After all, it's yours. Malabay, I mean. But we can go on flighty jaunts to spice things up."

"I suppose it is mine," she said.

She got into the bath. "I never thought about it," she said. "After all, it's got to belong to somebody. I would miss it. Let's make things up as we go along. Do you think that's silly?"

Tara got into the bath too.

"I think you're absolutely batty," he said. "But I don't give a damn. I'm crazy about you. Do you know how delicious you are?"

"Am I?" said Catherine. "Isn't it funny to have a bath together?"

"I don't see why."

Catherine got out.

"I meant all the time before when you've been here at Malabay and we didn't."

"I seem to remember giving you a good many baths when you were a little girl."

"That's what made it so odd. Now that everything's changed."

"What's changed?"

He laughed at her.

"Oh! SEX!"

She ran out of the room stark naked and went to put on her ridiculous clothes.

Pake looked up at them when they came into the dining room together very late. He did not treat them as though anything out of the ordinary had happened. He sipped his coffee slowly.

They heard the postman put down his bike and go into the kitchen by the back door.

Pake waited.

"I hear the bicycle of Mick-the-Post," he said.

Catherine smiled with relief. She got up.

"I'll go," said Tara. "I want to say hello to Mick."

He left the table and fondled Catherine's hair in passing.

Catherine blushed. She looked at Pake. He did not meet her glance. Neither of them spoke.

They heard the sounds of a conversation between Mick and Tara. They heard Tara laugh and then Mick's bike ride over the cobbles.

Tara was excited.

"We're going out tonight!" he said.

He stood behind Pake's chair and put the letters by his uncle's plate.

"Do you feel like coming, Pake? Mick's been telling me the most fascinating thing. We're going to look for gold!"

Pake felt for his spectacles.

Tara sat down beside Catherine. He buttered a piece of toast.

"What do you mean, gold?" she said.

"The man must have been at the bottle," said Pake. "There isn't a single goldmine in the whole of the country. Every fool knows that."

"That's just it," said Tara. "That's it exactly. It's fools' gold we're after."

"What are you on about?" asked Catherine.

"Well, he says," said Tara, "that if you go up to the peat hags late at night, you'll see all the gold in the world glittering at your feet."

"Go on!" said Pake. "Come off it! I've never heard that one before in my life. What's the fellow talking about?"

"That's just what I'd like to know," said Tara. "It sounds a bit like when you go swimming in the dark. Phosphorescence. It's very odd. We must find out. Will you come?"

He looked at Pake.

It was a challenge.

Pake put on his spectacles. He squinted at his correspondence.

"Letter from Poppy," he said. "I wonder what she's got to say. Have you seen her lately, Tara?"

Tara frowned.

Catherine waited.

"Yes," said Pake at length. "Yes, I'll come with you on this fools' errand."

"Oh, good!" said Catherine.

Both of the men turned to her in some surprise, as though they had forgotten that she was there.

"Did you get through any of your Greek?" said Pake.

"Not much. I got in a bit of a muddle. But can I take a holiday today?"

"Why should you?"

"It's special."

Tara and Catherine waited.

"You can have a holiday except for half an hour," said Pake.

He crumbled the remains of his toast on the edge of his plate.

"What's the half an hour for?" asked Tara.

"I prepared some slides this morning," said Pake. "Fairly elementary. It seems a pity to waste them."

"Can I see them too?"

"Yes, you can, Tara, if you don't interfere. In this case, Catherine is my pupil and not yours. You must promise not to distract her attention."

"Certainly."

"But it's my attention!" cried Catherine. "How dare either of you make a monopoly of it? You can't come, Tara. I'll never concentrate if you're in the room."

Both of them smiled at her.

"In that case," said Tara, "I'll just lead you to a fool's paradise this evening. But I'll come and hoik you out of your lesson, shall I? We might baptize the trimaran and take her out for a good sail."

"That would be brilliant," said Catherine. "Let's look at the slides now, Pake. Then I can start my holiday."

Tara watched them leave the room together. The similarity between them was quite striking. Catherine held open the door, to allow Pake to pass through first. Tara felt a pang as the door closed behind them. He knew that Catherine loved him. He knew that she would not have been the person she was if it had not been for the way in which Pake had brought her up. Moreover, he was very fond of his uncle.

He got up. He had a surprise for Catherine. He left the house and went down to the boatshed. He remembered her hip, thin and hollowed, the bone curved like a bird's and narrow like a boy's. He smiled.

After examining the slides through a microscope with Pake in his study, Catherine went down to the boathouse. She went into her room by the side door. She could hear Tara at work on his boat beyond the thin wall which divided the boathouse. She sat down at her table. The flowers in the jamjar were wilted. She opened the window and threw them out. She would pick more later. She began to write.

She had been writing for some time when she was interrupted by a knock on the door.

"Can I come in?"

She got up.

Tara came into the room. He caught her round the waist.

"Catherine! You're as white as a sheet!"

He bent over her.

"It's nothing," she said. "I often get giddy if I sit for too long."

He kissed her.

"Come outside," he said. "You'll feel better in the open. And I've got something to show you."

He led her through the other half of the boathouse and out into the fresh air.

"Look!"

The trimaran was afloat. She was moored to an old stump by the jetty. Her sails were white and blue and on the pennant flew a black swan. Her name, freshly painted in black letters on her bow by Tara that morning, was *Fionnuala*.

Catherine drew a deep breath.

"She's brilliant!" she said.

"Not bad, is she?"

"She's brilliant."

She hugged him.

"What made you think of Fionnuala as a name?"

"I don't know."

"I've had swans on the brain for days."

"Is that what you're writing about?"

"Haha! That's a secret."

"Here's another. I want you to launch her. Then she can wander forever across the lake. Like she did in the legend."

He bent down and fished out a bottle of Krug which he had hidden between the long grasses which grew round the base of the stump.

"What am I supposed to do?"

Tara gave her the bottle.

"Well, you smash the bottle over the bow and name her."

"Good God! Like the Queen of England? Seems a fearful waste of champagne. Can't we drink it and splash her with lake water instead?"

"What a greedy little alcoholic monkey you are! Just because we had some last night, it's gone to your head. You'll be gadding about with Mick-the-Post next thing. Come on: be grand! Isn't she a beauty?"

She smashed the bottle against the *Fionnuala* and the bottle exploded. Champagne gushed over the gunwales and ran into the lake.

He handed Catherine aboard.

She turned to Tara.

"Did I do it right? Is that what the Queen of England does?"

"I haven't got the foggiest idea what the Queen of England does. You did it with a flourish."

He was busy with the rigging.

"Hang on, Catherine. There she goes!"

The sail filled with wind. The *Fionnuala* flew across the lake. Wind and water sprayed their faces. They were ecstatic. Catherine turned to see the ripples in their wake.

"I'm going to take you round the island," said Tara. "She's going beautifully, isn't she? Hey, look in that locker!"

She rummaged.

"My God!" she said. "You do have style."

"Style," said Tara, "is essential. Open it."

"I never have."

"Well you'd better start now. Never too late to learn. You rip off that golden paper and unwriggle the wire. Then push up the cork with your thumbs and give it a little twist and try not to let it go off. You just want the smoke to come out, like the Pope when he gets chosen."

He smiled at her. She wore a yellow dress.

"There are glasses next to where the bottle was," he said.

"Got them."

She put them on the floor of the cockpit.

"Duck," he shouted. "Duck quick!"

The cork was half way out of the bottle.

"Duck, for Christ's sake! Duck! You'll get hit on the head! We're going to gybe."

The boom swung round.

Catherine ducked.

The cork came out.

Catherine poured champagne into a tumbler.

The *Fionnuala* flew on across the lake.

Catherine had not missed a drop.

She handed Tara a glass. She raised her own. They drank together.

"Well done!" he said. "You could get a job on the P. & O. as a purser in drag any day of the week."

"What's drag?"

"You're not serious?"

"What do you mean?"

"What does Pake think he's doing?"

"I don't understand."

"Messing about with Greek and old bits of mushrooms on slides and not knowing about drag. Honestly!"

"What are you talking about? What is drag?"

"Drag isn't much, really," said Tara.

He sipped from his glass.

"It's just dressing up as women."

"Can women drag up as men, too?"

"You don't drag up. You just drag. And it's in. Yes. They often do. When men are in drag, they're called transvestites."

"I would have understood that," said Catherine. "Drag just made me think of hunting. Do you think Sappho did, on her island? Put on whiskers and things?"

Tara laughed.

"You're impossible, darling. Who knows?"

They were very close to the island.

The island was not large. It was overgrown with wild woodland and fuchsias. Its outline was irregular, like the old tigerskin in one of the bedrooms at Malabay. It was a traditional holiday spot for the family as far back as anyone could remember. Birthdays were celebrated here. Bonfires were lit. Presents were opened. It was a place for special occasions. Catherine loved it. So did Tara.

This time they did not land there. The *Fionnuala*'s maiden voyage was of more interest to them. Tara tacked.

"I can't remember why she flew," he said. "Fionnuala, I mean. Didn't she have to fly forever?"

"No," said Catherine. "Not forever. She was a princess who went and got turned into a swan. I can't remember why. Something went wrong. Something always has to in stories, I suppose. When she got turned into a swan she was doomed to fly over the waters of all the mires and lakes and rivers."

"That's what I thought."

"But not forever. Only until Christianity came to the country."

"How awfully dull."

"I think that's just a modern ending."

"Christ!"

Tara leaped.

The wind had changed.

There was something wrong with the rigging. Tara just managed to right it. But only just. He headed back to Malabay.

Pake was in his study. He sat at his desk. He groaned. He did not see the sunlight that was flooding in through the windows which overlooked the garden. He was looking at an old letter. The ink was faded.

He read the letter a second time.

It was a love letter. He ran his fingers through his hair and then refolded the letter and put it back into its envelope. There was no stamp on the envelope. He put the envelope into a small drawer in his desk and locked the drawer.

After a while, Pake turned to his correspondence which had arrived that morning. He did not bother to open the manilla envelopes. He opened the letter from Poppy. He read it once. Then he got up and began to pace the room. He groaned again. He often groaned when he was alone. He sat down. He drew his pen-knife out of his waistcoat pocket, opened it and began to clean his thumbnail. This was unnecessary, but he continued to clean invisible dirt from under his nail for several minutes. He then drew a sheet of paper towards him and reached for his pen. His pen was old-fashioned. It was not a fountain pen. It had an ivory handle and a steel nib stuck into the socket. He dipped the pen into the inkwell. He blew across the nib. He poised the pen above the paper, looked at the ceiling and began to write. His script was minuscule, but very clear. His E's were Greek.

"My dear Poppy," he wrote.

He paused. He looked at the ceiling again. He continued.

"Your proposition is untenable. You know that I find most of your proposals unacceptable. This one is out of the question. Nevertheless, I am glad that you wrote. Otherwise, you might have taken matters into your own hands. This does not concern you. It is none of your business. Of course, I understand that you mean for the best. But I forbid you to meddle. Remember your promise. Keep it."

He paused again. This time, he looked out of the window.

He saw Tara and Catherine walking through the garden on their return from the lake. They held hands. Tara bent to Catherine. She laughed at what he said. They approached the house.

"The children seem happy," he wrote. "Surely that is the most important thing? There is no going back. We can merely hope for the future. Meanwhile, I send you my deep affection, as always."

He signed the letter and folded it into an envelope.

Tara and Catherine had disappeared from view. He could hear them inside the house.

He pushed his chair and got up. His movements were nervous. He left the study and went to fiddle with a fishing rod in the gun room. The rest of the day passed unusually slowly for him. But he spent it alone until dinner time, and so this went unnoticed by the rest of the inhabitants of Malabay.

The road leading up through the moors to the peat hags was lonely. They did not pass a soul on the way. Pake drove the Daimler. He drove it very slowly. He seldom ever used the fourth gear. Now he drove in second. Mick-the-Post sat in front beside him. In the back, Tara and Catherine did not touch.

"Is this far enough?" Pake asked.

"A little further," said Mick.

They travelled on in the darkness.

"Is this far enough now?"

"A little further yet," said Mick.

They crawled on.

No one spoke.

Tara leaned forward.

"Why must it be further on? Surely one bit of peat's the same as another?"

"Not this peat," said Mick. "This peat's peculiar peat. Take my word for it. But it's only peculiar when it's freshly cut. And the cutting will not be found until a little further on."

On they went.

"You can stop here," said Mick. "Do you see, now? This is where they've been cutting. It's clear as daylight, sure enough. But it's cats' eyes you need."

They all got out of the car. Pake bent back inside the Daimler to forage for his stick. It gave him a sense of authority.

The night was pitch dark. But it was clear and the stars were bright. A soft wind stirred over the moor. The air was very sweet. Everywhere, there was the faint sound of gently running water. The moors were full of water, often invisible, running underground for long stretches, then suddenly surfacing in unexpected places. There was black, brackish water in stagnant bogs. But when the water was sweet, it was the colour of beer.

"I brought a torch," said Tara. "Where is it? Hang on, Mick."

"Bloody useless a torch is here, if it's the peculiarities of the peat you've come to see," said Mick. "A torch is the last thing you need. It's only the use of your eyes you need, which you'd do as well to skin. Follow me now, like a file of filthy Indians for all they say they're red. Seeing's believing. An Indian I saw once was the colour of a pickled walnut. But watch your step, or rather mine. We don't want you tumbling down in the cuttings. You fumble with your stick, Mr Pake. The kiddos will find out their way."

He cackled. Then he vanished. He was swallowed up by the darkness.

Pake bellowed.

"Good God! What the devil do you think you're up to? I can't see a bloody thing and my stick's got stuck in the bog. What the hell do you think you are? Some vanishing act? Tara, bring the torch immediately!"

Catherine got the giggles. She could see clearly in the dark. She tried to stop laughing, but that just made her fit of the giggles worse. She sat down on the ground and laughed.

Pake was furious.

"Catherine, for God's sake, be quiet! Mick, come here. What is all this tomfoolery? Tara, muzzle that child. You've all gone mad and I can't see a bloody thing. Where are my spectacles?" Catherine shrieked.

"Fat lot of use they'd be!" she gasped. "Spectacles! Oh Pake! What an owl you are!"

"She's off again," said Mick.

He had re-emerged from the darkness.

"He's no owl, Catherine," he said. "Blind as a bat. Tara, where are you hiding yourself?"

"I'm having a pee," said Tara.

"Jesus, now you've gone and set her off again," said Mick. "There's no holding her. Pee up, man, as quick as you can slash. I never thought I'd be taking the three sillies up the mountain. Hush up, Catherine. Pretend you're a horse. Giddy up now, and stop all this hanky panky. Else it's your uncle who'll be having a fit next."

Catherine turned into a horse.

Tara joined them.

"Get me up," said Catherine.

Pake thumped his walking stick on the turf. It squelched. By now, he was in a thoroughly bad temper. He tried to disguise it by grinding his false teeth very quietly.

"Now that Catherine has calmed down and turned into a horse," he said, "let's follow you. But don't you go and vanish again, Mick. It's too dark. I'm too old for such capers."

Catherine clung to Tara's arm. She was still shaking from barely suppressed laughter.

Tara gripped her firmly.

Catherine understood.

They followed Mick.

Mick led them to the cutting.

Tara and Catherine allowed Pake to go first, partly out of politeness and partly because Catherine had developed hiccups. Tara dragged her to one side.

"Stand still," he said. "Stick your fingers in your ears and waggle them and swallow. I met a woman on a train once who cured me of the hiccups. Go on. Swallow like Billy Hoho."

Catherine did what she was told. It worked. She was astonished.

"What train?" she asked.

They caught up with Pake and Mick.

"Oh, some train going to Oxford," he said.

The peat cuttings were blacker than the night. Deep trenches had been dug into the moor, like slices cut out of a Christmas pudding. There was a strong smell of the freshly cut peat. By the side of the cutting, carefully stacked sods had been piled one on top of each other, like bricks. By now, even Pake's eyes had grown accustomed to the dark. The stars were very bright.

They all stood very close to the pit. Pake was close to the brink.

"What's this bloody trap?"

His stick banged against something hard.

Mick peered at it.

"Lazy sods," he said. "Gone and left their slanes all over the place."

He picked the object up.

He was right. It was a slane, a long-handled spade with two winged blades on the ends, rather like a pick-axe, but curved like sharp spoons.

"Nearly sliced my ankle off," said Pake.

But he was no longer grumbling. His voice betrayed a certain amusement. The expedition had begun to fascinate him. He groped in the dark.

Mick put down the slane. He began to ferret amongst the sods.

"This'll do," he said. "This'll do the trick. Now watch. Stand back a bit, Mr Pake. There's no need for you to be so near the edge. It gives me the heebie jeebies."

He bent down. He picked up a sod of dug peat. He held it between his hands and crumbled the packed, fibrous earth apart. Then he stooped and dragged it against the ground. The others watched. They saw his monkey-like silhouette against the sky. He began to run, rubbing the peat against the ground as he did so.

Catherine stood perfectly still.

As Mick rubbed the peat against the tangled roots of the heather and the short vegetation of the moorland, sparks flew. The sparks were tiny, short-lived lights, pale aquamarine. Flickers of vermilion light shone and scattered after the green sparks. They did not last for long, but as Mick continued to rub the peat against the ground, they continued in a trail. The stars were very bright.

"I want to try," said Tara.

They all tried. They helped themselves to bits of peat and imitated Mick. Sparks flew about all over the place.

"It's better," said Catherine, "if you do it really close to the ground."

"You're right," said Pake.

He had discarded his stick. In the starlight and the faint light of the moon, he cut a distinctly odd figure. He rubbed and scrubbed his piece of peat with an obsession.

"But blast it all!" he said. "Why doesn't mine work as well as yours, Tara?"

Tara was having a great success.

"Fetch another sod," said Mick. "Not all sods are the same as other sods. Some are more adjacent than others."

Catherine laughed. She fetched Pake another sod. This time, he had more luck. He was very pleased.

"Quite remarkable," he said. "Very remarkable indeed. To think I've never known of it. How did you find out, Mick?"

"I was surprised myself. It was an accident, you might say."

"But what on earth were you doing up here with the peat in the dark?" Tara asked.

Catherine kicked him in the shin.

"That would be telling, now," said Mick. "Avoiding a spot of trouble, you might say."

"Accidents," said Pake.

He stood up.

"Accidents are always interesting. Scientists seem to have them all the time, lucky fellows. But where would they be without them? Think of discovering the mould of penicillin and putting two and two together in such an extraordinary way. It's how the accidents are used which is so important."

"You mean like those cucumbers which failed to crop, but were supposed to store some kind of electricity?" Catherine teased him.

They had all got to their feet. Tara and Mick straggled behind.

"Yes," he said and smiled in the dark. "Always found that amazing, haven't you? To have had the idea of solar energy. Just the idea."

"I suppose it was in the air."

"Not a bit of it. I wonder what can be done with the peat?"

"Burn it, as usual. The sparks don't last long enough to light a match."

"Damn it, Catherine! I can't see a thing. Where the hell have the others got to?"

He shouted to them.

Mick and Tara came out of the shadows. Pake drove back considerably faster than he had come. It was downhill all the way.

"Let's go into the kitchen," said Tara, "and have a cup of tea."

He cleaned the mud off his boots on the scraper outside the kitchen door.

"No," said Pake.

He did not bother with the door scraper. He brushed past Tara.

"We'll go into the gun room," he said. "We don't want to disturb Nan."

He led the way. The others followed.

In the gun room, he opened a bottle of whiskey and doled out glasses which he kept in a cupboard full of old seed catalogues.

They sprawled into chairs. Mick, who had taken off his gumboots and walked behind the others in his socks, put his feet up on Pake's desk.

"Ta," he said to Pake. "Ta very much. Did you like the lights, now?"

He took a gulp of his whiskey.

"Very much," said Pake. "Fascinating."

"You know I don't like whiskey," said Catherine. "I'm going to get some water."

She left the room.

Returning with her glass of water along the passage towards the gunroom, Catherine heard the rise and fall of the men's voices. They were having an argument.

"I'll be damned if I won't!" Tara said.

"You'll be damned if you will!" Pake said.

Catherine walked into the room.

Tara was leaning against the fireplace with his back turned to the other two.

Pake sat at his desk.

Mick still had his feet on it, rather close to the inkwell. He took another swig of whiskey when he saw Catherine come into the room.

"What is it?" she asked.

"None of your business," said Pake.

"Rubbish!"

Tara turned and faced his uncle.

"It is Catherine's business. Of course it is. Very much so, if you ask me."

"There is something in that," said Mick.

"It's a question of the best man," said Tara.

Catherine laughed. She went over to the fireplace and put her arms on Tara's shoulders.

"But there's no question of the best man," she said.

"That's what I said," said Pake.

"You're the best man," she said to Tara.

"Stone the crows!" said Mick. "He can't have it both ways, can he?"

He cackled.

"It's not that kind of best man, Catherine," said Pake. "It's the other kind. For this wedding of yours, Tara is the groom."

"That'll be the day," said Mick. "Suibne's shed needs mucking out as it is. I'll be leaving. The lights aren't too bright on my bike."

He got up.

"Ta ta," he said.

"I loved the expedition," said Catherine. "Don't skid into a ditch. Nan'd never let us hear the last of it."

Mick left the room in his stockinged feet.

"Well, I still don't understand," she said. "I see about the groom. I'd clean forgotten about wedding formalities. Why are you so worked up about it?"

Tara turned to Catherine.

"I wanted Gerald to be my best man," he said. "You know Gerald."

"Well, no I don't," said Catherine. "But I know who you mean. That friend you've often talked about?"

"Exactly. Gerald's the best man. He's certainly my closest friend. That's what best men are."

He turned to his uncle.

"Isn't that so?"

Pake shifted in his chair behind his desk.

"Generally," he said. "But I'm afraid not in this case."

"What's different about our case?" said Catherine. "Why can't we be married properly with grooms and best men and things like everybody else?"

Pake sipped his whiskey and looked at his niece.

"Catherine," he said, "you know perfectly well that we don't have visitors at Malabay. I'm afraid I'm allergic to strangers. I'm very sorry for both of you. But there I draw the line."

"Yes, Pake," said Catherine. "You always said it was because of you having been locked up in that green cage during the war that no one ever comes to stay. It must have been quite beastly in the cage."

She left Tara and went to her uncle.

"Look out for the inkwell! Mick nearly kicked it to bits."

"I know," she said. "At least, I think I'm beginning to."

"What?"

"Understand."

"Understand what?"

Pake looked grim.

"Oh, Pake! Don't. Don't look like that. But I sort of understand that it must have been a nightmare locked up in that beastly cage all those years. You must have felt so mouldy, like teaspoons with verdigris. And the din I should think something fearful."

She looked at Tara.

"Don't you see, darling?" she said. "You've always known what a horrid time Pake had in that wretched cage. Don't let's make our wedding another kind of torture for him. Couldn't Mick-the-Post be best man instead? It doesn't really matter so much, does it?"

Tara put his arm around Catherine.

"All right," he said. "If Gerald is going to make Pake so unhappy by being the best man, I see that's only going to make you miserable too, and that's the last thing I want. But it's a pity. Never mind. Mick can do instead."

He kissed her.

"Thank you," said Pake.

He drained his glass.

"I'm going to bed," he said.

He put his nose round the door before he shut it.

"Mind the fleas don't bite," he said.

They heard him stalk upstairs to his bedroom.

"I do love you," said Catherine. "It was so nice of you to give up Gerald. I know you're terribly fond of him. But Pake has got these dreadful difficulties. He simply can't stand other people. It would ruin everything."

"I am afraid I do see," said Tara. "I see only too well. But what about you? Wouldn't you ever like visitors?"

"How on earth do I know? You're the only visitor I've ever had."

Tara laughed.

"Let's go to bed," he said.

"Don't! It hurts!"

She rolled her body away from his and curled up on the other side of the bed.

She was in tears.

Tara swore.

Catherine tried to muffle her tears. She sniffed.

"Oh God!" said Tara. "Don't cry like that. It's the most aggravating thing for a man."

"But if it hurts, then of course I cry."

"Well, stop sniffing at any rate."

Tara got out of bed. He looked for a cigarette. He found one, lit it and then sat down on the edge of the bed where Catherine had curled herself up.

He put his arm round her and stroked her back.

She burst into tears again.

He drew on his cigarette and inhaled deeply.

"Look, darling. I didn't mean to hurt you. Of course I didn't. I'm sorry. These things happen. You're just not used to it."

Catherine wiped her tears on the sheet.

"Have you got a hankie?"

He found her one.

She blew her nose and sat up.

"I don't understand," she said. "It wasn't like that last night, or this morning. Then it was delicious and you were so tender. Why were you so brutal to me?"

"Have a puff," said Tara.

He handed Catherine the cigarette.

She choked.

"That's the first cigarette I've ever smoked."

Tara stubbed it out on a shell which lay on the bedside table.

"It was like having a bonfire at the back of my throat," she said. "I quite liked it. Can I have another?"

He lit one and passed it to her.

"Don't inhale," he said. "Just be gentle."

"But why weren't you? When you were making love to me, I mean?"

"It wasn't just me making love to you," he said. "It was both of us."

"I didn't know."

"I think you felt like that last night," he said, "because it was the first time anybody had ever made love to you. And because I knew that, I was especially tender, and this morning. But tonight I forgot. You got me so excited."

"What do you mean, excited?"

"You're very sexy."

"Sexy? I don't know the first thing about it."

"Oh darling, I know. But you are. You'll find out. And it gets better, too, the more you do it. Here, give me a puff."

"I think cigarettes are the most wonderful new taste."

"Like sex? You're a natural. Things'll be all right, you'll see. I think you should go and run a nice hot bath. Then I'll come and dry you and we can be delicious, as you call it, again."

"And you won't be brutal?"

"Just go and have your bath."

"But Pake'll wake up. The plumbing's so noisy."

"Fuck Pake!"

She went.

Tara lay flat on his back in Catherine's bed. He listened to the sound of running water from the bathroom.

He imagined Catherine naked in the next room, dipping a toe into the water. He pictured her thin, young body in the steamy water. He lit a cigarette.

He thrust the covers off his body.

He put out the cigarette.

He thought of Stella.

He had an immediate erection.

Stella was naked. She bent over him. Her long blond hair brushed against his shoulders. Her clear blue eyes gleamed in the half light. She laughed.

"If you would have me, Stella."

"But I want your child, Tara. Give it to me!"

"Stella! Stella!"

She squirmed her body more firmly against his own. Her long legs gripped his thighs.

"You can have our child, Stella."

"Can I? Can I now?"

"Come quickly!"

"Yes!"

"When shall we marry, Stella? Now?"

Stella jerked her body away.

"Never! I only want the child."

She came.

So did Tara.

But they came apart.

"I hate your conditions," she said. "I despise them. You're like all men. You make nothing but compromises."

"I thought of the child," said Tara. "I thought it would be ours together."

"I never had that in mind. I don't need you. I just want a child. My child."

"You are so cold, Stella."

She left the bed and stood with her back to him. He knew her beautiful body off by heart.

"I'm going to leave you now," said Stella. "And I'm going to leave you forever."

She stooped. She gathered up her clothes which Tara had previously discarded on the floor.

"I shall never see you again in my life. From now on, I'm dead to you."

Very slowly, she began to dress herself. She drew up her knickers.

He watched her.

He could not move.

She drew the white silk up her thighs.

"As soon as I've gone," she said, "I shall go straight to my cousin. Yes, to Rupert. He will give me a baby. He will give me anything I want. He will know that I still taste of you. He will like it. I won't have to marry him, or anyone else in the word. I shall get my baby."

She dressed herself very slowly, deliberately in order to torture him. He could not take his eyes off her.

She spat. The spit landed at Tara's feet.

He never saw her again.

"Hurry up! I'm getting cold!" Catherine cried from the bathroom.

He tossed himself off.

He came.

Then he went to the bathroom and dried her.

They were extremely late down to breakfast.

"I'm beginning to get quite addicted to you," said Catherine.

They walked down the wide staircase hand in hand.

He laughed softly.

In the dining room, Pake had finished his toast. He had finished reading his correspondence, too.

They sat down.

The coffee had grown cold.

Pake did not look up.

His correspondence was to his right. To the left of the remains of his breakfast lay a curious assembly of bits of mud and moss and peat.

"I'll go and heat up the coffee," said Tara.

"Let me," said Catherine.

She wanted to get out of the room. She had never been so late for breakfast before. She was sheepish in front of her uncle.

"I'll go," said Tara.

He went.

Pake looked up.

"Come here," he said.

"What's all that muck?"

Pake took his magnifying glass out of his waistcoat pocket.

"That's just what I'd like to know," he said. "Come and have a look. I think it's much more interesting than it seems. Probably very interesting indeed."

"It just seems ordinary symbiosis," she said.

"It's a perfect example of that," he said. "But I'm up against a wall."

"What wall?"

"Bloody sphagnum. Let alone thacomitrum. I think I'm on to something here. But beastly B. & H. have left me in the lurch."

Tara came back with a jug of hot coffee.

"When did you last go to Bourne and Hollingsworth?" he laughed. "Or do you mean Boosey and Hawkes?"

"Don't be an idiot."

Pake brushed aside his correspondence. Most of it fell on the floor. He peered at the bits and pieces of mud and moss beside his plate.

Catherine sat down.

"I mean Bentham and bloody Hooker! They don't know. They're a fat lot of use. Bentham and bloody Hooker!"

He waved his magnifying glass ferociously in the air.

"But you've always sworn by them," said Catherine. "Called them the Holy Bible backwards."

"It's all right swearing on them as a Bible when they tell you something worth knowing. But they've given up the ghost. They're just plain baffled by cryptogams."

"What are you talking about?" said Tara.

"Moss and peat and stuff."

She bent down to pick up Pake's letters for him.

" 'However great'," read Pake from an old copy of Bentham and Hooker, " 'therefore, may be the present interest attached to them, they are beyond the scope of the present Flora.' Fat lot of use that is."

"Bibles aren't much use without ghosts," said Tara.

"Here's a letter for you," said Catherine.

She handed Tara an envelope.

Pake put down the Bentham and Hooker.

"Thank you," said Tara. "Have some coffee before it grows cold again."

"Clean forgot," said Pake. "Should have put it on your plate as soon as it arrived. I do apologise. I've been quite carried away by these cryptograms."

Tara looked at his uncle.

"That's perfectly all right," he said.

He drank some coffee and buttered some toast. He opened the envelope and began to read his letter.

"Perhaps it's not cryptogams," said Catherine. "Morphology might be in it."

"Bound to be," said Pake. "Morphology creeps into everything. But it's got to be something else, too."

Catherine reached for the honey.

"What I think is so queer," she said, "is that nobody round here seems to have noticed the peat sparks before. After all, they were quite spectacular, weren't they? You'd have thought they'd have given rise to all sorts of legends."

"It is rather peculiar," said Pake. "But what I want to find out is why this phenomenon occurs. I've got a hunch it might lead to something very exciting."

"It would be interesting to find out," she said. "But it is odd that no one seems to know about it. You'd think there would be all sorts of stories about people getting misled by fools' gold to some frightful elfin fate, or mythical mines of silver boasted of by some village idiot reeling down from the hags. Scattered gems and lost crowns on Beakus's Stump."

"Stick to the facts," said Pake. "We must enquire into crypto-gams."

Tara looked up from his letter and buttered some more toast.

"Moss Bros," he said.

"What's Moss Bros?" asked Catherine.

"It's where Gerald says I ought to get my wedding clothes." Tara poured out more coffee.

"Poppy knows all about cryptograms," he said. "Why don't you ask her?"

Pake grinned with satisfaction.

"Poppy knows nothing about cryptogams," he said.

"Poppy knows everything under the sun about cryptograms, Pake. You know that perfectly well. She's an official code-cracker."

"There are cryptograms and cryptogams," said Pake. "Poppy wouldn't make head or tail of ours. Ours are botanical and they are very difficult to determine."

Catherine looked out of the window.

It was pouring cats and dogs.

"Damn!" she said.

"You might well say damn," said Tara. "I was about to say it myself."

She smiled.

"Why?"

"Because it turns out I've got to go back tomorrow."

She was silent. She took a sip of coffee.

Pake looked at her.

She said nothing.

"I must, darling. It turns out there are all sorts of things I must arrange. And besides . . ."

Pake gathered up his letters and bits of moss and peat.

"I'm going to determine," he said.

He left the room.

"Besides what?" said Catherine.

"I didn't know you'd accept when I asked you to marry me, did I?"

"Didn't you?"

He kissed her.

"Let's go down to the boatshed."

"All right. But I'd better help Nan first."

"All right. Don't be long."

"Only as long as it takes. It won't be long."

Catherine and Nan had finished the housework. They were in the kitchen making the pudding for supper. It was apple crumble. Nan was making the crumble. Catherine pared the apples.

"Fairy lights, indeed!" said Nan. "Mick looked as though he was still seeing double when he tumbled off his bike this morning."

"Well, he often does, doesn't he?"

Nan sniffed.

"But the lights were lovely, Nan. They really were. Green lights with red and gold sparks like fire flies. You ought to get Mick to take you up there one night."

"I dare say. You're cutting the rind far too thick. There's no call for waste just because you spent all night and half the morning mooning about."

Nan fetched the flour from the great stone crock that stood in a corner of the kitchen. She put it into a wire sieve and held the sieve high over the pudding basin. She shook it from side to side. Only a very few grains fell on to the rim of the bowl, still fewer on to the table.

They stood opposite each other across the table.

"Have you thought about your wedding dress?"

Catherine looked up.

Nan held a lump of butter in one hand, a small knife in the other. The butter was sweet, unsalted. She had churned it herself. She cut small pieces off the lump of pale yellow butter, turning the lump as she cut, so that the pieces were cut at an angle. They clung to the blade of the knife and held together in a curved line of segments above the bowl. Catherine thought they looked like the Chinese paper cobra which swung in one of the attics.

"No, I hadn't."

The butter cobra landed in the bowl.

Nan put her floury hands on her apron.

"Well, you'd better start thinking. Think of your mother, now. You should have seen her."

"But I never did. Not to remember."

"She was pretty as a picture. Prettier than any picture I've seen."

Catherine went on peeling her apple. She peeled it very carefully, paring the rind as close as she could to the flesh of the fruit. She did it without a break. She held the coiled skin high over her shoulder and flung it down on to the floor.

"Bit late in the day for that kind of antic," said Nan.

Catherine stared at the skin.

"Can't see anything in it," she said. "Come and have a look."

Nan left her crumble.

The green appleskin had fallen into a curlicue.

"It all depends on which way you look at it," said Nan.

They walked round the skin, staring at it from different angles.

"But whichever way you look at it," said Catherine, "it definitely isn't a T. It isn't a letter at all."

"It looks a bit more like those half-moon E's you put on the Bakewell tarts that come out so strange," said Nan.

Catherine threw the skin into the chicken bucket.

"I think all pearly," she said. "And made of satin. Satin would rustle nicely."

"Sounds like a Pearly Queen, to me," said Nan.

"What's that?"

"I'm not too sure. I've seen them in the Sundays. Tinkers covered all over with buttons and pearls and shells. They cavort about in the streets of London and get their hands shaken by the Queen of England."

"What extraordinary things the Queen of England gets up to," said Catherine.

She had finished the apples.

"About the dress, though," she said. "Do you think that will do?"

"Sounds very nice," said Nan. "I think there's some satin I can look out for you."

"Let's make it as soon as Tara's gone," said Catherine. "He's going away tomorrow. I've done the apples."

She ran out of the room.

Tara was sitting on the stump by the jetty near the boathouse.

The rain had stopped.

He was dejected. He smoked a cigarette. He looked at the *Fionnuala*.

"What's up?" said Catherine.

She crouched on the grass beside him.

"Bloody rigging!" he said. "I'd meant to take you out in her today. I thought we might go for a long spree, past the Devil's Nose. But the wind's getting up. I think we'd better call it off for today."

"But there's always a bit of wind."

"Don't like the look of that cloud."

Catherine looked.

"It doesn't look all that ominous," she said.

"It's just I'd like to get the feel of her in good conditions. Without having to worry about the possibility of having to reef the sails. I'm sorry. But it's no go today."

Both of them were disappointed.

"Can I have a puff?"

Tara handed her the fag end of his cigarette.

She drew on it and then stubbed it out.

Tara got off the stump and stood beside her. He put an arm round her shoulder.

"I think I'd better fiddle about with the rigging," he said. "I think she's fairly stable. After all, she's a trimaran, not a cat. Still, you never know. But I think it's the rigging."

Catherine got up. She leaned against him.

"Listen!" she said. "Woodpecker."

They looked for it, but could not see it.

"Sounds like water being poured into an empty glass," she said.

"I suppose you could say that."

"But I did."

"You'd say anything."

They walked round the back of the boathouse. Catherine paused at the door of the room where she worked.

"I think I'll try and do a spot of writing while you tinker with the boat," she said. "I really ought to get down to my Greek. But I'll do that later, before my writing thoughts vanish."

"What do you mean, vanish?"

"Oh, they do, you know. Come and go. They're difficult to ensnare. I like to get them down first. Dreadfully ephemeral, my ideas. Like dreams. Difficult to capture."

"Do you write down your dreams?"

"Not exactly. Just stuff sieved out of them."

They went into the room together.

"I like this room," said Tara.

"So do I."

"It's like you."

"People's rooms often are. Pake's study is. Nan's kitchen."

"Yes. But this is very like you. It's odd, ramshackle, funny."

"Funny?"

"Why don't you use a more comfortable one up at the house?"

"Don't know. Prefer this. I like the view. And it's private."

"I'd better get on with the boat."

She heard him dismantling the mast outside. She looked at the writing in her exercise book.

'. . . the swans were craning.'

There was a blot. A line scratched out. She picked up her pen.

'An unfamiliar smell filled the air. They did not like the smell. They raised their heads and were still. They heard new, strange sounds. The sounds were noisy and discordant, noises of metal on metal, which jarred on them and disturbed the peace of the lake with a horrid dissonance. They hid amongst the reeds and waited. They strained their long necks and quivered in apprehension. But they kept silent and waited.

'The reeds were thrust apart. The unpleasant, fleshy smell was now overpowering. They saw a pink face staring down at them.

'Man had arrived.

'After that, things were different. The reeds were cut down. Building sites were marked out for bungalows to be erected on the shores of the wild and lonely lake. Metal cranes . . .'

She stared out of the window at the lake.

'One morning, the swans swam to the shore. They were too wretched to notice a skinny boy with mean eyes, sitting on the pebbles near the edge of the water. He scrambled up.

' "Look!" he screamed. "Swans!"

'He picked up a pebble and flung it at them. The pebble whizzed through the air. One white feather fluttered down and fell into the lake.'

"Hell!" Catherine said aloud.

Tara heard her. He came into the room.

"What's the matter?"

"I'm stuck. I can't write. It's all nonsense."

She scored a line through what she had written.

He sat on the edge of the table.

"It's all mouldy. It's no good. The things don't come out. I've got them in my head and they don't come out. At least, if they do they come out all wrong."

He sat on the edge of her table.

"Poor thing. I was talking to Gerald only the other day."

"Gerald?"

"Yes. He writes. He made writing sound like hell."

"It is when one gets stuck."

"He calls getting stuck the blank page malady."

Catherine laughed.

"But I suppose it's just like everything else. You just have to get on with it."

"But I can't! I can't! I'm stuck. Absolutely stuck. And it's all . . ."

"What?"

"It's all such nonsense, anyway."

"Well, I don't know anything about it. But I was in despair about that blessed rigging. I think I've worked it out, though. When I come back, we'll take her out again. I think you've done enough scribbling for today. Besides, you'll have all the time in the world when I'm away. Let's spend what we've got left together."

They walked up to the house. The sun had come out, but the grass was still wet. Catherine pointed to a clump of iris as they walked through the orchard.

"I've had an idea," she said.

"What?"

They had reached the walled garden.

"It's the garden," she said. "It's so tangly and overgrown. Pake never goes into it. I'd like to make it a real garden again. It must have been so lovely once. It could be, again. What do you think?"

Tara stood still. He looked at Catherine. He was smiling.

"Do you know, that's the first time I've ever heard you say you wanted to change anything at Malabay? Anybody else, come to that, except for Poppy. But then, she left it."

"Do you know what happened? Why did she leave?"

"Got fed up, I expect. I don't know. Things go wrong, sometimes."

"Pake said he's never been in love with her. Not properly."

"Poor old Poppy. Should think that's why she left. Can you imagine anyone living with Pake unless they were in love with him?"

"But wasn't she?"

"I can't imagine anyone wanting to live with Pake."

"She must have done."

"But imagine living with Pake!"

Catherine laughed.

"But I do," she said. "Live with Pake, I mean. I've never done anything else."

"But that's different," he said. "You're not in love with him."

"I should hope not! He's my uncle."

"He's my uncle too. But that's beside the point."

"I can't remember Poppy at all."

"You ought to meet her. I'm extremely fond of her. I'll take you to see her one day. I think she'd like you. Like you very much."

"I hope I'll like her. What do you think about the garden, though?"

They had reached the fish pond.

"I think it's an excellent idea. Excellent idea for a young sex-pot."

They went into the house.

"It's not the only idea I've had," she said. "I've got another I want to show you."

"You're not doing so badly for someone who's got stuck."

"But it's not for the lack of ideas that I'm stuck," she said. "It's just the putting down of them. But this one hasn't got anything to do with writing. It's an idea for you. Come upstairs."

Many of the rooms at Malabay were no longer used. Tara followed Catherine upstairs and along a passage that led into a small, neglected wing of the house. She opened the door. The light was dim, the windows shuttered. She went to open them. A bat lay on the sill. It trembled and then flew out of the window.

"They say that's a sign of luck," she said.

Tara stood by the doorway.

The room smelt of must and camphor.

"I don't like it," he said.

"The bat?"

"No. The room."

"It was my father's study."

"I know."

"I thought you'd like the room. I thought you'd like it to be yours."

"I didn't much like your father."

Catherine did not turn round. She stayed looking out of the window.

"I was only a child," he said.

"I was only a baby. I don't remember him at all."

Tara stayed by the door. He folded his arms.

"Come here," he said.

She left the window. She did not close the shutters.

He caught her by the hand and took her out of the room. He shut the door.

"This house is full of empty rooms," he said. "It's just that one in particular I don't like. I'm sorry. It was nice of you to think of it. But not that one."

"I don't see what's wrong with it."

"We ought to use all the rooms."

"All of them?"

"I don't see why not."

"What for?"

"To make it live. To come alive again. Like the garden. Let's go into the ballroom."

"The ballroom?"

"Yes. The ballroom. I want to fuck you in the ballroom."

Half way through the apple crumble, Pake turned to Catherine. His glance was full of reproof.

"I spent some time going over your translation," he said. "It's full of faults. You pay no attention to accidence. The syntax is bad. Herodotus was a lively fellow. Your translation is as dull as ditchwater."

Catherine put down her spoon.

"Everything I did today went all wrong," she said.

"Wouldn't say that," said Tara. "You did beautifully in the ballroom."

Catherine smiled.

"And you had one bright idea."

"What, may I ask, was that? Your one bright idea?" asked Pake.

"Catherine had an idea," said Tara, "about the garden."

"The garden?"

"Yes," said Catherine. "The garden. It needs gardening. Planting. It's lovely, in its sort of bedraggled way. But today I thought I'd like to make it like it must have been once. It must have been beautiful."

Tara helped Catherine to some more pudding.

"The garden," said Pake. "Yes, it was beautiful. It is neglected. Like your Greek."

Catherine held her spoon high in the air.

"Can I, though? Do the garden?"

"I see no reason why not. If you promise not to let it interfere with your studies."

"Why did you let it get tangled and weedy?"

Pake smiled at her.

"Why did you neglect your Greek?"

"I was lazy. And I got stuck. I gave up."

"So did I with the garden," he said. "But your Greek is just as weedy. You haven't got the hang of Queen Nitocris at all. She was a most distinguished woman."

"I did get in a muddle with all those mounds. But I liked what she did with the lakes."

"What did she do with the lakes?" asked Tara.

"She diverted the Euphrates," said Catherine. "She wanted to keep the Persians out. It didn't work out, her idea. Rather odd, Queen Nitocris."

"As I say," said Pake, "you haven't got the hang of her. We'll go over her again, when Tara's left for London. By the way, which train do you leave by?"

"The early one."

Catherine looked at her empty plate.

"Let's ride to the station," she said. "The horses haven't been out for ages."

"Good idea," said Tara. "How about a spot of port, Pake?"

"You have some," he said. "But I've got things to do. I want to go and see how my experiments with the peat are getting on. Don't give Catherine more than's good for her. And don't stay up too late, either. You'll have to make an early start if you're taking the horses."

He got up from his chair.

"By the way," he said, "when can we expect you back?"

"Night before the wedding."

Pake went off to his study.

Tara went to the sideboard.

"I wish he liked it better," he said.

"The port or my Greek?"

"Our marriage."

"I know."

"I don't suppose he wants you to marry anybody, really."

"What makes you think that?"

"Don't know."

"Perhaps he just thinks I'm a bit young."

"He does keep you to himself so."

"That's only because we lead such isolated lives."

"Exactly."

They drank the port.

"I can't see that it'll make much difference to him," she said.

"Won't it?"

He looked out of the window. He saw a blackbird on the lawn.

"You never know," he said. "It might. More than you think."

"I suppose," said Poppy, "that there's no help for it. People in love are such geese."

She stirred the lump of sugar in her tea. The spoon clanked against the side of the pale pink and white porcelain cup. Some of the tea slopped into the saucer.

"Damn!" she said. "They are a pair of geese and no mistake. It's one thing to be in love. That you can't help. I know to my own cost. But why marry? It's batty."

She took a sip of the Lapsang Souchong and put the cup and saucer down on the small inlaid rosewood table beside her.

"But you married," said Gerald. "Why shouldn't they?"

"They might have learned from my example. My marriage was an utter disaster. What's the point of being an old fogey if the younger generations refuse to learn from one's mistakes?"

Poppy was sixty-six. She looked more than her age.

Gerald helped himself to another ginger nut. It was a trifle stale.

"You don't mean to say you don't believe in progress?" he said.

"God knows what I believe in," said Poppy. "I don't."

Poppy was dwarfed by the chair she sat in. She was tiny and bony. She wore her hair in a short, frizzy halo. It was off-white. Her face was shrivelled and her complexion yellow. Her eyes were startling. They were very bright and did not miss a trick. She had a peculiar habit of swivelling them round very fast and suddenly arresting them on an object not apparently of any significance. Poppy had never been a beauty, but she had been considered extremely pretty and sexy in her youth. She still had very dainty ankles which she now crossed with a skittish movement. She glanced at her shoes and smiled. Her shoes were hand-made of green kid and they had scarlet laces.

The intimacy between the two companions was uncommon. It was not merely the discrepancy between their ages, but the fact that they paid it no attention. They knew each other very well. Glance and gesture were as eloquent a means of communication as direct speech and cross reference.

They were having tea in the drawingroom of Poppy's flat. Gerald lay stretched on a sofa which was upholstered in a loose cover of faded green and yellow chintz of a floral design. His feet did not touch the sofa. In Poppy's opinion, he had remarkably good manners for someone of his age. For even if he lay stretched on the sofa, one could not say that he sprawled. And although he did not sit, his manner was alert, his expression watchful.

He finished his biscuit.

"Do you mind if I smoke?"

"Do. More tea?"

"No thanks."

He shifted on the sofa.

His movement did not exactly convey restlessness, nor yet impatience. But it indicated that he was a busy man and that, although it was pleasant to dally on an elderly lady's sofa, the pleasure chiefly consisted in something else to which it corresponded. He did not have time to waste.

"When did you get back from Rome?" asked Poppy. "I don't suppose you've had time to see Tara?"

"No. But we're having dinner together this evening," he said.

"Are you going to the wedding?"

"I'm going to Mauretania. In any case, I haven't been asked."

"That's what I wanted to know," she said.

"Have you?"

"No. Nobody has, as far as I can gather. It all sounds very hole in the corner to me. The whole thing is too queer."

"Well," said Gerald, "since you seem to be so against the marriage, I don't suppose you'd have gone to it anyway."

"That's beside the point," said Poppy.

She swallowed a little tea.

"It's quite different to be able to refuse an invitation. That would be one thing. But not to be asked at all is altogether different. I just feel miffed. But at least I don't have to worry about a wedding present. I'd always meant to give Tara my Byron if he went and got married. I don't think I will now, after all."

She glanced at her first edition, twelve volumes bound in blue calf, amongst the many books on her shelves.

"There doesn't seem much point to a wedding without presents," she said.

Poppy's drawingroom was beautifully proportioned. The two French windows looked out on to a small, now shabby Georgian square. But the room was so full of various accumulations that it seemed to be smaller than it was. The walls were a faded yellow, the kind of yellow used frequently in the glaze of eighteenth-century china. Not much of the walls was visible. They were mainly obscured by bookshelves crammed with books very catholic in taste; pictures, mostly good of their kind, by far the best of which was a small Delacroix, badly in need of cleaning; old looking-glasses, ornately framed, which lent deceptive reflections; a collection of fans; butterflies in glass cases and a square piano built for the daughters of George the Third.

The surfaces of the several tables were scarcely more visible than the walls of Poppy's drawingroom. They were cluttered with books, old letters, vases of flowers, sheets of music and a great many ash trays.

The one thing which all the objects shared in common was that none of them seemed to be what they were. Everything masqueraded as something else. The book ends were ebony elephants with ivory tusks and howdahs of mother-of-pearl; the legs and arms of the furniture were carved to resemble the heads of lions and other wild beasts. The picture frames were peopled with cupids. The very vases were fashioned in the forms of dolphins, mermaids and nymphets. Even the ash trays were cast in the moulds of fantastic and unlikely flora, ranging from ladies' fingers to cabbage leaves.

Gerald flicked ash from his cigarette into a green and purple china cabbage leaf.

"You know," he said, "it's odd when you come to think of it. But I scarcely know anything about Catherine at all."

"Catherine!"

Gerald raised one eyebrow.

"Curiosity killed the cat," said Poppy. "You are a nosy parker, aren't you? But then, friends always are. I suppose it's only natural. Where would friendship be without curiosity? I'm afraid I can't let any cats out of the bag about Catherine. Except I can't help wondering why Tara doesn't marry someone more original, if he will insist on getting married."

"Isn't she? Original?"

"Original? I haven't got the faintest idea. She may be original as sin, for all I know. It just seems to me beside the point to go and marry someone you've known all your life. Besides, it's well known, I believe, that cousins shouldn't marry."

"When did you know Tara ever stick to any rules?"

"This is taking anarchy too far. Besides, his idea of anarchy doesn't even stick to any other anarchist's view. Of course, he'd say that was true anarchy. But hasn't he ever spoken to you of her?"

"Very seldom. Of course, I've always known of her existence. Known he's always spent a lot of time at Malabay. Even when he was hooked on Stella. But Catherine can only have been a child then. No, I haven't got a clear picture of her at all."

Poppy glanced at the carpet.

"Hasn't he ever asked you to Malabay?"

"No."

"Or talked to you about it?"

"Hardly ever."

"In that case you really have been kept out of the picture. Hobnobbing away, the pair of you, for most of your lives, as thick as thieves. He's a darker horse than I'd thought. If you had some idea of Malabay, you would have some idea of Catherine."

"I'm afraid I don't quite follow you."

Poppy turned her attention to an ivory fan.

"Well," she said, "I wouldn't imagine there was an atom of difference between them."

"But Malabay is a house."

"That's what you think. Yes, Malabay's a house all right. There's no denying that. But it's a very potent house, if you see what I mean. It has a very strong effect on some people. And Catherine has never been out of it. She's been brought up there entirely alone by that ridiculous old Pake. She's got Malabay in her blood. And that lot, that family, they have the most tenacious corpuscles going. I can tell you. I wasn't married to Pake for nothing. Once they get something in the blood, they simply cannot get it out. There just isn't a vaccine strong enough. That was partly the trouble between Pake and me, you might say."

She smiled a smile tinged with malice.

She stood up and began to gather together the dirty teacups.

Gerald helped her. He carried the sugar bowl and the milk jug into her poky kitchen. He knew where the things lived. He started to put them away. It did not take them long to do the washing up together. Poppy washed and Gerald dried.

When Gerald had put away the last saucer, he walked over to the window and looked outside.

"It's a lovely evening," he said. "Why don't we go and sit in the Square garden?"

"That's not a bad idea. Except I feel rather in need of a drink. I expect it was the subject. But I've got some work to do later on."

"Interesting?"

"Don't you find work always is?"

Gerald smiled. He turned towards her.

They exchanged a conspiratorial glance of amusement.

This was one of the things they were firmly agreed on. Work, in their view, was something tantamount to an ethic, to which they both clung with an almost Evangelical fervour.

Poppy was a code cracker for the Secret Service. Gerald knew this. He never mentioned it to her specifically. Poppy seldom enquired after his career.

She looked at his hands.

"You have the most delightful ears," she said. "So sharp."

"We could take a look," he said.

"It's not what it seems. I've got Clementina tomorrow."

Gerald was foxed.

"Why don't we take a drink with us," he said, "and drink it on that bench beneath the trees?"

"There's a bottle of Vouvray in the fridge," said Poppy. "That would be suitable, don't you think?"

"Highly. You go first. I'll follow with the bottle and glasses on a tray. Your neighbours will think you've gone and got yourself a butler."

Poppy giggled.

"I wouldn't bank on that," she said.

"Thanks."

"Do you object, young man?"

"On the contrary. I find it most intriguing."

"Gerald, you are absurd!"

"So are you, Poppy."

Poppy selected a hat from the dozens which dangled from a coatstand made of bamboo. The coatstand imitated a giant stag. She chose an old straw hat decorated with dahlias made of raffia. The hat had strings of emerald ribbons. These she secured beneath her chin in a large bow which she tied up very firmly.

They sat on an iron bench underneath a sycamore tree. Gerald had been right. The evening light was delightful. It was golden, hazy and almost warm. It was kind to the dusty, dilapidated Square. An old couple walked slowly to and fro. They cast discreet but inquisitive glances at Poppy to whom they were accustomed. They cast less discreet ones at her companion.

"How nice this is," she said. "How very nice. It might be nicer if it wasn't quite so nice. But that's only hypothetical. At any rate, the wine is good."

"Yes. The wine is good. You always have very good wine."
"I know. It's important, don't you think, to choose well?"
She sipped the Vouvray. She held her glass up to the light.
"Tell me more," he said. "I want to know."
"What do you want to know?"
"About the set up."
"The set up?"
"Catherine."
"So you call Catherine a set up?"
"Oh, Poppy!"
"You asked for it."
"Your hat is so very nice."

It was relatively quiet in the Square. The garden was screened by grimy sycamore and plane trees. The lay-out of the garden had not been altered since the eighteen-eighties. Vestiges of a formal Victorian scheme for bedding plants remained between the now-untended gravel paths. They were no longer strictly adhered to. The standard roses were in need of pruning. Geraniums and pillar-box red tulips stood to attention between the buddleia and the weeds.

Poppy darted Gerald a wicked smile.
"But I don't know where to start," she said.
"You could always begin at the beginning."
"My dear Gerald! How can you be such a goat? One would think you were still in the nursery. There is no beginning. There never is. Ends, if anything, are more common. But beginnings, they are so frightfully tangled. Surely you know that? Origins are so misty. One can't really entertain the idea, really. You might as well listen to twaddle about woods full of owls, or still waters where fish do nothing but sleep. Why don't you do something more sensible, like filling up my glass?"

He filled it.
"You leave me in the dark," he said. "I'm not at all clear why she was brought up by Pake. What became of her parents?"
"They got lost."
"Lost?"
"Yes. Lost. Lost at sea. Terence and Nellie. They'd gone out night fishing. For mackerel. We often used to do that at Malabay. It always put me in a filthy temper for the rest of the next day. But they all

adored it. The sea was rough. It was perfectly ridiculous. And really quite unnecessary."

"How dreadful."

Gerald drank some wine.

"Yes. It was. It was all very dreadful. They were both good sailors. There seemed to be no reason. It was wretched. The waiting. And then no corpses. It's difficult to believe in death without a corpse."

"I hadn't thought of that."

"Take my word for it."

Gerald lit a cigarette.

"That must have been just before you and Pake got divorced?"

"Yes. Bad timing. Divorce took much longer then. Things were still so disrupted. It was just after the war. I wanted to leave before. But there were difficulties."

"Difficulties?"

"What with one thing and another. I don't think Pake ever got over it."

"The divorce?"

"You could say that."

She looked away. Gerald refilled their glasses.

"Tara told me he had a bad war," he said.

"He had an absolutely frightful war. He was a spy, you see. A brilliant spy. But he got caught. No fault of his own. That was a set up, if you like. He got bunged into an appalling fortress worse than the Château d'If. They put him into a green cage made of iron. I can't go into the ins and outs of it. And I don't know why it was green. But it was. Bottle green. It was ghastly for him and made him more peculiar than ever. He'd always been a bit odd. But then, spies are, I find, generally speaking. After the war, he went to Malabay. He insisted. I told you they have it in their blood. And then after Nellie's death . . ."

"Nellie?"

"His sister. Catherine's mother. They were very close. Oh, close isn't the word for it."

"What is, then?"

"The word for it?"

"Yes."

Poppy shifted her situation on the bench.

"I really couldn't say," she said. "But the situation was impossible. Untenable. No, it was out of the question."

"But you say so little."

"So little of what you want to know?"

"You say so little of Catherine."

"But I know so little of her. She was only a baby. Terence had made Pake her guardian. Terence was no great loss. I always thought him rather a dull old stick. There was a point to him, though. He was loaded. Stinking rich. Jago had gambled. Gambled badly. There wasn't a brass farthing left."

"Jago?"

"Pake's father. Nellie's father. Tara's grandfather. Lost every penny at the races. A darling man. Very like Tara. I told you they'd do anything for Malabay. Oh, there's no doubt that Nellie married Terence for his stocks and shares. To keep it going. And Catherine, of course, has inherited it. Lock, stock and barrel."

"And you've never seen her since?"

"I've never been back. No, I've never seen her since. I keep in touch with Pake, so to speak. We correspond."

Gerald looked past Poppy, beyond the branches of the planes and sycamores, through the iron railings of the Garden to the street behind the Square. Through the branches, he could see the passing traffic. A young girl hailed a taxi. She wore a blue skirt. The taxi stopped. She got in. The taxi drove on.

Gerald glanced at his watch. It was a beautiful watch. Its face was inlaid with lapis lazuli.

"I must go," he said. "It's later than I thought. I'll take the glasses, the tray, this empty bottle up for you. Do you want to stay?"

"Oh, I'll stay," she said. "I've got one or two things to ponder. And then there's Clementina. She will insist on Anglo-Saxon with modern Danish. Here's the key to the flat. How very thoughtful you are."

He stood up. He put the empty bottle and the glasses on the tray. He stooped and kissed Poppy lightly on the cheek.

She touched her cheek where he had kissed it.

"I'll bring back the key," he said.

"Don't bother. Leave it under the mat. I liked seeing you. Give my love to Tara."

"Yes. I'll send you a card, if such a thing exists, from Mauretania."

They smiled.

He walked away down the path and disappeared from Poppy's view. He shut the gate and glanced back. Poppy had left the bench.

Tara was late. Gerald sat in the lobby and ordered a drink. He took a small notebook out of his jacket pocket. He sipped champagne. He jotted down queries about gazelle hunting in Mauretania. He lit a cigarette. He glanced about the lobby. He recognised a man he disliked. He looked away and asked for a second glass of champagne.

Tara was soaked to the skin.

"Terribly sorry to be so late," he said. "Couldn't find a taxi anywhere. I got caught in a downpour. Walked. I'm drenched."

"You look like a drowned rat," said Gerald.

The head waiter had noticed Tara's arrival. He brought a glass of champagne.

"Let's take them to the table," said Gerald.

They followed the head waiter. He glanced about the diningroom as though he had added a new and exquisite dish to the menu. In a way, he had. He knew perfectly well that the mere presence of the two young men would enliven the atmosphere. He was right. A well-known publisher who, for the last half hour, had been mesmerised uncomfortably by his adolescent son excavating a lobster with an embarrassing lack of success, now discovered a new amusement in watching the boy desecrate the coral. At another, larger table a group of Americans who had been lavish in their orders and puzzled by the faded décor, now believed themselves to be in the centre of the real thing. Tara and Gerald were unaware of any effect they might have.

Towards the end of their dinner, the head waiter smiled benignly at them. They had eaten well. They appeared to be engaged happily in conversation. But he was wrong. They were on the verge of a quarrel.

"But why should you mind so much?" said Tara. "You don't know anything about it."

"Do you?" snapped Gerald.

His voice was savage.

"You don't seem to have any idea of what you're doing at all," he said. "It's monstrous."

"Monstrous, is it?"

"Catherine is only a child."

"Catherine will be seventeen the day we get married."

"She's a baby. Why don't you wait? Let her grow up."

"You've never met her."

"But what are you getting married *for*?"

"There's never been any question of anything else!"

Gerald pushed away his plate and lit a cigarette. He very seldom smoked during a meal. He was surprised by the violence of his own attack. He felt exhausted.

"Look here," he said. "You say it's none of my business. Perhaps it isn't. But you are my friend. And anyway, don't you see, it's the principle of the thing."

"What principle?"

"I can't see the point."

"Why should there be a point? I'm not marrying Catherine out of principle."

"I'm not joking, Tara."

Tara burst out laughing.

The other people in the restaurant turned round to look at him. They smiled. They liked the sound of his laughter. They wished they could share the joke.

"I know you're not joking," said Tara. "But it can't be helped. Things won't change that much. Not between us, I mean. Why should they? Let's have some pudding."

Gerald signalled to the waiter. The waiter never failed to be impressed by his gesture. It was a simple one, but he seldom saw it so well executed. He shuffled a couple of menus together and walked to them without any hurry.

"What's the pudding?" said Tara.

He did not open the menu.

"The summer pudding is very good this evening."

"Bit early in the year for summer pudding, isn't it?"

"Nothing is impossible. The fruit was flown in this morning. I recommend it."

Tara smiled. So did the waiter.

"Two summer puddings, please," said Gerald.

The waiter took the order and walked away with a singular feeling of satisfaction.

"You never mentioned love," said Tara.

"No. I didn't."

The waiter returned with the puddings, crimson, scarlet and ruby-red, smothered in thick cream on white plates.

Tara tasted it.

"But it's delicious!"

The waiter beamed and left.

"But it's absolutely delicious," said Tara to Gerald. "It's quite amazing. We've eaten the most colossally expensive fish that tasted of nothing at all. I can't think what we ate it up for. But this pudding is exquisite. It tastes just as it should, and smells of the country. Try it."

He watched Gerald taste it as though it was a matter of great importance.

"Isn't it good?"

"Very. You're quite right. It's first-rate."

Tara was delighted.

"How long are you going to be away for?"

"Hard to say," said Gerald. "Depends on how things go. And there's something I haven't told anybody yet."

"Oh, good! I want to be the first to know."

"I've gone and bought an island."

"Very unprincipled. Where is it?"

"In the South. It's very wild."

"It's what you've always dreamed of. I remember you saying once at some party how you loathed the hugger mugger and longed for an island of your own. Wasn't it at one of those awful parties Bob Mallet used to give?"

"I dare say."

But neither of them could remember.

"Then you'll give up hotels and write on your island?"

"I shan't give up hotels entirely. But I can do as much as possible on the island. There's a tower. It's a ruin."

"Habitable?"

"Primitive. But I have plans. I shall build."

"A hotel?"

Gerald laughed.

"I wondered if you'd like, both of you, to borrow it after the wedding?"

"My dear Gerald," said Tara. "That's most extraordinarily kind of you. Yes, I think we'd love to."

"Do you often say we?"

Gerald signalled for the bill.

"Oh no," said Tara. "Not this time. This time it's on me."

He whipped out his cheque book.

"I won't look a gift horse in the mouth," said Gerald. "Thanks."

"It's not a gift horse," said Tara. "Gift horses are sight unseen."

"You're the oddest kind of anarchist I've ever come across."

"That's what you think. Can an anarchist stick to conventions, even of anarchy? One must go against them, here and there. I'm a seventh degree anarchist. I'll let you know when I get to the ninth, extended."

"I don't understand."

"I didn't think you would. It was just a reference to patterns in music."

The waiter was sad to see them go.

The night was warm. The streets were still wet. The rain had only just stopped.

"I'm staying at Bob Mallet's flat," said Gerald. "Let's walk. It isn't out of your way, is it? I don't want to be late, else I'd ask you in for a night-cap. I've got a plane to catch at some unearthly hour in the morning."

"I'd love to walk. Don't want to stay up late either. Actually, that's not quite true. I love staying up late. But I'd better not."

The two friends walked through the familiar streets. For a while, they walked in silence.

"It's not true, what you said," said Gerald.

"What isn't?"

"That things won't change. Of course they will."

"I dare say you're right. But they might change for the better. You mustn't feel excluded. It's just that Catherine is now included."

They strolled on.

"How is the book going?" asked Tara.

"Not too bad."

Tara understood he meant it was going very well.

"It's coming out in the autumn."

"Same publisher?"

"Yes."

"I've been having great fun with my trimaran. Did I tell you?"

"Yes. But what does Catherine do?"

"Do?"

"Yes. What does she do?"

Tara laughed.

"God knows," he said. "She doesn't do anything, really. Potters about. Translates a bit of Greek. She's nuts on botany. She never went to school. Pake gives her lessons. Oh, and she writes a bit."

Gerald turned to Tara.

"What does she write?"

"I don't know."

"But doesn't it interest you?"

"I dare say it might if I read it. I can't tell."

"I mean, don't you encourage her?"

"I did try the other day. I told her about your blank page malady. I think it rather cheered her up."

Gerald was silent. They strolled on. Gerald lit a cigarette.

"Like one?" he said.

"Yes. I meant to ask you, where did you get that jacket?"

"Sweden."

Tara stopped. His match had gone out. Gerald held out his cigarette. Tara took a light from it.

"I don't understand," said Gerald. "I don't understand how you can get along without working. Don't you feel a lack of structure?"

"Structure? I don't need your opium."

"Damn it! I know you don't. I wish you did. We've never seen eye to eye about that."

"No. There has always been that. That difference. I don't suppose we shall see eye to eye in a month of Sundays. It's not that important."

"Don't you think so?"

"No. No, I don't. I think our feelings for each other are much more important."

Gerald smiled. He did not agree. In the dark Tara did not see his smile.

"Stop."

"What's the matter?"

Tara's shoelace had come undone. He groped and tied it up.

"I hope you're not offended," he said, "not to have been asked to the wedding, after all. You got my letter asking you to be best man? But Pake won't have it. No one has been asked. It's going to be a very quiet affair."

"I'm not offended in the least. I think Poppy is a bit, though. Miffed, she said."

"So you've seen her?"

"I always do when I'm in town. You know that."

"She does get the bit between her teeth."

"That's only because she worships the idea of you."

"Telling me it's only the idea. Fuck, my cigarette's gone out."

He threw the stub into the gutter. Gerald gave him another. Tara tapped his heels against the pavement. It was a jazzy step, a trick he had.

"I'll try and pacify her," he said.

"Might not be a bad idea."

"Hang it all!" said Tara. "She's my aunt, not yours."

They had reached the crossroads. Neither of them wanted to separate. They stood on the pavement, hesitating in the dark. They turned towards each other. Tara's cigarette glowed. They clasped each other in an embrace which surprised them both. Tara pressed Gerald's arm ferociously. With an abrupt, desperate gesture, he strode off into the night.

"It's no use," said Nan.

She had pins in her mouth.

"You'll have to get on to the table. I'll never get the hem of your blessed train straight like this. It's half-way into the chicken bucket as it is. What you want such a length behind you for, I don't know."

"I want to rustle," said Catherine. "I want to rustle up the aisle."

Catherine climbed on to the table. She stood straight as a die, her hands folded on top of her head. Nan crawled about the kitchen floor. She pinned up the hem and snapped off bits of tacking thread.

"What was my mother's wedding dress like?"

"Nellie's? Hers came from Paris in a box full of tissue paper."

"But what did it look like?"

"It was the colour of milk, made of satin. She liked to rustle too. Satin covered with lace. Flowers, the lace was made to look like. They didn't look like any flowers I've ever seen. You've got the same colouring, Catherine. The same dark hair and green eyes. Runs in the family."

It was evening, an hour before dinner. Dinner was safely in the oven. The cat sat close to the range. Outside, it was raining.

"Tara says we might go to Paris and . . ."

"Does he, now? There, I've done the pinning. You'll have to do the hemming. I've got other fish to fry."

"What fish?"

"The cake."

"Oh, a wedding cake!"

"Of course I mean a wedding cake," said Nan. "You can't have a wedding without a cake! You and Tara can hold hands and plunge in the carving knife and wish."

"Do you know why Tara didn't like Terence?"

"Didn't like Terence?"

"Yes. He said he didn't like my father very much."

"I dare say he was a bit hard on him. Tara always was in mischief."

"What?"

"I couldn't say. If it wasn't one thing, I suppose it was another. You slide out of that confection, now. And do your best hemming. Not worth doing a thing unless you do it properly."

"You say that about everything, even dusting the chairs."

"Well, it's true. I've got to get the dinner ready."

Catherine pulled on her old green cotton dress. She gathered up the yards of satin in her arms.

"I'll go and start now. I'll do it in the ballroom."

Nan looked after her. She shook her head. She had let the dinner over cook.

Tara came back to Malabay the night before the wedding. Catherine, Pake and Tara lingered over the remains of dinner. The curtains were not drawn. The lights had not been switched on. They sat in the dusk. None of them spoke. Pake fidgeted. Tara drained his glass. Catherine watched them both.

"So everything is in order for tomorrow," said Tara.

Pake picked up a crumb from the tablecloth. He glanced at his nephew.

"I left all the arrangements to you," he said.

Catherine looked at Tara. He laughed.

"That's all right. I think I've arranged everything except for a mere formality."

"What is that?" asked Pake.

"Oh, just a mere formality," said Tara again. His tone was light. "Just the question of the witnesses. I hoped, in fact I assumed, Mick would be one and you would be the other. I thought it only polite to ask you. That is all right, isn't it?"

Pake did not answer immediately.

"It's never wise," he said, "to make assumptions. It's a form of gambling."

"What's so terrible about gambling?" said Catherine.

"Gambling is an activity which runs in the family," said Pake. "Or certainly, it would appear to. Your grandfather Jago gambled away his interest in Malabay. Tara seems to have inherited this characteristic."

"Well, but my father saved it," said Catherine.

There was a very long silence.

"No," said Pake. "Thank you for the invitation, Tara. But I will not be a witness to your wedding."

Tara scraped back his chair. He got up and walked over to the sideboard.

Catherine kept perfectly still. She felt chilly. She did not understand this turn of events. She waited.

Tara fingered the decanters on the sideboard. His back was turned to the others.

"Can I pour either of you a drink?" he asked.

He did not turn round.

"I think a glass of port," said Pake.

"I'd like some too," said Catherine.

Tara brought the decanter to the table. He passed it to his uncle.

"Why not?" he said. "Pake, why won't you witness our wedding?"

Catherine took a large gulp of her port.

Pake lit a cigar. He did not look at Tara or at Catherine. He looked at a spot on the wall beyond their heads. He puffed out smoke.

"Never mind why not," he said.

"But if you won't," said Catherine, "then who will? We must have witnesses. Oh, Pake! Why will you be so cagey?"

He looked at Catherine with mild amusement.

"My dear child," he said, "you are perfectly right. I admit it. I am extremely cagey. It's hardly surprising."

He waved his cigar in a semi-circle.

Tara lit a cigarette. He would not look at Pake. Catherine held out her hand to Tara. He took it. She could feel that he was shaking with fury.

"But I'll arrange matters," said Pake. "Will you excuse me a moment?"

He got up and left the room by the door that led into the kitchen.

Tara and Catherine could hear him talking to Nan. They heard Nan's voice raised and the sounds of argument. Then they heard footsteps. A door shut.

"He's got her in the gun room," said Catherine. "That means business."

Tara was silent.

Catherine was on the verge of tears.

"What's it all about?" she said. "I don't understand. And you are in such a fury."

"I don't know what it's all about," said Tara. "Let's have some more port. I don't understand Pake. He always puts everything down to having been in that infernal cage."

"Blast the cage! But it must have been ghastly."

"I dare say it was," said Tara. "But it's over. It's all so long ago."

"That doesn't make it less beastly for him."

"But what about us? It's our wedding. I'm sick of other people's pasts."

Tara refilled their glasses. He kissed Catherine.

"Whoever invented kissing had a brainwave," said Catherine. "If only Pake wasn't coming, we could go on kissing forever."

"It's delicious with you. But not with everybody. Some people have mouths like sandpaper."

"Don't talk to me about other people's kisses. I don't want to know."

"That's not true."

Catherine turned away.

"Well, yes," she said. "I want to know everything. But the idea of you kissing someone with lips like sandpaper makes me feel sick."

Pake came back into the room. He leaned against the door. He looked very tired.

"Mick-the-Post and Nan will both witness your wedding," he said.

"I suppose you won't even give me away," said Catherine.

"Oh, my dear, what does it matter? I'll give you away if you want."

Pake looked ill. Catherine flinched.

"It's time I went to bed," Pake said. His voice was threadbare.

They heard him stomp up the stairs.

Catherine burst into tears.

"For Christ's sake stop it!"

Tara set down his glass.

"Stop it! Shut up! I can't stand it when you cry. You make me want to hit you."

"Do! I don't care. Do what you like. I've never been so unhappy in my life. I don't give a damn what you do. Nothing will ever make any difference."

"Don't be so stupid. You know that's not true at all. But do stop crying."

"If you kiss me."

Tara laughed. Then he kissed her.

They climbed the stairs together.

"No," said Catherine when they reached the landing.

"You're absurd, you know."

"I didn't think of getting married. You did. Let's do it properly."

"Left it a bit late for that, haven't we?"

"It's just . . ."

"I know."

"I love you."

"I know."

He closed the bedroom door.

The wedding was over. It was pouring with rain. They stood on the steps of the church. Catherine's train was wet.

"Do you feel different?" she asked him.

"Don't be silly," he said. "You didn't think all that mumbo jumbo would make any difference to my feelings for you?"

"That's not what I meant," she said.

Many people had turned up for the wedding. Uninvited guests, stray people from Ballingstown.

Nan came bustling up to Tara and Catherine.

"Get out of the mud. All that satin in the mud! Get into that old rattletrap. Half of Ballingstown is here and the better half of that looks like it'll want cake."

She shooed them, like two wet chickens, into the Daimler.

Catherine and Tara sat in the back. Their knees were swathed in lengths of wet and muddy satin. The windscreen wipers screamed on the glass. Pake turned the Daimler into the avenue. Tara reached for Catherine's hand.

"Bloody party," he whispered. "Never mind. Let's just cut the cake, take some champagne and disappear. They won't notice. Not once Mick–the–Post starts making speeches."

Catherine hesitated.

"I know it's a bore," she said. "But I think we ought to be there, really, even if we don't stay for very long."

Tara sighed.

"Well, you know as well as I do," she said, "that the last thing we want is any trouble from the boys from Ballingstown. You can never tell what might happen with them."

He swore.

"To hell with them!" he said. "It's our wedding, not theirs. You're talking as if you lived the other side of the border."

"It's not as simple as that," she said. "You can never quite tell in these parts. You know the place well enough. No one's been altogether easy here for over eight hundred years. Everyone's just had to live with it. These days, it's not a joking matter. And Pake's such a goat, he could pay to keep them quiet, but he won't. But I dare say you're right. As you said, it is our wedding. So don't let's bother."

Tara picked up her left hand and kissed the ring which he had slipped on to her finger such a short time before.

"Come on, darling," he said. "We're here."

★

Much, much later they were wakened by the sound of a door slammed, voices, a car driving off into the rain.

"Last guests," said Tara.

Catherine stretched.

During Tara's absence, Catherine had prepared her mother's old bedroom for them both. It was a fine room, large and with lovely proportions. It overlooked the lake. It was much more comfortable and more beautiful than her old room. The bed was huge, made of walnut and hung with faded blue curtains. This was the first time she had ever slept in it.

She turned over on to her tummy and nuzzled Tara's ear.

"Do you know something?" she said.

"What?"

"I'm starving."

Tara laughed.

"So am I," he said. "Let's go and see if there's any cake left."

Catherine's wedding dress lay on the sofa at the foot of the bed. The train spilled on to the floor. The satin gleamed in the dusk. They lay naked in the bed.

They dressed hurriedly in their ordinary clothes.

Tara turned on the light in the ballroom. The party was over.

"Christ! What a mess," he said.

"Thank God we didn't go to it, the party. Look what they've done to the cake!"

"It's awfully good, though."

They ate ravenously, cramming the food into their mouths with their hands. They drank champagne, too.

"Let's go out," said Tara.

He laughed. He had a distracted look. He was slightly drunk.

"Let's take the horses and go for a gallop."

Through the long windows, Catherine could see that it was blowing hard. It had stopped raining.

"You're mad," she said.

"Are you scared?"

She rose to his bait.

"Why not?" she said. "Come on, then. Let's go now."

The night was wild. They were caught up by the wind. It blew them down to the paddock. They had taken the bridles from the stables with them. They had not bothered with saddles.

"Oh, look!" said Catherine. "I'm so glad you thought of coming."

They stood still and gazed at Suibne and Eorann who were grazing under the apple trees in the small paddock. The wind had blown away the clouds. The stars were very bright. Both the horses looked up, shook their manes and walked towards Tara and Catherine. They bent their heads and allowed themselves to be bridled with an unusual docility. Catherine sprang on to Eorann's back, Tara on to Suibne's. They let themselves out of the paddock and rode side by side down the avenue.

"Where shall we go?" Catherine asked.

"Beakus's Stump," Tara said.

They turned off towards the moorland in the direction of the Stump. As they left the avenue and the protection of the trees, the wind rose against them. Instinctively, they buried their heads in the horses' manes. They urged the horses on. They rode fast until they reached the Stump.

Beakus's Stump, the cairn on top of an old barrow on a particularly lonely part of the moor, seemed unearthly in the moonlight. The moon was full. It shed a cold light, sometimes hidden by the clouds blown across its face by the wind.

Tara dismounted. Catherine remained on Eorann. She looked up at the moon.

"I never thought," she said, "how heavy the moon must be. It just looks like a ball of silver, with the face of the man in the moon all crumpled. But really, it is a mass of energy whizzing about, so far away. I can't understand why it doesn't come crashing down and blow us all up."

"Come down," said Tara.

She slid off Eorann's back.

"The horses won't stray. Look at them," she said.

Suibne and Eorann were huddled against the mound of stones. The stones protected them from the wind. They cropped the short turf.

"Come," he said.

Their voices were blown away.

Tara reached for her and led her to the cairn. They had to fight against the wind, pushing with their knees and flailing with their arms. They reached it. Tara pushed Catherine in front of him. Inside there was peace.

They stayed there for a long time. They made love to each other again and again.

Afterwards, they lay quietly and listened to the wind howling over the moor. They gazed up through the stones and looked at the stars.

"How bright they are tonight."

"Yes," said Tara.

Catherine leaned her head against his shoulder.

"At Malabay," she said, "I thought you were daring me to come out into the night with you. As though you were testing me. You thought I'd think it too wild. You don't know I'm wilder than you. But you're right. It is beautiful, isn't it?"

"I was testing you. You're right."

"But why? What for? Why should you want to test me?"

"I wondered if you had spirit."

She laughed.

"I was a bit drunk, too," he said.

She laughed again.

"The spirit!" she said. "My God! If I didn't love you, I'd bite you!"

"Some people do both," he said.

"Some people would do anything from what you say. At least my kisses aren't like sandpaper."

He kissed her again.

"No. No, they're not like sandpaper. Not in the least."

"What did you say to the girls with sandpaper kisses? Or did you like the rasping of their tongues?"

"Laid off them when I didn't find the sandpaper suited. You are absurd, Catherine."

"How can I help not being?"

"Absurd?"

"I have nothing to go by."

It started to rain. They did not move. Eorann drummed her hoof on the turf.

"But I have a secret," he said.

"What?"

"It'll keep."

"Not in this weather. It'll just get soggy."

"This secret is waterproof. It'll keep."

"Till when?"

"I'll tell you on my birthday. Let's have a picnic on my birthday. On the island. I'll tell you about it then. It's an island secret."

"Pact. I've got one for you, too."

"Come on, then. Before we catch our deaths."

They rode downhill slowly. Catherine turned her face back to the cairn. For one moment, it was lit up by moonlight. Then a passing cloud obscured it. She turned away.

"I don't want to go on with my lessons."

"Do you mean that you wish to be uneducated?"

Pake stood with his back to Catherine in the gun room.

She sat in the chair facing his desk.

"But I'm married now."

"Yes," he said. "You're married now. But your education is incomplete."

"You've always said one's education is," she said, "incomplete. That one could never stop learning."

"I'm glad you remembered that. That's not an easy lesson to learn."

He turned from the window and sat opposite her behind his desk.

"To tell you the truth, I'm not sure I have. It's just that it gets so awfully in the way."

"I'm so glad you said that," he said.

"I mean, oh I don't really know what I mean."

"No. How should you know?"

"It's not that I don't want to go on knowing more. But just at the moment it's so frightfully inconvenient. Tara gets annoyed when all my time gets taken up."

"All your time?"

"I have no time."

"There is no time."

He looked at the clock.

"It's tea time."

He stood up.

"How is your experiment with the peat and stuff going?" she asked.

"It takes up all my time."

"You just said there wasn't any."

"I meant there is never enough."

They left the gun room arm in arm.

"But it's going well?"

"Oh, it's going. It's going, all right. But I haven't the slightest notion where. I hope it might be a source of energy to stop the clock, so to speak."

"Will you explain exactly?"

"Later. Later. Now it's time for your tea."

"It all looks like nothing, to me."

Catherine linked Tara's arm.

"Oh, no," she said, "but don't you see?"

"But there isn't anything to see."

"But there will be."

She had spent a lot of time in the garden. She had cut things back, right down to their roots. She had weeded, hoed and pruned. She had sent off for catalogues.

"No," she said. "There is nothing to show for it yet. But there will be."

"What?"

He looked disconsolately at the border.

"Look at the seeds I planted," she said. "Morning glory, honesty."

"Honesty?"

"Yes. And Chinese lanterns. You can't hope for it all to spring up at once."

"I suppose not."

"Bother it all. You are all in such a hurry!"

"All?"

She trudged along the path.

"Yes. Pake says there is no time. You are in such a hurry. I can't keep up."

She fled into the house.

Catherine had finished her dinner. She sat in her chair and watched Tara and Pake eating cheese.

"I can't make up my mind about it," said Pake. "It could be beetles in the heather. But I doubt it. Definitely not St Elmo."

Tara looked at his uncle.

"St Elmo?"

Pake smiled at him.

"More cheese? Yes. St Elmo. Patron saint of navigators. Hope he stands you in good stead. But I don't know whether he'll be of more use to me than desiccated beetles. But surely you've heard of St Elmo?"

"Never in my life."

"I believe Darwin saw flashes. Sailors are reported to have seen flashes of light streaking out from the tips of the masts, sparking off the yard arms. But that is usually during storms. In this case, it doesn't apply. A pity. Probably just a case of beetles. Bioluminescence. Pity, because I have a weakness for old Elmo. But I'm more interested in the truth of the matter."

"Do you mean like the light of mycelium?" Catherine asked.

"Yes," said Pake.

"What's that when it's at home?" Tara asked.

"Just what it sounds like," said Catherine. "Slimy. Spawn. Actually, it looks like the finest gossamer cobwebs if you put it under a microscope."

Pake poured out more wine.

"It might be that," he said. "Or it might be the static electricity fired up when the peat is dragged against the heather. I don't know. I've written off to Kew. They're generally very helpful. But I want to harness it."

"Harness it?" said Tara.

"Yes."

Pake looked at Catherine.

"I've set up slides," he said. "Ramsbottom's very good on the subject. Excellent man, Ramsbottom. But now they say he's a bit out of date. I'd like you to look tomorrow at what I've got going in progress. Spawning away like God knows what."

"But Pake!" said Catherine.

"What is it?"

She looked to Tara.

Tara looked away.

"I can't possibly do it tomorrow."

"What's so special about tomorrow?"

"Tomorrow is Tara's birthday. Surely you haven't forgotten?"

"Tomorrow and tomorrow. Tomorrow never comes."

He pushed away his plate. He looked resignedly at the tablecloth.

He could not see a crumb to pick.

"No, but don't you remember? I told you. We're going off to have a picnic. On the island."

"I had forgotten. The day after tomorrow will do just as well."

He walked out of the room.

"Oh Christ!" said Tara.

"Don't."

They left the table together.

Catherine slept badly. Tara was so fast asleep that she did not like to wake him. She watched him for a long time. His toes stuck out of the sheets. She could have nibbled them. She could have nibbled his ears. Instead, she crooked her elbow against her chin and waited until he woke up.

"Happy birthday!"

But she had said it too soon. He grumbled in his sleep.

She turned over. She felt disjointed altogether. The morning light was distracting. It was not at all what she had imagined.

"Come here."

"I'm so tired."

"No. You're just daft. Come here."

"Always? Always when you want?"

"Don't you?"

"You'll always get the better of me, Tara. I was watching you, in your sleep."

"Did I twitch, like you?"

"No. Not a bit. You just lay still. I could have hit you."

He smiled.

"You can't resist, can you?"

They were very late down to breakfast.

There was no sign of Pake. An empty egg shell, some crumbs of toast, nothing else but his empty chair.

"Elmo's got him hook, line and sinker."

"Coffee?"

It was a glorious morning.

"Toast?"

"Look out."

"What is it?"

"I just mean," said Catherine, "look at the day. Isn't it lovely for your birthday?"

"I love you in green," he said.

"I'm off," she said.

"What about me?"

"It's only for you that I'm off. I'm going to get a picnic together."

He scrunched up toast and honey. She licked him behind his ear.

"Oh, but you have no idea!" she said.

He watched her dance out of the room.

She had collected everything. The picnic in a hamper, her fable of swans. She set off in the old rowing boat towards the island. She had cast off the boat and was back paddling with one oar. She looked across the lake. She saw the sail of the *Fionnuala* on the horizon. Water slopped into the tub. She stayed the oar. The sail had disappeared. She smiled. She rowed towards the island. A strong wind rose up and blew her there in no time.

Catherine moored the boat. She carried the hamper up the path to the spot where picnics were always held. Flat stones remained an indicator of previous picnics enjoyed by other generations. Tara and Catherine had often picnicked there before. She remembered roasting potatoes and chestnuts. Once, a pigeon's egg had exploded in the flames of a bonfire. It was the perfect place for a picnic. Willow trees grew down to the shore of the lake. Behind was a clearing where one could lie in the sun. Through the trees, from the picnic site, the lake was visible and the orchards of Malabay beyond.

Catherine prepared the picnic with great care. She laid it out with pleasure, absorbed entirely with what she was doing. She spread a white cloth under the shadows of the willow tree. She had stolen a bottle of white Montrachet from Pake's cellar. She put it to cool in the gully. She laid the cloth with plates of blue and white china, silver cutlery and cut glasses. She stood back. She criticized. She re-arranged a fork.

She had bribed Mick-the-Post to fetch up crayfish to the boatshed. She had scolded Nan to make a cherry tart. She would make the mayonnaise. Later, they would boil water over the fire and have coffee. After that, she would give Tara his surprise.

She set about collecting dry sticks, wood and tinder to light the fire. There was a heap of old brushwood lying about under the trees. It kindled immediately. Thin vermilion flames flickered between the twigs. A line of blue-grey smoke signalled to the sky. There was no wind.

Catherine looked across the lake. She could not see the *Fionnuala*. There was no hurry. She knew that Tara would not keep her waiting. He was never late for her.

She sat on a stump underneath the willow tree and began to make the mayonnaise. She cracked the egg against the rim of the basin and threw away the white into the bushes. The yolk dropped into the bowl. It was a splendid yellow. She stirred it gently. She added a little mustard, salt and pepper. She dripped olive oil down the back of a wooden spoon. The mayonnaise began to take and to turn into a thick unguent. She added lemon. She tasted it. It was delicious. She licked the spoon. A bird sang. She turned her head. The mayonnaise had curdled.

He was late. She looked at her watch. He was late.

She stood up and walked down the gully to the strand where the waters of the lake lapped the small white pebbles and the grey sand. She looked out across the lake. There was no sign of the *Fionnuala*. There was nothing to be seen on the lake at all. It was empty. The waves lapped insistent on the shore. The strong wind, which had risen so suddenly, had died away completely. There was not a breath. She had never known such stillness on the lake at Malabay. She did not like it. She did not like it at all.

Even as she stood by the edge of the lake the sky, which had been so perfectly blue, darkened. The wind whipped up. She felt it gather. She shivered. The surface of the lake broke and the waves which had been so gentle now beat against the stones.

Something moved. She saw something move on the jetty by the boathouse on the opposite shore of the lake. From such a distance, it was difficult to make out what it was. It jerked up and down, gesticulating. It was a figure. A puppet. It was manic. It was mad. She knew it was not Tara. She would have recognised Tara from no matter where. Something was wrong. She did not understand. She threw up into the lake.

From the tail of her eye, she caught sight of the *Fionnuala*. It flew across the lake like a comet. The speed was dreadful. The *Fionnuala* was heading straight into the wind. Catherine vomited again. Then she jerked up her neck. She saw the trimaran broach. She saw the boom swing out. She saw Tara stagger at the helm. The boom hit him on the nape of the neck. He fell. The *Fionnuala* pivoted. Then she capsized.

The rowing boat was heavy. It leaked. Catherine pushed it out across the strand. The bottom grated against the stones. She was clumsy. She was slow. The oars would not fit. The rowlocks seared. She strained at the oars. Very slowly, the boat pulled away from the island. She seemed to be making no headway. The sweat poured down her back. Her arms ached. The wind was against her. Once, she looked over her shoulder and saw the three overturned hulls.

Catherine was icy cold and soaked in sweat by the time she reached the trimaran. She had a terrible pain in her solar plexus. She feathered the oars, then shipped them. She reached out with one hand to gain a purchase on one of the overturned hulls. There was no sight of Tara. She bent over the gunwale of the rowing boat. Through the refracted light beneath the surface of the water, she could see the distortion of the broken mast. The blue and white sails were furled around it. They trailed in a slow dance, wreathing in the water and shrouding the boom. She peered into the water.

"Tara!"

She called into the water.

"Tara!"

There was no sound.

She kicked off her shoes. She could not undress. She ripped the placket of her skirt. It took too long. She tore at her clothes. It was hopeless.

She dived.

The sails sagged. They were intolerably heavy, weighed down by water. The light was dim. The mast was stuck fast into the mud.

Catherine swam in between the sails, deeper and deeper down. At the bottom of the lake, half hidden by the sail and pinioned by the boom, she found Tara. He did not move. He lay with open eyes; only his hair stirred in the water.

She forced her way down to him. She tried to take him in her arms. He fell away. She knew that he was dead. She had to come up for air.

Mick-the-Post had run from the jetty when he saw the trimaran capsize. He took out his own dinghy. He rowed as he had not rowed for years. He cursed when he saw Catherine dive. When he reached the trimaran, he found her drooped over the hulls. She had been down several more times to try to free Tara. She was utterly spent. He lifted her into the dinghy. She was light as a cobweb. He wrapped his jersey round her. She crouched motionless where he had put her. She was bloodless, white and cold. She stared in front of her with eyes that did not see.

Mick-the-Post knew that there was no hope. But he took off his boots and went down. When he surfaced, he wasted no time. He rowed hell-for-leather back to Malabay. They were both drenched and frozen. They did not speak. He half carried Catherine up the steps of the jetty. She could scarcely walk. They took the short cut over the rough pasture and through the orchard up to the house. They stumbled over the tussocks. They did not notice their naked feet were cut and grazed as they staggered up the hill.

By the time they reached the house, Catherine was barely conscious. She never remembered what happened for several days after that.

On his return to England from Rome, Gerald went to spend a long weekend in the country with his friends the Mallets. He was pleased that his book was finished. His agent was ecstatic. It had been a difficult book to write, his most ambitious so far. It was pleasant to enjoy the relative dullness, comfort and amiableness of the Mallets' household.

He came down to breakfast late. He was not in the best of spirits. He was annoyed by a mild hangover from drinking too much whisky with Bob the night before and sitting up too late. The conversation had not been worth it.

Bob and Antonia Mallet sat in the kitchen of their converted farmhouse. They had already finished their breakfast. They were only waiting for Gerald to appear. Their daughter Swizzle, a child of thirteen, scraped back her chair when he came into the room. Gerald winced at the noise.

"I'm going to practise," she said.

"Not the piano," said Bob.

"No fear. Gymkhana's tomorrow. I'm going to practise an imaginary egg-and-spoon. I bet Iris and Arthur and Ella May that I'd bag all the prizes. We've got heavy stakes in this gymkhana. I can't afford to lose."

"Ella May's far too young to gamble," said Antonia.

"That's what you think," said Swizzle. "She's precocious."

"You haven't joined the pony club in my absence, have you?" said Gerald.

Swizzle laughed at him.

"Don't be daft," she said. "I wouldn't be seen dead in one. This is a private job."

She slammed the door behind her.

Gerald sat down. He poured himself some coffee.

"Toast?" asked Antonia. "It's cold. I'll make some more."

She walked over to the Aga.

Bob got up.

"I'm going down to the five-acre," he said. "See you later. Want the paper? Come and join me after you've finished breakfast. Might as well go over to the White Hart and have a hair of the dog. It's a lovely day. Do you good to get out."

"Fine. Antonia, your coffee is as good as ever."

Bob left the room.

Gerald watched Antonia. She stood with her back to him, making toast. He picked up the paper. He did not follow the English press very closely. He did not spend enough time in England to read it regularly. And when he did, he disliked what he considered to be its insularity, its chauvinism. He read half the leader, a book review which determined him not to buy the book, and turned the paper over.

He buttered his toast and spread it thick with Antonia's home-made jam.

She sat beside him. She poured herself another cup of coffee. She laughed.

"Good Lord!" she said. "Bloody fortune for a villa for eight in the Med. Can you imagine? Double beds in broom cupboards, the heat, too much sour wine. Sounds hell."

Gerald did not reply. He took the paper away from Antonia. He had seen the announcement of Tara's death. An image of Tara laughing over a non-sequitur flashed through his mind. He put the paper down.

"What's the matter?" said Antonia. "You look dreadful."

"Bad news, I'm afraid."

He pushed the paper into Antonia's hands.

"Did you know him? I'd always heard."

"Yes. I'll have to go, I'm afraid."

"A very special person, people said. Bob said. Were you very close?"

Gerald did not reply.

She put an arm round him in a clumsy attempt to embrace him.

"I'm so sorry. That's such a silly thing to say, I know. The funeral's not till Friday, it says," she said. "Won't you stay? I don't know what to do. Gerald, you look completely done in. Let me give you some whisky. Medicinal."

He tried to collect himself.

"Sweet of you. Can I phone?"

"Of course. You know where it is. In the hall, unless you'd prefer to use the one in our bedroom."

He carried the whisky with him into the hall.

He telephoned Poppy.

Her voice had a cracked pitch.

"Will you be going?" she asked. "It's this terrible business of funerals. They'll be burying, not incinerating. There's no crematorium in Ballingstown. In any case, I gather Catherine goes in for the church and such rubbish."

"I think I will, Poppy."

Gerald stared at a hunting print, badly hung, on the Mallets' wall.

"Can I take you?" he said. "I wondered. Partly why I rang. But I want to see you."

"Perhaps somebody should go. Does it matter? I suppose you'll do just as well as anyone. Much better than most. I shan't go. I'm allergic to such things. Even Tara, damn him. Besides, it'd just be plain indecent. I got excommunicated in my heyday."

"You can't mean that, Poppy."

"I don't know what I mean."

"I'm coming up to town straight away, Poppy."

"Take me out to lunch," she said. "I'm all at sea."

"I'll meet you at the hotel at one, if you're really sure you feel like going out."

"Dead sure. Where are you?"

"With the Mallets."

"What on earth possessed you?"

"They're soothing."

"They're dull. I call them ditchwater. And at a time like this. Don't stand me up."

"Have I ever?"

Poppy hung up.

Antonia had stacked the washing-up machine with the dirty breakfast things. The machine made a droning noise which got on Gerald's nerves. He had to raise his voice to make himself heard above the sound. He was exasperated. He seized Antonia by the wrist.

"Come out," he said. "Out into the garden. We can't talk here."

Antonia looked surprised. She blushed. She offered him her bland and kindly face. Gerald realised that she had misunderstood him. She wanted to be kissed. He let go of her wrist.

He led the way into the trim and unsurprising garden. He lit a cigarette, then turned with an apology and offered her one. She accepted and smiled at him with a look of complicity which made him want to knock her on the head. He lit the cigarette for her.

"I must leave at once," he said. "I must go and see Tara's aunt."

"But you'll come back after, won't you?"

"I can't. It's one of those things, you know."

"Life," said Antonia.

She looked away.

"I'm sorry," she said. "I didn't mean . . ."

She wore a yellow dress sprigged with daisies.

"Been awfully nice," said Gerald. "I would have."

He kissed her on the lips and despised them both.

"So you see," he said.

"Of course. But you'll let me know? I mean, keep in touch, so to speak?"

"You'll tell Bob?"

"I'll tell him why you've had to go."

"Thanks," said Gerald.

He threw his cigarette into Antonia's herbaceous border.

"Yes," he said. "I'll keep in touch, so to speak."

Gerald's car was luxurious. It was an even greater luxury for him to be alone. He slowed down to turn out of the Mallets' drive. He opened the roof and felt the wind stream through his hair. The minor road he took towards the motorway was full of bends. It passed through fields and woods. The countryside was undulating, gentle, very English. He had not gone far when he saw Swizzle in a small field, riding her fat pony bareback. She held the reins in one hand, the other she held out, balancing an imaginary egg-and-spoon. He stopped.

Swizzle dropped out of the race. She cantered over towards him.

He leaned out of the window.

"You're disqualified," he said.

She let her pony graze.

"You're all packed," she said.

It was an accusation.

"You're leaving, aren't you? Were you sneaking off?"

"No. Something cropped up. Unexpected. I have to go."

"The others will be furious. Ella May wanted you to umpire. But Arthur said you ought to be the prize giver. Said you'd give much the best prizes."

"Did he, now?"

"Iris said you didn't know one end of a horse from another. But Arthur said that didn't matter. He said the prizes mattered."

"What did you say?"

"I said it all depended on who was the winner."

"You should have warned me. But it makes no difference. I have to go."

"What's the point of grown-ups unless they come in handy? Did you have a row? Your voice has all changed."

"It's another world," said Gerald. "Here, this is the first prize."

He handed her a pound.

"And this is the booby."

He gave her a ten shilling note.

"And half-a-crown each for the piggies in the middle. Mind you don't cheat."

"Golly! Thanks. Why more for the booby than for the pigs?"

"Pointless being in the middle. You're either tops or so bottom it's below sea level. The middle is just a lot of slime."

"Yuck!"

"Exactly."

He turned on the ignition.

"Good luck!" he said.

Swizzle pocketed the money and grinned at him.

"Watch me jump that log," she said.

Gerald waited and watched her pick up the reins and set her fat pony to the jump. She gave the beast a couple of savage kicks. It picked up speed and grudgingly cleared the log at the far end of the field. In the distance, Swizzle looked like an obstinate elf. She looked back at him, glinting with triumph. Gerald waved. He drove on.

Poppy had already arrived at the hotel. She was sitting on a green brocade chair in the corner of the lobby. She did not see him come in. She was dwarfed by the chair she sat in. She sat shrunk, crouched in misery. She toyed idly with a glass of champagne. Gerald was shocked by her appearance. She seemed to be much older. Her face was creased with undisguised pain and unhappiness.

He walked up to her. He bent over her and kissed her. She looked at him. Neither could bear to see the other's expression.

He pulled up a chair close to her. He took her hand and held it. She let it rest in his. It was small, shrivelled, limp. Her finger nails were painted scarlet.

Gerald signalled for a waiter. The head waiter walked over. His deportment was impeccable, but Gerald could see that he already knew of Tara's death and, under the professional mask he wore, that he was shattered.

"Please accept my sympathies," he said in an undertone to Gerald. "Shocking. Very shocking. He'll be greatly missed."

Gerald nodded. They said nothing more. They knew it was not the time. They understood each other very well.

"We might as well have more champagne," he said. "And your quietest table."

"I've already seen to it, sir," said the head waiter.

Poppy could not decide what to eat. Gerald ordered gulls' eggs and smoked salmon for them both. He watched Poppy bang the shell of her egg against the rim of her plate. She was incapable of peeling it. He took it from her and peeled it for her. She stared at it, translucent and bald. She rolled it on her plate and made no attempt to eat it.

"Tell me," said Gerald. "Tell me how it happened."

"It's inconceivable. I don't know the faintest thing about boats. An accident. They will happen. They run in that family."

"But he was such a good sailor, I always thought."

"That's what they said about Nellie and Terence. Don't ask me."

Poppy's voice was odd. It still had the same shrill pitch which Gerald had noticed on the telephone.

"I can't eat this egg," she said.

"No. Stupid of me. How about some scrambled ones with the smoked salmon?"

"I'm not very hungry."

"But you ought to eat something. So should I."

They sipped the champagne. The head waiter removed the gulls' eggs and returned with scrambled eggs in a silver dish.

"And Catherine? I suppose you've been in touch with Pake?" Gerald said.

"He says very little. After all, there's nothing to be said. I mean, what's the point?"

"But he said nothing about her?"

"Who? Oh, Catherine. God knows. She's only a child."

"I know."

Poppy poked at her scrambled eggs.

"At least she's quite well off, I gathered," Gerald said. "Did Tara leave a will?"

"Yes. Oh, yes. Tara left a will. I witnessed it. He wanted my advice."

"Sensible."

"Of course, he knew my passion for codicils. It's the codicils that fascinate me."

"So I suppose it's full of them?"

"Codicils?" said Poppy. "No. None at all. I was quite peeved about it. He wouldn't put in even one. Took all the zest out of it. But what sticks in my gullet is all this religious hocus pocus. Bloody priests! I tried to get Tara to do the same as me. But he wouldn't. Said it would only upset Catherine."

Gerald refilled their glasses.

"You see, I did the only sensible thing. Left my body to the Nation," Poppy said.

"The Nation?"

He drank some champagne.

"Yes, the Nation. They can do what they like with it. It's all the same to me. I'd rather be of some use than none at all. Think of my eyeballs and kidneys. Any old organ. I'm told they whip them out and give them to some deprived person. I don't dislike the idea of bits of me continuing to function after I'm dead. And it sort of sabotages God a bit. Makes Heaven more democratic."

"I thought you didn't go in for all that."

"I don't. I wouldn't be seen dead with J.C."

"You're too vehement to be convincing, dearest Poppy."

"That's what Tara said."

The head waiter took their plates away.

"No; it's the bits of bodies that interest me," said Poppy. "Like the best murder cases. I follow the law reports, you know, most carefully. They put Agatha Christie in the shade. Of course, there'll never be anything like the Bodkin Adams case again. Things are not at all what they used to be."

The head waiter hovered tactfully.

"I couldn't eat another thing," said Poppy.

She had not eaten anything at all.

"I don't know what we're doing here, Gerald. I must have been mad to have thought of it."

Gerald asked for the bill.

"It's the shock," he said. "It's only natural."

"I dare say. But I'm furious. I'm absolutely furious with Tara. How dare he go and die before me? Now I'm all alone. I haven't even got anybody to leave anything to any more."

"I thought you'd left things helter-skelter, you told me once, to all sorts of people."

"Yes. I've labelled everything. That's to beat the death duties. Everything is ticketed. Even the china."

"The china? Oh, why not the china? You have some beautiful china."

"I know. When I can't sleep I lie in bed dreaming up new codicils. Then, in the morning, I re-label all the cups and saucers. My solicitor is most understanding. Tara always used to turn over his soup plate to see if it still belonged to him."

Poppy's face crumpled.

"I think I've lost my wits, Gerald. Every time someone I love dies, part of me dies too. And I loved Tara. Oh, Gerald! I loved him more than anyone."

"I'm going to take you home," he said.

When they got to her flat, he telephoned her doctor. The doctor gave her a sedative and his presence had a calming effect on her. Gerald had been planning to spend the night at the Mallets' flat. But he slept on the sofa in Poppy's drawingroom and did not leave her until after lunch the next day.

★

Since Tara's death, Catherine refused to leave her bedroom. Not her old bedroom, but the one which had once been her mother's and which she had shared with Tara. The doctor from Ballingstown was worried. She had developed a mild fever. Her blood pressure was very low. Nan brought her meals upstairs on a tray. Catherine seldom touched them. She did nothing. She lay in bed and stared at the ceiling. She dragged herself from the bed only to go to the lavatory and to wash. She washed herself far more than was necessary. She took several baths a day and then returned to the bed, limp and exhausted. For a few days the sun came out and flooded in through the windows. Then she drew the curtains and lay in the dark. Several times, Pake came into the room. He sat on the end of her bed. He could find nothing to say. She refused to speak to him. She turned her back and hid in the bedclothes.

On the morning of Tara's funeral, she woke early. It was pouring with rain. She ran a bath and lay in it, staring at her body with dislike. The bathwater grew cold. She dipped her head back and immersed it in the water. Then, very slowly, she climbed out of the deep copper bath. She stood on the cork mat. She bent her head forwards and plaited her long dark hair into a single thick braid. She did not dry herself. She walked to the washbasin. Water dripped from her body on to the floor. She took a pair of scissors. She grasped her wet plait and cut it clean off.

Much later, Nan found Catherine's hair lying on the bathroom floor. She folded it in tissue paper and put it away in a drawer. Catherine never asked what had been done with it.

Gerald arrived at Ballingstown by the slow train. There was no taxi at the station. He did not know that the only taxi at Ballingstown doubled as a hearse. He walked from the station to the church. He walked slowly. The church was built on a small flat hillock overlooking the straggling town. The churchyard was surrounded by common land where the grey-green grass was cropped short by grazing sheep. He was struck by the difference between the countryside he had left so recently where he had been staying with the Mallets and this place. It was mainly, he thought at first, the quality of the light. Here the light was dim, diffused. It was not only because of the rain. He had a sense of timelessness. He trod through the mud up the path that led to the church. He noticed the odd hummocks of land, the moors beyond, the lake. The unfamiliar landscape, the wildness of its aspect, made it seem more foreign than the distance he had travelled warranted. He felt a complete stranger. He thought of Tara. The strangeness of the place made him aware only too acutely of how much Tara had hidden from him, how much he would never know, how much he had not known. For he equated this path, those moors, that lake with the side of Tara which he had never discovered.

By the time Gerald reached the church, the funeral service was over. He walked into the churchyard and stood to one side, in the shade of an old yew tree. He watched the small procession leave the church and file slowly in the wake of the coffin. The coffin was simple, black and anonymous. It seemed absurdly small. It had been covered with weeds and wild flowers; mallow, daisies and yew. He could scarcely believe that Tara's body lay inside. For a moment, he turned away.

The procession was led by a young girl followed closely by an elderly man who shuffled with a walking stick. The man was dressed in old tweeds. Gerald supposed him to be Pake. The girl he knew to be Catherine.

She was very thin and extremely pale. She wore an old schoolgirl's navy blue mackintosh. The mackintosh made her look even younger than she was. She had a black cotton scarf wrapped loosely round her head.

"She looks scarcely older than Swizzle!"

He watched Catherine follow the coffin to the grave. The wind caught at her scarf and blew it back to reveal her head of unevenly cropped dark hair, the ends jagged, showing the nape of her neck curiously white, vulnerable, horribly exposed. He understood, in a flash of intuition, that she had cut off her hair in a demonstration of utter desperation. He stood appalled.

He leaned against the tree. He watched the thin line of mourners follow Catherine and Pake to where the coffin had been lowered into the grave. An old priest, his black vestments flapping in the wind, spoke. His words were blown away. Gerald saw Catherine stoop and pick a handful of grass which she threw into the grave. She turned. For the first time, he saw her face.

He was astonished by her beauty. It was as shocking as Tara's had been. But what shocked him more was the frozen blankness, the deadness of her expression. Her face recalled Tara's. He tried to banish the memory. But he could not help remembering Tara's liveliness, his gaiety. He could imagine this pale unhappy girl smiling, laughing, her sad green eyes dancing with mischief and fun. But her movements, her gestures, the way she walked made her seem as though she was not there.

"Every time someone I love dies, part of me dies too."

Catherine looked more dead than alive. A ghost. Gerald was revolted. He was revolted that this beautiful child should have been numbed, nipped in the bud. It horrified him. It was against Nature. He understood why Poppy had cursed Tara for dying. But she had not thought of Catherine at all. She had thought only of herself.

The other mourners, dressed in black, their Sunday best, followed Catherine and Pake at some distance. Gerald remained where he was by the yew tree. As she passed within a couple of feet of him, Catherine lifted her eyes and looked at him directly. She stopped. She made a strange gesture, half extending her hand towards him. For one moment, her face was illuminated by the most beautiful smile he had ever seen. Then she looked down and walked slowly on. He was not sure that she had seen him at all.

He stared after her. He wanted to stop her. He wanted to touch her. He wanted to try to comfort her. He wanted to tell her that he had loved Tara too. He wanted to evoke some response. But he could not. He stood where he was, paralysed. He could not intrude on such a private, wild and desperate misery. There was nothing that he could do.

He watched her climb into a very old Daimler. He saw Pake get into the driver's seat. A stout woman of indeterminate age, dressed in black, and a peculiar-looking skinny little man got in the back. The car jerked off and drove away down the hill in the direction of Malabay.

Gerald waited until the other mourners had left the churchyard. He walked between the grey tombstones to Tara's grave. Two old and decrepit gravediggers were heaping up the soil with spades into the grave. They looked up as Gerald approached. One of them leaned on his spade.

"A terrible business," said the gravedigger.

"Yes," said Gerald. "It is a terrible business."

The old man looked him in the eye.

They both knew that there was nothing more to be said.

Gerald stooped, as he had seen Catherine do. He picked up a fallen leaf from the grass. He dropped it on to the half-covered mound. Then he walked away. The rain had not stopped. He was soaked by the time he got back to Ballingstown.

Gerald walked up the main street of the town. It was deserted. The modest houses, none of them more than two-storied, had their blinds drawn down. He was unnerved by the benighted look of the street. There were only a few shops, and they were shut. He hated the noise his feet made on the empty road. He knew that he was being watched from behind the blinds. There were more pubs than shops. Only one, The White Strand, advertised accommodation. No trains left from the station until the next day. He was forced to spend the night. He went into The White Strand.

It was dark inside. There was a reek of cabbage and furniture polish. The place was horrid. At the end of the narrow hall was a desk with nothing on it except for a telephone. No one was to be seen. From the other side of a closed door he heard the sound of men's voices. He opened the door and went into the Saloon.

Several men stood at the bar. A few sat at tables. They were all dressed in black. As Gerald entered, they fell silent. They stared at him. He went up to the bar. They all went on watching him. None of them said anything. Gerald tried to put a bold face on it.

He asked the barman for a whiskey.

The barman poured the whiskey into a tumbler. Gerald added water from a jug on the counter.

"I'm hungry," he said.

The barman took the money.

"I suppose there's no chance of my getting any dinner? I thought I could smell something cooking in the hall."

The barman hesitated.

A titter of amusement went round the pub.

"If it's dinner you're wanting, that's only for guests."

"I'd be more than willing," he said, "to spend the night. I noticed you advertise rooms."

A man at the far end of the bar snorted.

Gerald looked about him. He recognised one of the gravediggers.

"It's a great reputation she has," the gravedigger said. "The lady of The White Strand. That is to say, if you have a taste for kale."

The gravedigger muttered something to his neighbour. Gerald did not catch what was said. But he was aware that some piece of intelligence about himself was being passed around the pub like a game of Chinese whispers.

"It spells nothing but trouble," said the gravedigger's neighbour. "Nothing but trouble at all."

"I don't mind kale," said Gerald to the gravedigger.

Someone laughed. The atmosphere relaxed. Conversation was taken up again.

Gerald carried his glass of whiskey over to an empty table. He sat down. He was very tired. His journey had been long, difficult and uncomfortable. He was much more upset by Tara's funeral than he had expected. He had expected the tragedy to have been masked by the rites. He had been wrong. He had seen something else. He thought of Poppy. He reflected on what he had seen of that shambling old man, Pake. He tried not to think of Tara. He could not help thinking of Catherine. He lit a cigarette. He asked for another whiskey.

His supper was brought to him at the table in the bar room. It did not look very appetising. It was a plate of boiled cabbage, boiled potatoes and boiled mutton.

He did not notice what it tasted of. It was hot. He was hungry. That was all. He found himself asking for a bottle of stout. He did not know why. He finished his dinner. He lit another cigarette and drank the rest of the stout.

He was very much struck by the faces of the men in the bar. Their expressions betrayed next to nothing. Close. Close, he thought, thin, gaunt, their cheeks lined, their eyes narrow, guarded. Yet they shared a common dignity, almost, he thought, a nobility. From time to time he caught a sudden gleam of life, curiosity, a wink, a joke he did not understand. And these were the men whom Tara had known since childhood, of whom he had never spoken. He began to realise more and more of how much he had never known about Tara. He gulped down his stout.

The barman directed him to his room.

He spent a wretched night. The mattress was lumpy. The bed-clothes were unaired. He woke several times from unpleasant and disturbing dreams. As soon as he heard the sounds of people moving about in the inn, he dressed and went downstairs. There was no sign of the barman. He made his way into what turned out to be the kitchen.

It was a poky room, ill-lit, badly equipped and dirty. A small woman, so small that she was practically a dwarf, stirred a pan of porridge on the stove. She looked over her shoulder at him. She had a nasty squint, a sympathetic smile.

"Is it breakfast you'll be after?"

He smiled.

"You might as well have it in here," she said.

"Yes. I'd much rather."

"You can sit down there," she said.

She pointed to a couple of chairs drawn up to the kitchen table. The table was covered in American cloth patterned with faded carrots and cherries in green squares. The cloth was greasy.

He sat down. She put a bowl of porridge in front of him and poured out a mug of tea. The porridge was surprisingly good.

"I'd like to use the telephone," said Gerald, "before I leave."

"Unless it's foreign parts you want to ring," she said. "For the operator as she calls herself won't be in till after she's finished feeding her chickens. And that won't be till after the end of the morning, with all the fowls she has."

"It's only a local call," he said.

"You'll find the instrument in the passage."

He dialled Malabay. He waited for a long time before there was any answer.

Pake answered.

Gerald identified himself.

Pake refused to recognise the identification.

"I know," said Gerald. "I know it's a bad time. That's why I'm here. I'd like to see you. I'd like to see you very much. Otherwise, I wouldn't have come. I wondered, is it possible? I could come over before the train?"

There was a very long pause at the other end.

"There is a taxi," Pake said finally, "at the other end. Your end. You'll find it from the sweetshop on the corner of the high street. Tell the man to wait. Our meeting won't take long. I hope you understand."

He hung up.

The driver never said a word. Gerald sat in the front because he wanted to have the best view possible of Malabay and its demesne. He was grateful for the driver's silence. Suddenly, he felt sick. There was a ghastly smell of rotten flowers: dead flowers and Jeyes' fluid. He wound down the window. He turned back and caught sight of petals of dead wild flowers lying in the boot. He knew that the taxi had been Tara's hearse.

"Stop! I'll walk."

"It goes."

"You'll wait?"

"I'll stop."

He could not help being impressed by the façade of Malabay. The house was far larger than he had imagined. It had an odd mixture of grandeur combined with a ramshackle kind of simplicity. There was no denying that it was gracious. It was dilapidated, certainly, but unpretentious. He fell in love at once with its grey stone walls, the French windows, the avenue, the view, the lake.

The driver overtook him and drew up in the courtyard. The driver looked away. Gerald crossed the sweep of grey flagstones. He went to the front door and knocked. As soon as he had done so, he realised his mistake. Clearly, the front door was never used. The knocker was mildewed, the step overgrown with moss and mould. It was too late for him to beat a retreat. He heard the clank of a bolt drawn open, of a key being turned on the other side of the lock.

The door creaked. Pake swore. The door opened.

He went inside. He stood in a hall floored with grey flagstones, panelled walls, an elm staircase. Portraits on the walls, gumboots in a corner. And a pervasive smell of wood fires, apples, toast and soap. Gerald liked it.

Pake looked as though he had not slept. He wore the same tweeds. They shook hands.

"I didn't know about the door. Foolish of me."

"Too late. Too late for that. Too late for anything. Follow me."

Pake turned his back on Gerald. But Gerald had already taken in a strong impression. An impression of an unhappy man, a fine man.

He tripped over a scraper.

"Frightfully sorry," he said. "I didn't see it."

"The scraper? It's got no business in the hall. God knows, God knows what's been going on. I haven't kept up."

"No, of course not."

"But why is the scraper inside the hall? Damn it! The scraper . . ."

Gerald followed Pake down the length of a dusty passage. Pake kicked open the door of the gun room.

The gun room was dark. The shutters had not been unbarred. Gerald stood by the door in the gloom and watched Pake wrestling with the bolts. He went forward to help him. Pake grunted, but did not try to stop Gerald.

Pake sat behind a large desk and indicated a leather armchair beside the fireplace for Gerald. The fire was not lit. He sat down. The room was irrefutably masculine. It smelt of tobacco, linseed and leather. There were guns in racks and several fishing rods in a tall rush basket. Gerald noticed that the desk was littered with a jumble of twigs and earth. An old-fashioned microscope stood on one corner of the desk. Then he realised that this jumble was, in fact, arranged very methodically. He did not understand its significance.

He looked at Pake, waiting for him to speak. There was no denying that he looked a distinguished man, but there was something so reserved in his bearing that Gerald became more and more uneasy. Pake picked up a magnifying glass from the desk. He peered through it at the arrangements of bark and twigs. Then he looked at Gerald. His eyes were remarkably like his niece's. There was an expression in them that made Gerald look away at the unlit fire.

"I've seen Poppy," said Gerald.

"Poppy! But she's not here."

"No."

"And I cannot think why you are here. At a time like this."

"It's because it's a time like this that I am here," said Gerald. "I came, I suppose, to see if I could be of any help. To offer my sympathies."

"I find," said Pake, "that since Tara drowned, I have become increasingly less sympathetic. Towards him. Towards the world. It's the effects, perhaps, more than the loss. I cannot bear to see what it has done to Catherine. But I see very little of her now. She keeps herself to herself and doesn't want to see or be seen. I don't know what the best thing is to do. I'm not sure that I believe in the best any longer. You are too young to understand that."

Gerald crossed his legs.

"But you must make her do something," he said. "Something. Anything. Why don't you take her away?"

"Where to?"

"Does it matter where?"

"If it doesn't matter where, then why go anywhere? I never go anywhere."

Pake stood up.

"It's a pity," he said. "It's a pity about St Elmo. Did you know that he was the patron saint of navigators?"

Gerald stared at him.

"But this," said Pake, holding up a twig of heather, "is clearly a case of bioluminescence. It is why dead bodies glow. Dead fish, dead beetles, dead bodies. In the end, we are reduced to nothing but bacteria. And then, perhaps, we glow."

He smiled.

"Where is Catherine?" Gerald asked.

"I'm on the verge of an important discovery."

"I suppose I could see Catherine? I was a great friend of Tara's, you know."

"Catherine is under mild sedation. The doctor has been. He had to come in any case, for the inquest."

"What was the verdict?"

"Accident. Conditions were deceptive."

"Deceptive?"

"Yes. Conditions here at Malabay are frequently deceptive."

"Do you mind if I smoke?"

"Not at all, not at all."

Gerald lit a cigarette. Pake lit a cheroot. Gerald noticed it was the same brand that Poppy smoked.

"Catherine ought to get up."

"That's one point of view. There's time for you to have a drink before you leave for the station. Do you care for whiskey?"

"Yes. I'd like some very much."

Pake walked over to a cupboard. He fumbled for glasses and brought out a fine pair of old rummers. He put a half empty bottle of excellent malt whiskey on the table. He filled Gerald's glass to the brim. Gerald noticed that Pake had liver spots on his hand and that his hand shook. But the whiskey did not spill. Gerald accepted the drink.

Pake drank. Then he crossed over to the window. He stood with his back to Gerald. He appeared to be inspecting the garden.

Gerald felt flat up against an impenetrable wall of stone.

"It's time for me to leave," he said.

He swallowed some of his drink.

"Yes," said Pake. "Yes. It is time."

He did not turn from the window.

Gerald knew that he would not turn. He saw a spasm across the old man's shoulders.

Gerald walked out of the house.

He left the front door open.

It was night. Catherine lay in the large bed of her mother's old room. Her sleep was heavy, induced by the drugs the doctor had prescribed for her. She dreamed.

She was in a foreign land, far away in the frozen tundras of the north. A wide river with a strong current, bordered by pines and maples, broadened out into the mouth of an estuary. She stood in the snow in the long grasses which grew on the dunes by the estuary. She watched the waves break against the dunes. The sky was white. It was very cold. Thick flakes of snow began to fall.

Coming down the river bank towards the sea, she saw two men in a small cart pulled by an old white horse. The men had guns and three black retriever dogs. When they reached the dunes, they saw her and stopped. The tracks which they left were clear-cut in the snow.

"Come with us," they said. "Come with us, or you'll freeze to death."

She was reluctant. They insisted. The men got out of the cart and walked towards a low hut woven out of the reeds which grew in the dunes. It was so well camouflaged that Catherine had not noticed it before. She went inside it with them and the dogs followed.

The hut was warm. Catherine was grateful. The wind outside was very cold.

The men wore thick jackets lined with fur. They left Catherine in the hut and busied themselves outside. From the cart, they lifted out many white clay birds and put them in a great cluster on the shore. These clay birds were large and very beautiful. Some of them had eyes and feathers painted on them. They looked strange on the sand. Then the men returned to the hut. They began to load their guns.

They were kindly men. She could not understand everything they said, but she liked them. They joked between themselves and spoke to her in a friendly way. She patted the dogs and they wagged their tails. Occasionally, the men offered Catherine a nip of strong spirits from a hip flask. To keep out the cold, they said.

Catherine looked out at the white sky and the grey waves breaking on the shore. The sky was filled with large white birds flying in a wide formation. Catherine marvelled at their beauty.

The men began to emit strange sounds, queer honks imitating the cries of birds. The birds were attracted by the noise and by the sight of the clay birds sitting on the sand. They flew low over the hut where Catherine and the men were camouflaged by the reeds.

The men levelled their guns, took aim and began to shoot. They shot again and again and each time they fired, another bird fell dead on the snow. The noise of the shooting and of the live birds honking cries of mad distress was deafening.

The dogs left the hut to retrieve the birds. The men grew very excited. The slaughter of the birds had gone to their heads. One of them ran out of the hut and began a crazy dance on the dunes. He waved a rag of white cloth round his gun. The birds were attracted by the waving white rag, for they mistook this for one of themselves. The man fired again and again and the birds fell down. When the men stopped shooting, the remaining birds tried to regroup themselves into their old formation. But the formation was not the same, for they were decimated. The surviving birds flew on in silence.

Catherine left the hut.

She saw quantities of dead birds lying on the snow. White and grey feathers lay scattered round them. Blood had spilled and it had already frozen. The men began to heave up the bodies of the birds which the dogs had retrieved and they flung them into the cart. The dead birds were very heavy and they fell into the cart with a thud. Then the men began to collect up the clay birds.

"Coming with us?" one of the men asked.

Catherine shook her head.

She watched them leave the way they had come.

She stared at the blood and feathers left on the frozen shore.

"They were alive and they were beautiful. Now they are dead."

She saw one dead bird remained, forgotten by the men.

She struggled to wake up. But each time she tried, Catherine was sucked down again by sleep. She stood shivering on the shore of the lake beside the forgotten bird.

Her face was wet with tears.

Her face was covered with kisses.

She felt a hand between her thighs.

"Oh, darling. Now you've come back, I never want to wake again."

She parted her legs.

She felt the weight of a man's body on hers.

She woke up. She was not alone.

Pake was with her in her bed.

She screamed.

He did not stop. He began to babble into her ears.

"Ah, my darling. How I've missed you. Now I've found you again I'll never let you go."

He stank of whiskey.

She fought him. She hit out wildly. She wrenched her body free from his and got out of the bed.

She stood at the foot of the large fourposter. She grasped at the coverlet and flung it round her naked body. In the dim light, she stared at Pake. She watched him writhing on the bed. She took one step towards him and hit him. She hit him very hard indeed.

"Get out! Pake, get out at once!"

He moaned.

She hit him again.

He opened his eyes and saw Catherine.

He covered his face with his hands.

Catherine threw the sheet across his withered body.

"Get out!"

Pake stumbled out of the bed. He clutched the sheet close to him. She watched him shamble from the room.

For some time, she stood leaning against the bedpost.

Then she went into the bathroom.

She was violently sick.

Afterwards, she ran a bath and washed every crevice of her body, every strand of her cropped hair.

She went into her old bedroom and lay curled up in a small ball on the single bed. She saw the light begin to rise. Then she began to cry. She had never cried like that before. It was the first time that she had wept since Tara's death. She did not stop for a long time. When morning came, she left the bed and dressed. She went down the main stairs and left the house. From the stables, she unhooked a bridle from a nail on the wall. She ran, sometimes stumbling through the long grass, down to the paddock where the horses were.

Suibne and Eorann were grazing close together. They looked up at her. Eorann turned away, but Suibne lifted his head and walked up to her. She bridled him and then jumped up on to his back.

It was a beautiful morning. The air was filled with the smell of the sea and the smells of the wild flowers of summer. Catherine, who had not left the house for days, except to go to Tara's funeral, was giddy from the freshness of the air. A soft wind blew from the sea. It caught at the curls of her short hair. She left the paddock and rode Suibne down the avenue.

She had made no plans where she was going to. At the end of the avenue, she hesitated. She was half tempted to go up to the moors, to revisit Beakus's Stump. But Suibne was unwilling to go in that direction. Instead, they rode along the lake, across the flat land that led to the sea. When they came to the long stretch by the shore of the lake, Catherine put Suibne to a fast gallop and they did not stop until they reached the sea.

The tide was out. She raced Suibne across the empty strand. Startled gulls flew overhead, shrieking as they flew. Camomile and thrift grew on the sandbanks which sloped down to the sea. Suibne stopped, spent by the race, when they came to the outcrop of slate and coloured rock which jutted out into the sea.

Catherine bent forward and draped her arms round Suibne's neck. He was hot and his neck was damp with sweat. She buried her face in his mane.

A fine white spray broke against the outcrop of rock. Through the spray, Catherine could see the pale aquamarine waves reflect the colours of the sky and glitter where the sunlight caught the crests. She lifted her head and breathed in deeply. The salt air made her feel clean and rinsed and strong. She inhaled avidly.

Then she turned Suibne round and they rode back. She trotted

Suibne gently through the water in the shallows where the sea met the strand.

Coming back to Malabay, Catherine overtook Mick-the-Post pedalling up the avenue.

He stared at her. He was surprised to see her out and on horseback too. His crooked face broke into a jagged smile.

"I'll take the letters from you," she said.

"Ta," he said. "It's grand to see you out."

"It's a grand day," said Catherine.

Suibne pawed the ground.

Catherine gave him a light flick across the shoulder with the reins.

"No point in speaking, Catherine," said Mick. "There's no words. You know what I mean."

"No," she said. "There's no point."

"Don't forget the letter, now. There's only one today. It'll save some time. I'd best be off."

"What's all the hurry?"

"Least said. But there's more than some confusion down in Ballingstown."

"That's nothing new."

"It's trouble that I'm speaking of."

He handed her a letter addressed to Pake. She stuffed it into her pocket. They smiled. Mick zig-zagged down the avenue at an uncommon speed.

After she had rubbed him down in the stables, Catherine led Suibne back to the paddock. Eorann lifted her head and whinnied when she saw them. Catherine turned Suibne loose. She watched the horses rub their heads together and then flirt off down to the far corner of the paddock.

She leaned over the gate.

"Why, Eorann, I do believe you're in foal!"

She was immensely pleased.

Then she sighed. She felt very tired. She turned and walked slowly back to the house.

They were late, Nan and Catherine, with the dinner. Catherine had gone into the kitchen to help. But she did not concentrate. She got in

Nan's way. Usually, Nan would not have hesitated to mince her words. But she was so pleased to see Catherine downstairs again that she did not even grumble when Catherine burned a sauce. She threw the remains into the chicken bucket and, after one look, the saucepan too. She set about making a fresh sauce herself.

Catherine fiddled about with the spice jars ranged in a rack near the stove.

"It's odd," she said, "how fond I am of nutmeg. And the silver grater. I used to think, when I was a child, that the grater was my special friend."

"You and your fancies. You used to chatter away to the dustpan and brush, come to that. Funny kid, you were."

"They used to tell me the most extraordinary things, the dustpan and brush."

Catherine laughed.

"Nobody could understand their language, except for me. That was half the interest. Such crumbs of scandal."

Nan stirred the sauce.

"If that doesn't go to show," she said.

"Show what?"

There was a knock at the back door.

"Who on earth is that?" said Catherine.

There was another knock.

Neither of them moved.

The door burst open.

Mick-the-Post flew into the kitchen.

"What the hell do you think you're doing?"

He was frantic.

"What the hell do you think you're doing?" said Catherine.

"Bursting in on us before we've even had our dinners!" Nan said.

"You're daft, the pair of you!"

"What's come over the man? Get out of my way," said Nan. "Else it'll be the second sauce this evening thrown for the chickens. And no extra eggs to show for it."

Mick-the-Post jumped up and down on the door mat.

"For the love of God, will you stop gabbling on like a pair of women?"

Catherine began to laugh. She thought the man was drunk.

"But we are a pair of women," she said. "What else do you take us for?"

Nan laughed too. But she kept her eyes on the sauce.

"I'm not joking Catherine. Have your fads and fancies if you like. But I never took you to be crazy entirely. It's not the time to go cuckoo now!"

He banged the kitchen table with his fist. A tin spoon fell on to the stone floor.

Catherine stopped laughing. She turned and stared at him.

"What's bitten you?"

"Can't you read, Catherine? You with your nose stuck in a book half the living day? Did you never read the letter I handed you this morning?"

"Oh, my God!" said Catherine. "I clean forgot. But it wasn't addressed to me. It's still in my pocket."

She fished it out. It had got crumpled.

"Fine bloody postman you'd make! Never should have left it with you. The one and only time I've failed to deliver to the house direct. And you go and forget! Forget!"

He was beside himself.

"Well, I'm sorry," Catherine said. "But why all the song and dance? It's not the end of the world."

"It may not be the end of the world. But I think it may be the end of you!"

"Come off it! What the hell are you on about? You know perfectly well that Pake takes ages to answer his letters. Anyway, how the Devil did you know he hadn't got it? And what's it got to do with you?"

"I'm not saying. But I happen to know, on account of what it's got inside it. Rip it open, Catherine! Rip it open!"

"Have you gone mad, or what? This letter is addressed to Pake. I'll go and get him. Hang on."

"For crying out loud, Catherine, there is no time to be hanging on. Tear open that envelope. It's trouble inside it. Trouble. Now do you understand?"

Catherine understood.

Nan left the sauce unguarded on the stove.

"Better do as he says," said Nan.

The kitchen was suddenly very quiet.

Catherine fumbled with the letter.

"Fools!" muttered Mick. "It's bloody fools you are. And all for the want of reading a letter written as plain as a pikestaff. Fools! Fools! Fools!"

Catherine tore the letter open. She stared at it.

"But what does it say, child? What does it say?" said Nan.

"It's a warning. A serious warning. It's telling us to get the hell out." Her voice shook.

"Get out of what, for the love of God?" said Nan.

"You'd better spell it out for her," said Mick. "Although I don't know what's come over you, Nan, to turn as thick as a bloody doormat. Haven't you ever heard of trouble in these terrible times we live in? Does that mean nothing at all to you, woman?"

Catherine leaned against the back of a kitchen chair. She trembled from head to foot. She could not keep her voice steady.

"'You've always refused to pay,'" she read. "'Now you must pay with the house. There's three of our boys killed on the border. The house goes up tonight.'"

Nan looked at the clock.

"Hell!" said Catherine. "Pake has never paid attention. He's never paid. And now we're all going to have to. And with Malabay! Oh, Malabay!"

Mick picked up the tin spoon and began to rap it against his knuckles.

"What shall we do, Mick? What shall we do?"

He said nothing.

"It isn't a joke, is it?" said Catherine. "It's not one of those pranks of the boys down in Ballingstown? Tell me! You must tell me if it's serious!"

"Do you think I'd be here if it wasn't?"

The passage door opened.

They all looked round.

It was Pake. His hair was wild. It had twigs in it. He clothes were rumpled. His eyes gleamed strangely. Moss and twigs clung to his tweeds. He held a piece of mud in his hand.

"I've found it!" he said. "I've found it! I've found the root of it!"

They stared at him.

Mick looked at Pake. He looked away. He spat on to Nan's spotless floor.

"This is a fine time for that!" he said.

He crossed the room and shook Catherine by the elbow.

"What the Devil's going on?" said Pake.

"It's trouble, Mr Pake," he said. "And if you ask me, it's only yourself to blame. For it's what you haven't done. What you haven't done, Mr Pake, adds up to more than all the mischief you could ever have made, however much you set your mind to it."

Pake groaned.

"Oh, for Christ's sake, don't start groaning, Pake. Mick says it's trouble."

Nan took the saucepan off the stove. It was burnt out.

"The best thing," said Mick to Catherine, "in fact, the only thing, is for you to get yourselves off and lie low in the boathouse. You've got a couple of hours, more or less. Probably less. I wouldn't like to put too fine a point on it. Their sense of timing is not reliable, entirely. But there's no time to dither in."

No one moved.

"It's not you, Catherine. But the way you're not doing anything is exasperating to a degree to drive one mad. I was only now down in The White Strand. And of course it was the only topic of their conversation. For they'd been waiting and watching and couldn't make out why you hadn't stirred yourselves. That was why they sent the letter. For there's nothing against you, Catherine. It's not that. That's not in question."

"What is?"

She leaned against the Aga.

"That's another question. It's one that only Mr Pake can answer, and he doesn't look capable. Oh, but there's an awful lot of gelignite to spare. And they're frightened it might get damp and go to waste, you see?"

"And there's no stopping them?"

"There's no stopping them now. If you'd not forgotten the letter, you'd only have had more time. It's too late. You must hurry. Good Jesus, when I think of those sweet explosives, it beggars all description. And they have to be economical for they can't afford not to get rid of it."

Catherine laughed again.

"Give the girl a drink!" he said. "There's no stopping her, once she gets started. And this time, she won't turn into a horse. I can tell by the look of her. But go easy, Mr Pake, now."

Nan fetched the bottle. She filled a tumbler with whiskey. Catherine drank it straight off.

"At this rate," said Catherine, "we might as well all have a drink. It's sobered me up."

She watched them drinking. Pake and Nan stood together near the stove. Catherine walked up and down the room. Mick perched on the kitchen sink. To her, they seemed dwarfed, shrivelled either by her shock, or by theirs. She could not tell. Nan leaned against the range as though it might save her. Pake stood bolt upright. Even in his madness, there was a remarkable dignity about him. His dark green eyes were very bright. But she knew that he was no longer there.

She took another swig of whiskey.

"You're right," she said to Mick. "We'd better stir our stumps. But you'd best be off. I can't thank you enough for coming. Too dicey for you to stay."

He did not move.

"You'd better take Nan with you."

"I'll not be stirring."

"But you must!"

"No."

"But Nan?"

"Do you think I'll leave you now?" said Nan.

Catherine threw her glass into the sink. She felt rather drunk.

"All right, then. But if you won't leave, then buck up and get some blankets or bread and cheese, or God knows what. Something sensible. And bring it down to the boathouse. We must hurry."

"Those poor chickens," said Nan.

Pake drained his glass.

"Yes, of course," he said. "Of course. Nan, you must do the best you can. But I've got other things. Things of the utmost importance. My whole experiment is at stake. Vital, vital. My slides! My God! My microscope! The whole caboosh! I must collect it all. All the evidence!"

He scurried towards the door. His trousers caught on a nail as he passed.

"Damn it! How many times have I told you, Nan, to hoik out that blasted nail? It rips my clothes to shreds. I won't have a stitch to wear."

A leaf fell out of his hair. He left the room. They heard him muttering wildly as he went along the passage.

Catherine gazed after him. She was very close to tears. Then she went over to Nan. They clasped each other, briefly.

"Blankets you may call handy," said Nan. "But have you given a thought to the valuables? All that French china they say is so precious? Not to mention the silver?"

"Hang the valuables!" Catherine said. "They're of no importance. I don't care. Do as you like. But get yourself down to the boathouse as fast as you can, and see that Pake gets there too."

"No! Not till you tell me where you're off to!"

"Tell her then, Mick! Tell her I'm going to fetch the horses in."

He did not move.

"Of course I'm going to fetch the horses in. They'll be crazy with fear. And I think that Eorann may be in foal. Oh, hang it all!"

"I'll come with you," said Mick. "You'll never manage them both by yourself. Nan, promise that you won't loiter?"

"And Mr Pake?"

"There's no accounting for him," said Mick.

Mick and Catherine went out into the yard together.

There was no time to say anything. Catherine could never have put into words how grateful she was to him. It had flashed through her mind in the kitchen, that if only Tara had been there, they could have seen to the horses together. But Mick-the-Post was as familiar with Suibne and Eorann as she was. With him, there would be no difficulty.

They snatched halters and bridles from the stables.

Mick picked up a couple of empty sacks. He paused.

"Seems a shame to say goodbye to those," he said.

He gathered the saddles and hoisted them over his shoulders.

They ran through the orchard to the paddock. The light was fading fast. The going was not easy. They were both reminded of that other, dreadful time when they had crossed the same ground after Tara's death.

"Poor bugger," said Mick. "God rest his soul. But if we don't get a move on, it's ours He'll have to be resting too."

Catherine took one of the saddles from Mick.

"Evens the load," she said.

They reached the paddock and dumped the saddles over the post. Mick swung open the gate.

"Damn!" said Catherine.

"Hell's bells!" said Mick. "This is a fine night for capering."

The horses were going to be difficult to catch. Catherine thought she had never seen them so beautiful. But there was no time to watch them. Suibne and Eorann were gallivanting in the shadows, executing a wild and cavalier dance.

"Not a squeak," said Mick. "Not a squeak of a weasel out of you."

He stole through the paddock towards the horses, uttering a low whinny as he went.

Catherine watched him. He cast a crooked shadow on the grass. The horses saw him. They kicked up their heels and raced away in separate directions. Catherine followed Mick into the paddock. She fastened the gate behind her. She carried a halter, out of sight, behind her back.

She crept along the side of the low grey stone wall that bounded the paddock. The horses cantered to the far end of the field. She hoped that Mick would be able to corner them there. Mick turned his head. He winked at her. He knew what she was up to.

Catherine took a chance.

She called out in the special tone that she always used for Eorann. Eorann pricked up her ears. She trotted towards Catherine. Catherine stood still and waited until Eorann stopped beside her. She grasped a tuft of her mane and slid the halter over Eorann's nose. Catherine held her very firmly under the chin. For a moment it looked as though Mick would have the same success with Suibne. Then Suibne reared up on his hind legs. He gave out a wild and quite eerie shriek. Then he began to leap and to tear round and round the paddock.

Mick went over to where Catherine stood with Eorann.

Eorann was struggling to be free. She was trying to join Suibne. It was difficult for Catherine to hold her. She leaned all her weight against Eorann's flank.

"Take her, Mick. I can't hold her any more. Take her down to the boathouse."

Mick-the-Post took hold of the halter.

"You'll never catch him," he said. "He's gone clean off his rocker, if you ask me. You haven't got a hope in hell. He's crazy. He knows what's in the wind as well as you or I."

"I don't care," Catherine said. "He may be mad now, but he wasn't mad this morning. Go on. Take the saddles with you. But leave me a sack, just in case."

She watched Mick lead Eorann away.

Then, she turned to look at Suibne.

He was still careering wildly round the paddock. At intervals, he began to buck and rear and to give out his shrill, hysteric cries. They sent shudders down Catherine's spine. Then, he halted and faced Catherine.

In the moonlight, the stallion looked ordinary. But Catherine knew that he was not.

She let the halter drop on to the grass. Very slowly, she walked up to him. She held out her hand. He nuzzled her palm. With her other hand, she stroked his forelock. He bent his head against her cheek. She took his head between her hands. Then she breathed into his nostrils. A spasm ran through his body. Catherine breathed into his nostrils again. Then she stood back. Suibne waited.

"Yes, you are mad. You are raving mad, my darling Suibne. Off with you! Bolt! Be a mad horse!"

Suibne snorted. Catherine felt a wave of his hot breath over her face and through her hair. Then, he reared. He cantered off and headed for the wall. He picked up speed as he approached it. He sailed over it, clearing it with a lunatic ease. He vanished. Catherine knew that she would never see him again.

She walked down to the boathouse.

Tears were streaming down her face.

She went straight into the shed which housed the boats. Mick had already led Eorann into the shed and tied her up to a post. He had covered her head in a sack. He was crooning to her, calming and stroking her. Eorann was docile. But there was something unspeakably sad in the droop of her neck. Catherine put her hands into her mane.

"I let him go," she said. "Suibne. He flew over the wall."

"Only thing you could do. He'd gone bonkers. Any other time, you'd have had to shoot him."

"Never!" Catherine said. "He's got the same right to be bonkers, mad, as you have to be sane, if that's what you think you are. Are the others down?"

"Nan's next door. Mucking about with her indispensables."

"And Pake?"

"Listen. That's him now. He took his time, didn't he?"

Catherine opened the door that led into her work room.

The first thing which caught her eye was the brown teapot from the kitchen which Nan had put on her desk. Even then, it struck her as being incongruous.

Pake was puffed. His arms were burdened with his boxed microscope and sheaves of papers and files of documents. He piled them on to Catherine's desk.

"Good work!" he said to Nan.

Nan was sorting out bundles of miscellaneous objects. She had already made a neat pile of blankets.

"One last trip to do," said Pake. "Only the microcrystallines. Those, and other odd papers. That should do it."

"But Pake!" said Catherine. "You can't go back. It's out of the question. It's too late."

"Don't be silly, Catherine. One more load, and I'll have the backbone of my thesis. Of course, there's an awful lot I'll have to leave. Pity. But it can't be helped. Bloody idiots! Should have given us more warning."

"But the whole thing might go up any minute!"

"Nonsense. Don't panic. Keep calm, that's the main thing. Keep calm and don't panic. Here, have a sip of this."

He brought a bottle of whiskey out of his jacket pocket. He handed it to Catherine.

She took a swig and gave him back the bottle.

"I'll have one for the road." He laughed.

He stuffed the bottle back into his pocket.

"But Pake!"

"Don't worry," he said. "I made sure Nan brought a good supply down here. By the way, Nan, have you remembered my wax balls?"

Nan took a small silver Georgian snuff-box out of her apron pocket.

He opened it with care.

"Just in case," he said. "You never know. I might get blasted half-way down the hill."

He stuffed two pink wax balls into his ears.

He made for the door.

"Pake!"

He did not stop.

"Pake!"

"Deaf as a post. Can't hear a thing."

He dashed out of the boathouse.

Nan and Catherine could hear him laughing. But it was a mad bellow of the deaf.

She fled through the door into the boatshed.

"Mick! Mick! When is this thing supposed to go off? Pake's gone off back to the house. Should I follow him?"

Mick did not stop to soothe Eorann.

"Bloody barmy," he said.

He put down Eorann's hoof. He looked at Catherine.

"Cuckoo, isn't it, Catherine. One thing is for sure. And that is trouble is trouble. But Pake is just asking for it."

"But when? When will it go off?"

"I told you they were not reliable. Do you think they're just armed with stop clocks?"

"I'm going after him."

"Catherine, you will not be doing any such thing!"

"Oh, yes I will!"

"Oh, no you won't. What the hell do you think this is? Some bloody pantomime?"

He drew a pistol from his pocket and aimed it straight at Catherine.

"You stir anywhere and I'll shoot you through the head."

"Good God!" She laughed at him. "No, Mick! You'd never do that. But where on earth did you get it from?"

Eorann stamped. Mick held her fast. He still kept the gun pointed at Catherine.

"All right," she said. "I won't move. But do, for heaven's sake, put that thing away. For what does it matter? We'll probably all get blown up in any case."

He put the pistol back into his pocket.

Eorann tried to leap.

They both held her fast.

"But you know that pistol wouldn't have gone off," she said. "You got it out of Terence's drawer, didn't you?"

Eorann shrieked.

The explosion went off.

Mick would not let Catherine or Nan leave the boathouse. They spent the night, all three of them, very uncomfortably on the piles of blankets. Mick snored.

When Catherine woke, she was stiff and sore and very cold. She had a bad headache. It was late. She drank some tea from the thermos she saw on her desk. The tea tasted sour. It was tepid. She went into the boatshed.

Mick-the-Post had already taken Eorann back to the paddock and turned her loose. From the doorway of the shed, Catherine saw Mick and Nan sitting on the bollard by the jetty. Their backs were turned to her. They were gazing out at the lake. She went towards them.

None of them spoke.

They followed her up the hill towards the house.

The garden was looking lovely. Catherine noticed several of the flowers she had planted were already beginning to shoot up. A trowel she had forgotten to put away still stuck out of one of the borders.

Malabay was no longer there.

There was a great heap of smoking rubble where the house had been. Iron balustrades, a cracked marble fireplace, pieces of a chandelier were just recognisable in the smoking ruins. There was nothing left. There was nothing left at all.

"Pake?" Catherine asked.

"They took him to the church," said Mick. "His remains."

The remnants of a faded damask curtain furled round an iron bedstead. It stirred very faintly.

The smell of the smouldering fire was strong and acrid.

Pake was buried the next day.

Catherine sat with Mick and Nan in the small, seedy waiting room at the station at Ballingstown. The train was late. She got in. She leaned out of the window. None of them waved. The train left the station. Catherine sat back in the corner seat.

ASYLUM

"It's very good of you," Poppy said to Gerald several years later, "to bother to visit."

She was sitting up in bed. She had been reading before Gerald came into her room. The bed had an orthopaedic frame. The book was Gerald's latest novel, which had just come out.

She wore a blue bed jacket trimmed with peacocks' feathers. Her eyes were very bright.

The view from Poppy's windows was of mountains covered in snow, dark outlines of coniferous trees and a pale expanse of frozen lake, the lake discernible from the land only by its more shadowy tone of white.

"I thought that I was at the other end of the world," she said. "From anywhere."

"Not from where I'm staying," said Gerald. "My hotel's not far off."

"Thought you'd given up hotels. Thought you did all your writing on your island in your tower."

"I do, most of it. But I've got started on another book and I've got some research to do."

"Research? Apart from the Clinic, I thought this place was just a minor ski resort."

"There's a very good university in the town, didn't you know? It's got an excellent library. Most distinguished, of its kind.

Specialises in just what I'm burrowing after. My hotel is rather grand. But I like the snow. I went skiing yesterday."

Poppy tapped the novel with her finger.

"Absolutely frightful cover," she said. "Enough to intimidate the most tigerish of bookworms, I'd have thought. Says a lot for the public spirit that it's a bestseller. But my dear Gerald, quite apart from that, for that's of no consequence whatsoever, it really is very good indeed. Your best yet. You've captured Tara to the life. It's extraordinary. I don't know how you managed it. I congratulate you."

"Thank you. You know that you're the only critic that I really rate."

He was better pleased than he cared to show.

"It wasn't easy," he said, "to write about Tara."

"No. I don't suppose it was."

He had brought her presents: flowers; a novel; American and English newspapers; a jigsaw of Versailles; a bottle of wine.

"Thank you. Isn't Versailles ugly?"

"Your room's not too bad."

"No. I was relieved when I arrived. The view."

"So was I."

He got up from the chair. He went to find a vase for the flowers. He saw Poppy's reflection in the glass: a withered monkey with eager eyes propped up against a barrage of pillows.

"But it caters," she said. "It caters for all sorts, a nurse told me. The Clinic, that is. Think it started off as a T.B. place, but then T.B. went out of fashion, so they had to expand. Swop livers and hearts and all sorts of things. They even have a bin."

"You think shrinks moved in with the decline of consumption?"

"What is it about mountains? Always in the mountains. Or was it the gold standard? Did T.B. go out with the gold standard? Gold pumped in the veins used to be considered the best cure. Or do you think it's the inbreeding in the mountains that accounts for the number of loony bins?"

"I wouldn't have thought that most of the patients were local," he said. "Mountain air is very healthy, so they say."

"They'll say anything. But this bin is fascinating. Some of them, the lunatics, are out-and-out nutters in straitjackets. That's what the nurse said. But most of them are harmless. I've found out where they're kept. I've even got to see them playing tennis."

"My dear Poppy! Surely you're not supposed to gad about the place? I thought that you had to stay in bed?"

Poppy laughed.

"That's what you think!" she said. "I'm only practising. And I haven't had it yet, the operation, I mean."

Poppy's legs were still elegant. She swung them out of the bedclothes. Her nightdress was made of blue silk and went very well with her bed jacket of peacocks' feathers. She felt about with her feet for a pair of magenta mohair slippers. She found them underneath the bed and put them on.

"No," she said. "As you say, it's not a bad room. Pity about the furniture. But that can't be helped. Did I tell you I've ordered a great many trees? They'll make all the difference."

"Trees, Poppy?"

"Yes, trees. Very tall ones. All sorts. In tubs. Then, I shan't feel so exactly as though I were here. I do like things to be different from what they seem, don't you know?"

She reached for an ebony stick with a silver knob which was propped up against the side of her bed. The silver knob was engraved to resemble the feathers of a cockatoo.

She hobbled over to the window. She looked out. She stood with her back to Gerald.

"I thought," she said, "we might go and watch the lunatics. Playing tennis. For a spot of entertainment."

"Anyone else might consider you ghoulish, Poppy."

"Don't be so conventional! I think I'd like a drink."

She remained with her back to Gerald.

Gerald walked over to a small refrigerator, half hidden in one corner of Poppy's room. He put the bottle of wine he had brought her inside. He noticed that it was filled with bottles of well-chosen wines, mineral water and champagne.

He opened a bottle of Quincy.

"But you seem to be in the lap of luxury," he said. "It's more like a hotel, really, than a clinic."

"It has a certain reputation," she said. "That's why I chose it."

She was put out.

"Don't get in a huff, Poppy. But you must admit, it's an odd form of amusement to watch lunatics playing tennis."

She grunted. But she turned from the window.

"I'd call it a mild form of sport," she said.

She sipped the Quincy and gave Gerald a condoning smile.

"After all," she said, "there's not much difference between them and anyone else as far as the eye can see."

"Then what is the point?"

She waved her glass at him.

"Precisely that. Because they don't look like what they think they are," she said. "They don't look in the least like teapots or Napoleon. They just look like perfectly ordinary tennis players in white shorts. They might even be at Wimbledon."

"How do you know that they think they're teapots or Napoleon?"

"I don't. It's all in the mind. Of course, that's where the fascination lies. But it doesn't put them off their stroke."

Gerald was concerned. He did not like to see Poppy so stiff and in such obvious pain.

"I suppose it's all right?" he said. "They don't mind you roaming around?"

"Don't see why they should," she said. "After all, I'll be entirely at their mercy once they've hacked me up."

Gerald looked out of the window.

The snow glittered. There was, he thought, no such thing as pure white. There were so many different whites outside. He remembered how glorious he had felt in the shower after having been skiing.

"All right," he said. "If you're sure it's not too much for you."

"There's a lift," she said. "It's huge. For the stretchers. It's got hundred of knobs. It's so difficult to remember which one to press. That's how I discovered the lunatics. I poked the wrong knob by mistake."

The tennis courts were laid out underneath a glass dome through which the white mountains and the frozen lake were clearly visible. There were five hard courts, only two of them occupied. The players were dressed as Poppy had described, in white aertex shirts, white shorts, white socks, white tennis shoes. The surfaces of the courts were a dull pink, the nets green, the balls an acid yellow. Facing the courts was a series of raised benches, presumably for spectators. These were empty.

Poppy led the way with a proprietorial air.

"Damn!" she whispered very loudly. "The teapot isn't here. Nor is Napoleon. But I like the look of that couple, don't you?" She pointed her stick at one of the courts.

"Let's watch them," she said. "That young woman clearly thinks she's God. I suppose that's what comes of female liberation, although they've been at it so long, you might have thought they'd have arrived by now."

She sat down on a bench. Her stick clattered to the ground. Gerald sat beside her. They watched the game.

"I must say, the standard is quite high, considering. I told you it was almost like Wimbledon. Except it's a pity there isn't any grass. But do look, my dear, at God's opponent!"

Gerald looked.

"Have you ever seen such fangs? He looks quite like a werewolf. But I expect they're only false. Dentures. Probably thinks he's Dracula."

God's opponent did have teeth which stuck out in the most fang-like manner. He also had a peculiar haircut with a tuft on the top of his head.

"Lobotomy job, I wouldn't be surprised," said Poppy.

Gerald took her arm.

"Don't think we ought to talk," he said. "Don't want to distract them."

The acoustics in the dome made Poppy's voice carry with a piercing clarity. The man did look like a werewolf. God was playing with uncommon authority. There was something familiar in God's gestures: her slams, backhands and volleys. God was winning, hands down.

Both of them were startled when God, who had just scored a point, let off a bleep. The bleep was followed by an indistinct voice which seemed to come out of the pocket of her shorts.

"Good heavens!" said Poppy. "One of God's messengers."

God smiled at the werewolf and put down her racket.

The werewolf shrugged his shoulders.

As God left the court, she saw Poppy and Gerald sitting on the bench. She marched up to them.

"Can I see your pass?" she said. She had an English accent.

She stared at Gerald.

"What on earth are you talking about?" said Poppy.

"What are you doing here?" asked God.

"Who do you think you are? God, I suppose," said Poppy.

"I am Doctor Mallet."

"Swizzle!"

"Gerald! Is it really you? Where on earth have you sprung from? I thought it looked like you, but I couldn't believe it. It's been such ages."

They kissed briefly, on the cheek.

Gerald was uncomfortably aware that Poppy cut a curious figure, to say the least, in her bed jacket of peacocks' feathers, her azure nightgown and magenta slippers.

Swizzle cast Poppy a professional glance.

"What's your room number?" she said.

"I'm not sure," said Poppy. "It's got a yellow door. Of course, all the doors are yellow. But it's quite easy to find. It's the last one along the corridor on the left."

"You'd better come with me," said Swizzle.

She brooked no argument. She led the way out of the arena. They followed.

Gerald offered Poppy his arm.

"Who is this creature?" she whispered loudly enough to be overheard by Swizzle.

Swizzle led them down a corridor of a nasty shade of green and then into a small office. She unhooked a white coat from behind the door, slipped it on and sat behind a desk which was covered with a variety of telephones.

"Do sit," she said. "Sit down. I must call."

She picked up one of the telephones.

"Mallet speaking," she said into the telephone. "Can you get Cohen to take over 107 for me? Something's just cropped up. Thanks."

She opened a thick blue file. She rummaged in it and shook her head. She leaned on her elbows and stared at Poppy. Then she looked at Gerald.

"I'm afraid your friend is not on my files."

Gerald had not seen Swizzle since that summer's day when she had been a child of thirteen, riding her pinto pony bareback in an English meadow. He had avoided the Mallets since that visit. The memory of it left an unpleasant taste. There had been no quarrel. He spent so little time in England. He thought of her now as she had been then: a slender imp with corn-coloured hair, racing against imaginary ponies with a non-existent egg and spoon in one hand.

He smiled.

"You've changed," he said.

She laughed.

"Hardly surprising," she said.

Swizzle had developed into a sturdy young woman. There was nothing left of any impishness, no suggestion of anything imaginary. She shone with self-confidence. Her hair was short and well cut. Her hair shone too. She was not unattractive.

"But are you really a doctor, Swizzle?" Gerald asked.

Swizzle looked slightly embarrassed.

"I haven't finished all my qualifications yet. It does take years, you know."

Poppy scanned her.

"Yes," she said. "Not a bad thing either, when you think of it."

"I'm training, you see, to be a psychiatrist."

"I see," said Poppy.

"But there are endless exams," Swizzle said to Gerald.

"I suppose a psychiatrist is the modern equivalent of God," said Poppy.

Swizzle gave Poppy a professional, blank look.

The room they sat in was bleak. There were no pictures. The walls were lined with filing cabinets. A pot of African violets stood on the sill. They were in need of watering.

"But what interests me," said Poppy, "is that if you turn out to be a budding shrink, what is that werewolf in disguise?"

Swizzle looked to Gerald.

"You still haven't explained," she said.

Gerald burst out laughing.

Both women stared at him.

"Oh, Poppy! Swizzle! It's ridiculous! Of course Poppy's not on your files. She's in another department altogether. Nothing to do with you. Orthopaedic."

"Are you sure?"

"Oh, I'm quite sure, Swizzle."

"But, look here, what on earth are you doing down here, if you're supposed to be up there? It's strictly against the rules."

"I'm paying for it through the nose," said Poppy. "This whole operation is hideously expensive."

"But how did you get in?"

"Quite easy, my dear. Child's play, really. I just poke the knob when I have the inclination. The knob marked X. Zooms me straight down. But now, I want to know all about you."

Gerald explained.

"I thought the Mallets' daughter was a mere child," Poppy said.

Gerald lit a cigarette.

"People do grow up," said Swizzle.

"Some people do," said Poppy. "Others don't. But who is the werewolf?"

"She means your tennis partner," said Gerald.

"Of course I do," said Poppy. "Who else? His teeth."

"He's a dentist."

"What, with fangs like that? A dentist? You mean to say he's not a lunatic after all?"

Swizzle hesitated.

"He's a patient," she said. "We don't call them lunatics."

"Why not?"

Swizzle was silent.

"I suppose," said Poppy, "it's like rat catchers. You have to call them rodent inspectors. Nobody calls a spade a spade these days."

Swizzle crossed her ankles.

"So what," she said, "are you here for?"

"Oh, hip and heart and this and that. Orthopaedic. Didn't you register?"

Swizzle's bleeper buzzed inside the pocket of her white coat.

"I must go," she said. "Duty calls you know."

"Christ!" said Poppy.

"By the way," said Swizzle to Gerald, "I haven't got time now, but there's something I'd like to talk to you about."

"Are you free this evening? Why not come and have a drink at my hotel after work? I'd ask you to dinner, except I've got an awful lot of catching up to do."

"Fine. What time?"

"How about seven?"

He named the hotel.

"Perfect," said Swizzle.

Gerald and Poppy left Swizzle's office. He took Poppy back to her room. He stayed with her for another fifteen minutes. She asked him to read Horace aloud.

"A very bad translation," she said.

He agreed.

He left. Her operation was scheduled for the following day. He made arrangements to visit her as soon as was convenient afterwards.

Swizzle toyed with the cocktail stick. It pierced a stuffed olive in her glass.

The gesture reminded Gerald of Antonia.

"And so, you see," she said, "I couldn't help wondering. I only put two and two together when I saw you. You were a friend of his, weren't you?"

"Yes," he said. "You could say that. A friend."

He lit a cigarette.

The hotel was expensive and very ugly. They sat in a secluded corner of the bar. The carpet was green with yellow diamonds on it.

Swizzle popped the olive into her mouth.

"I've always read all your books," she said. "Oh, I'm a great fan of yours!"

She giggled with the olive in her mouth.

"I shouldn't say so, though. Yet why not? It's true. I liked the last one specially."

Gerald looked at her legs. They were strong and muscular. She wore flesh-coloured stockings.

"But what is it," he said, "that you wanted to tell me?"

"I ought to tell you."

"Ought?"

"Well, yes, I think so. Catherine is a patient."

"Catherine?"

"Yes. She's in the bin. I thought you ought to know."

Swizzle finished her olive.

Gerald sipped his drink. He watched Swizzle try not to smile, a fleeting upward quirk, a smile of triumph. He had seen a bad conjuror smile like that when he had been surprised by the success of a trick with a rabbit, a top hat and a silk scarf at a children's teaparty.

"But how strange of you," he said, "not to have told her aunt."

"Her aunt?"

"Yes, her aunt. Didn't you know that Poppy is her aunt?"

The treacherous little smile vanished altogether.

"But surely she mustn't be upset on any account? She seems, the aunt, not quite all there."

Gerald looked at Swizzle. She wore a plain and sensible dark red dress. It was not unbecoming.

"Oh, Poppy's there all right," he said. "It's just that you are so frightfully here. Are you in charge of the case?"

"Good Lord, no! I'm not nearly high up enough."

He smiled.

"But I'm making a special study of it, though."

"How long has she been there?"

"A long time. She doesn't seem to be responding. Not in the way one would like."

Gerald inhaled.

"I'd like to see her," he said. "If you don't think that would be too upsetting."

"I'll arrange it," she said.

"Tomorrow?"

"I'll have a word with my boss. I told him I'd seen you and wanted to talk to you. Otherwise, it wouldn't have been ethical."

"Did you win that race?" asked Gerald.

"What race?"

"That gymkhana with your friends when you were so high?"

"Oh, that!" Swizzle laughed. "Fancy you remembering that! No. I got the piggy prize."

He glanced at his watch. He stood up.

"See you tomorrow," he said.

"Thanks awfully. Thanks awfully for the drink."

Gerald got into the lift. He carried a bunch of wrapped flowers. He pressed the button marked X. He found Swizzle waiting for him in her office. She led him along the corridor. The walls were beige, the linoleum grey. Along the corridor, all the doors had small panes of glass let into them so that one could keep an eye, Swizzle explained, on the patient. She stopped outside Room 107. She peered through the pane.

"I think she's asleep," said Swizzle. "But you can never tell with her. She often just lies there for hours with her eyes shut. I'll tell you what. Why don't you just go in very quietly and sit beside her until she wakes up?"

"You don't think you'd better tell her? After all, she may not want to see me."

"She knows already that you're coming. Professor Shubin told her this morning."

"Who's Professor Shubin?"

Swizzle looked at him in surprise.

"Professor Shubin," she said with emotion, "is the Head of the Department. He is . . ."

"Your boss?"

"Yes. My boss. He is one of the most distinguished psychiatrists in the world. I'm surprised you haven't heard of him."

"It's not my department, Swizzle."

"No. I suppose not."

"And he was in favour of my seeing her?"

"She was. And he could see nothing against it. Hypothetical, really. Who can tell?"

He hesitated.

"There's a buzzer by the bed, if you want me."

"All right."

Swizzle left him. He heard her sensible shoes clack on the linoleum.

He looked through the pane and all he could see was a narrow bed. Catherine lay with her back turned to him, half covered by a single sheet. Her dark hair fell across the pillow, exposing the nape of her neck. Her left wrist was attached to a drip suspended by the bed. She did not move. He hesitated. He glanced down the corridor. A maid was polishing the floor. He opened the door.

The room was small. There was a window, shut, with a meagre view of other wings of the gigantic Clinic, and of a small patch of garden covered in snow. He sat down on the aluminium chair beside her bed.

She was not fully awake. She muttered something in her half sleep which he could not catch. Then she turned towards him. She opened her eyes and stared. She did not seem to see him. Then she smiled.

"Gerald?"

"Catherine."

"I wondered if it was really you. The doctor said that you would come. I fell asleep."

"I brought you some flowers."

He handed her the bunch of freesias wrapped in fancy paper.

"Sorry about the wrapping," he said. "And that awful ribbon. They would insist, in the shop."

She looked at him shyly.

"It's rather sweet in its silly way," she said. "But it is a funny thing to do to flowers, to muck them about with salmon-pink ribbon and polka-dotted paper."

She undid the ribbon with her free hand. The paper fell on the floor. She buried her nose in the flowers.

"They're exquisite," she said. "The smell. I'd forgotten."

Gerald walked over to the window. The view was not inspiring. He realised that Catherine was close to tears. He could imagine that she did not want to cry in front of him.

"I'll go and see if I can find a jug," he said.

He left the room.

Catherine combed her hair.

He came back with a steel vase. He filled it with water from the basin in the corner. He sat down again beside the bed. He watched her arrange the flowers. She did this with great care, placing each stem singly in the ugly vase. He took the vase from her and put it on the locker by her bed.

"I often wondered whether we would ever meet," she said. "It's a pity about the surroundings."

"They could be better. But never mind. At least we've met at last."

"I ought to tell you," she said, "that I read your book. One of the doctors lent it to me."

She smiled at him.

"I think it's very good," she said. "I mean, it's very like; very evocative. But it never occurred to me that you and Tara were lovers. It was very unimaginative of me."

"But we weren't!" he said. "Not in real life. Of course, we were the greatest of friends. Of course I loved him. I'm quite sure he loved me, too. But we never had a sexual affair, as I made it seem in the book. Not even when we were at school. No, I made it like that in the book because in every relationship there is always an element of sexual attraction, some ambiguity. I just put it in, I suppose, to make the book more convincing. Life, you see, is often far more subtle than fiction."

"Yes, I see that," said Catherine. "But you certainly had me convinced."

"Would you mind if I had a cigarette?"

"No, of course not."

"Would you like one?"

"I haven't got any."

"Have one of mine."

She took one. He lit it for her.

"But there isn't an ashtray," said Gerald. "Perhaps we're not supposed to. Is it against the rules?"

"I don't know. It either is or it isn't. It must be one or the other. Probably against the rules. Rules are nearly always beastly. Perhaps one ought to invent them. Make them up as one goes along. In any case, all the doctors smoke like chimneys. Look, there's that tin thing they keep the thermometer in. We could always use that."

"I don't agree," he said. "I think rules are very important."

But he fetched the kidney-shaped basin and put it on Catherine's bed.

She flicked ash into it.

"It must have been rather odd for you to have read it, my novel."

"Yes, it was. To tell you the truth, I found it very upsetting. I'd spent so much time trying to forget it all. It was impossible not to recognise that it was all about Tara and you and me. But you invented me."

She stubbed out her cigarette.

"Odd how right you got it, though. Ending me up in a bin. Just where you've found me. But there's one thing you got wrong."

"What was that?"

"A mere detail. My mack was navy, not dark green."

"So it was," he said. "You're quite right. I'd forgotten."

There was a knock at the door. A nurse came into the room.

"Thank God!" said Catherine. "You've come to take the drip out?"

The nurse smiled.

"I'm afraid I'll have to ask you to leave the room," she said to Gerald. "Won't take long. If you'll just step outside."

He waited in the corridor. When the nurse came out of the room, she winked at Gerald.

"Nice for her," she said, "to have a visitor. Anything for a change. She's looking ever so much better for it."

He watched her walk away down the corridor.

Catherine was sitting up in bed. Her arms were crossed behind her head. She smiled and held out her free hand. He took it and held it.

"That happened before," he said.

"What did?"

"You held out your hand just like that."

"That was just in your book."

"No. In real life. You held out your hand to me."

Catherine stared at him. She did not let go of his hand.

"I put it into the book just as it happened."

"So you really went to Malabay?"

"Yes. I went to Tara's funeral. I went to the house later, the next day. You were still in bed. Everything, just as I wrote it, that part, was true."

"You really went to Malabay!"

She burst into tears. He let her cry. He gave her his handkerchief.

"Wipe up," he said.

"What?"

"Up. Wipe up, not down. Otherwise you'll get the most dreadful wrinkles."

Her tears turned into laughter.

"Now you've got hysterics. Tara once told me the only thing to stop you having hysterics was to get you to turn into a horse. But I don't think that's the answer here."

"There's not much he didn't tell you. And there's not much you left out in that book of yours. You didn't leave anything out, but you went and put in an awful lot which didn't happen but which, as you say, might have."

Catherine was calmer.

"It's a damned nuisance," he said. "I would like to stay. But I must leave now. I'd like to come and see you again. Can I come tomorrow?"

"If you're sure you'd really like to. Yes, I'd love you to."

He stood up.

"Is there anything you'd like me to bring?"

She considered.

"The thing I'd like best," she said, "is an exercise book and a pencil. I'd like that very much, if it's not too much of a bother."

"Of course not. And don't worry. I'm sure things aren't as bad as they seem."

"Do they seem very?"

"Bad? They can only get better, Catherine."

He closed the door behind him and then tapped on the little pane. He grinned at her. She smiled back, pointed to the flowers and waved.

Gerald had a good many notes that he wanted to sort out before continuing the research on his current novel. He was behindhand with his work. He knew that he had no time to waste. He knew that the sensible thing to do was to take a taxi. But he was agitated. He decided to walk back to his hotel.

He had walked quite far before he realised that he had taken a wrong turning. He was on the other side of the lake. The light was fading. He did not know where he was. He was hungry. He was tired. He was cold.

He saw a neon light illuminating a dismal bar attached to a filling station. He went inside. It was empty except for a couple of boys who thumped a one-armed bandit. He noticed that the calendar, decorated with a photograph of a Persian cat with a blue ribbon tied around its throat in an enormous bow, was out of date. A very fat woman came through an interior door, its glass panels hung with dirty synthetic lace.

He asked for beer.

He could see behind the bar, which was lined with looking glass, the reflection of the fat woman's shoulders, the bottles, the beer pumps, the boys. He could see his own reflection. He looked away.

The fat woman laughed.

"What's up?" she said. "Might as well drink up. You look fed up."

She sliced the foam off the top of the tankard with a plastic spatula.

"How much?"

He put the money down on the counter and left the bar.

It was cold outside.

He followed the road which led around the edge of the lake. He increased his pace in order to keep warm. Then he stopped. In the half light, he saw a small throng of children skating on the lake. They skated with facility and skill. They were skating a game, a kind of dance, probably ages old. He saw that they were repeating a pattern on the ice, threading in and out, leaving the marks their skates had cut behind them. Then one of the children went out of turn, slid and fell. The thread was broken. The game stopped. The other children swooped on their friend. They laughed. They wobbled on their skates, clinging to each other in a group to support themselves. Then they resumed the pattern of their game exactly, so it seemed to Gerald, where they had left it off.

He moved on.

When he got back to the hotel, he went straight to his room. He wrote late into the night.

Catherine was sitting at a small table in the foyer where some of the patients in Ward X were allowed to assemble. She was sitting with the dentist. The dentist was solving a crossword. Catherine was cleaning the leaves of a dusty rubber plant which stood in a pot beside the table. She wiped each leaf separately with a twist of moistened cotton wool. The dentist sighed.

"No luck?" asked Catherine.

He shook his head. He seldom spoke. He was self-conscious about his teeth. Catherine was one of the few people to whom he did occasionally speak.

"No. I've got stuck."

He handed the crossword over to her. She puzzled over it.

"Why do you clean the plants? The nurses ought to do it."

"You know as well as I do that they never do. I quite like doing it. At least, I partly like it. It reminds me of being out of doors. I've got it. It must be resonance. The clue, I mean."

"Of course!"

He was animated by the answer. Very carefully, he filled in the empty boxes of the crossword. He wrote with a blue ballpoint.

"Now I see how to finish it," he said. "I say, I've noticed that you never eat any breakfast."

"No," said Catherine. "I never do."

"Well then, do you think . . ."

He hesitated like a sheepish wolf.

Catherine waited.

"Would you give me your butter?"

He brought this out with great difficulty.

"My butter? Yes, of course."

She was surprised when he put out his hand. She shook it.

Gerald, who was on his way to visit Catherine in Room 107, was surprised to see her shaking hands with the werewolf. He had not thought that she had any contact with the other patients. She looked quite different from the previous day. She had not seen him. She was livelier. She smiled gaily at the werewolf. He stood and watched her. After shaking hands, the werewolf picked up his paper and walked off. Gerald watched Catherine go on wiping the dust off the rubber plant. She looked around. She saw him. She smiled. She made no attempt to disguise her pleasure at seeing him.

"I'm so pleased you've come! I've been looking forward to it all day."

They walked together down the corridor arm in arm. This did not go unnoticed by the nurse who passed them half way down to Catherine's room.

Catherine shut the door.

"What on earth were you doing with the werewolf?" asked Gerald.

"The werewolf?"

"That man you were shaking hands with. The one with the teeth."

"The werewolf! He has got fangs, hasn't he?"

Catherine burst out laughing.

She began to tell him about the butter. Her laughter was infectious. Gerald laughed too.

They were interrupted by the nurse, whom neither of them had noticed in the corridor.

"Drip time," said the nurse.

Both of them tried to stop laughing.

"You do seem to be enjoying yourselves," said the nurse.

She was not unfriendly.

"I suppose I'd better leave," said Gerald, who was still laughing.

The nurse nodded. He left.

When he was allowed back in, Catherine's wrist was strapped up again to the needle inserted into her vein, attached to the drip installed beside her bed. She was lying down.

"But how did you know," she asked, "about his fangs? You didn't see them, did you? He had his mouth shut."

"It was Poppy's name for him."

"Poppy?"

He sat on the edge of her bed.

"Poppy's here, too," he said.

"What's she doing here? She hasn't gone off her rocker too?"

He explained.

Catherine was silent. Gerald lit a cigarette.

"Can I have a puff?" she asked.

He handed it to her and lit himself another.

"Why didn't you tell me you knew that Mallet person?"

He blew out smoke.

"Professor Shubin told me this morning that she was a friend of yours."

Gerald laughed quietly.

"She's just Swizzle."

"Swizzle?"

"Yes. That's her name. I used to know her when she was a little girl. Her parents are old friends. Rather dull. Haven't seen them in ages. It was she who told me that you were here."

"I'm afraid I don't like her very much, this Swizzle of yours."

"Swizzle isn't mine."

"No, but you know what I mean."

"Why don't you like her?"

Catherine looked away.

"Difficult to say. I don't suppose it's her fault, really, but she makes me feel as if she's on the hunt. Partly because of what she does to me."

"What does she do to you?"

She did not answer.

Gerald stroked the palm of her hand.

"Tell me," he said.

"It's so disgusting."

"Tell me."

She made an effort.

"She has to stick tubes down my throat. To get samples. It's quite beastly. I hate it. Anyone would. It makes one feel very sick and the whole process is horribly humiliating. Once, she couldn't come. Another doctor took her place. Then, it was all quite different, much easier. It didn't hurt nearly so much. And then she keeps bursting in on me and questioning me. It's like the Spanish Inquisition. No; I'm exaggerating. She can be quite human sometimes. She was nice enough to give me a copy of your book. But then I wondered if it was because she guessed that you'd drawn Eleanor from me. And now I see she knew all along. I don't know, I think she's like a spy. But you probably think that's batty of me. And quite right too, I dare say. They say I'm as batty as a fruitcake. Has she sent you to spy on me?"

"There is a difference," he said.

"What?"

"Fruitcakes are nutty. Not batty. I'm not sure you're either."

"I'm not sure of anything."

"I am."

"What's that?"

He leaned over and kissed her. He ran his fingers through her hair. They kissed for a long time. Catherine was the first to draw away.

"Fuck!" she said.

"We can't," said Gerald. "Not here. Perhaps you are crazy, after all."

"No, I don't mean fuck, Gerald. I mean fuck!"

"Fuck what?"

"Fuck Swizzle!"

"You must be out of your mind!"

"So they say. I don't mean fuck her, either."

She laughed.

"I mean fuck!" she said. "I just saw her. She was looking at us kissing through that pane of glass in the door."

"Oh, fuck," said Gerald. "Fuck her!"

He stood up.

He went towards the window.

"Poppy's got a much better view," he said. "Are you really sure you saw Swizzle?"

"Yes."

He lingered by the window. He saw a bird peck forlornly at a twig covered with rime. He was not much good at birds. He could not identify it. He just saw it as a dismal little bird.

"I quite forgot," he said. "I brought you the exercise book. Here."

He gave her a small parcel.

She unwrapped it. Her fingers were unsteady. She tore at the paper.

"It's too much," she said.

"It's nothing."

"Thank you very much. It's lovely. How did you know I would love it, that green?"

"Don't know. Just guessed. Seemed the right colour for you."

"And the pen, too. A real pen. Can I try it now?"

He watched her unscrew the top of the pen. She fitted it on to the end. She licked the nib, then wrote her name on the fly leaf of the exercise book. There was something, he thought, pathetically childish in the pleasure she took in making her mark with the pen on the paper.

She smiled at him. She was radiant.

"You've made me so happy," she said.

"What's in that thing?" he asked. "The drip plugged into you?"

Catherine looked askance at the drip.

"That contraption!" she said. "I'm not sure what's in it today. If it's not one thing, it's another. They keep trying all sorts of things out."

"But why? What for?"

"To make me better, I suppose."

"But what is wrong with you? Why are you here? What have you got to get better from?"

She closed her eyes.

He waited. She did not move.

"If you can't tell me," he said at length, "then how can I help you?"

She opened her eyes.

"You?" she said. "You, of all people help me? You put me in the bin in your book. I got into one in real life for very much the same reasons. I'm told I'm depressed. That doesn't cheer me up very much. I led a very wild kind of life after Tara died and Malabay got blown up. I dare say it was stupid, self-destructive. It's easy to say that. There was nothing left, you see."

"There was you."

"But I didn't count myself. I would rather have done without myself. Or done away with myself, to put it bluntly. I'm surprised you don't seem to cotton on to what I'm saying. You write so very clearly about it in your book."

"But the book is fiction, Catherine. You are real."

"But I didn't want to be real. I can't go into all the details now. I will try and tell you. But not just now. Come here, will you?"

He sat very close to her on the bed and put his arm round her.

"It was a bit of a liberty, you know," she said, "to write that book. To write about me and Tara. You never even asked me. It was as though I didn't exist at all. What you wrote was very perceptive. But as you say yourself, it wasn't the whole truth. Don't get me wrong, though. I'm not in this bloody bin because of what you wrote. Gerald, please be patient."

"I am not a patient man."

"But I am a patient."

"So they say."

"People will say anything. It's odd, you know, last night I remembered that Tara . . ."

"Don't stop."

"That day, his birthday, the morning that he got drowned, he said he had a surprise for me. I never knew what it was. But in this book of yours, you said that we were both going to visit you on some island with a tower."

"I wish I'd never written that goddamned book," he said. "You're right. It's too close to the truth. I didn't think about you. Forgive me."

"Forgive you? Don't be silly. But was that true, about the island and everything?"

He sighed.

"This kidney basin's getting awfully full of stubs," he said.

He lit another cigarette. This time, they shared it.

"Yes," he said.

"And it exists, this island?"

"Yes."

"What's it like?"

"I'm not going to tell you. I'm going to take you there."

She wiped her eyes with the back of her hand.

"What the Devil did I do with that handkerchief you lent me yesterday? I don't know whether you make me cry or laugh the most. Kiss me again instead. They won't let you. They won't ever let you take me away from here. I'm stuck. No, of course it's not your fault. Not the book. Don't be silly. It's not really mine, either. It's just the consequence of such a long chain of events which I can't break. I don't know how to."

He kissed her again. They clung to one another.

"You must go," she said.

"I'll be back."

"I hope so. You have lovely eyes. Brown, with violet rings round your irises."

"Yours aren't too bad, either. Green goggles. Do you trust me, in spite of the book?"

"Yes. Do you?"

"Yes."

"I'll be back tomorrow."

After Gerald left, Catherine lay quite still until the nurse arrived to remove the drip.

This time, Gerald took a limousine from the Clinic straight back to his hotel.

On his return, the porter handed him a message. The message was from Swizzle. She had left a telephone number and had asked him to call her. He sighed, put the scrap of paper into his jacket pocket and took the lift to his room.

He poured himself a glass of iced mineral water. Carrying the glass, he went straight to his bed. He kicked off his shoes, lay on the bed, took a sip of water, put the glass on the bedside table and fell fast asleep.

He dreamed of Tara.

Much later, he woke up with a crashing headache.

He reached out for the telephone and asked the switchboard operator to put him through to the number which Swizzle had left.

"Gerald?"

"Swizzle."

"Oh, good. You got my message?"

He found her voice repugnantly cheery.

He looked down at his feet in their grey silk socks.

"Yes?"

"The line's not too good," he said.

"Oh? Pity, I hoped you'd've rung earlier. Never mind. But I want to see you. It's not really anything one can talk about over the telephone."

He did not reply.

"Will you be free tomorrow, perhaps?" she asked. "In the evening?"

He made an effort.

"Would you like to have dinner, Swizzle?"

"That'd be terrific."

"Well, turn up here, then. Before eight."

"Lovely. See you then."

She rang off.

He went reluctantly down to the hotel restaurant. There was nothing on the menu that appealed to him. He scarcely noticed what he ate. He went to bed unusually early without doing any work at all. His sleep was interrupted by the most hellish nightmares.

Gerald decided not to give Swizzle dinner at his hotel. He met her in the lobby and offered her a drink.

"I thought it'd be more fun to go to a small inn I discovered the other day. It's quite high up the mountain, on the other side of the lake. How does that sound to you?"

Swizzle looked about the hotel.

"I'm so bored with this place," Gerald said. "It's not really my kind of hotel at all."

"It's very luxurious," she said.

"It's luxurious all right. But it's so anonymous. It could be anywhere. I'll order a taxi to take us to the inn."

"Don't do that," said Swizzle. "I've got a car."

She drove very efficiently in her little white car through the snow up the mountain to the inn.

It was a simple, unpretentious place. It was scrupulously clean. There was not a speck of dust to be seen anywhere. It was run by a plump and kindly looking woman. The cooking, like the place, was simple but good. They were the only guests.

"I know the décor is really hideous," said Gerald. "But I can't help feeling rather fond of it. It's so peculiar."

Swizzle inspected the room.

The walls were painted pink and mauve. They were hung about with wooden carvings of grotesque men, beer mats, pewter tankards, and dolls and angels twisted from dried wheat.

"Everyone to his taste," she said.

It was clear that she did not like the inn. She would, Gerald realised, have preferred a more swank and tasteless dinner at his hotel. He remembered Catherine laughing over the ridiculous polka-dotted paper which her flowers had been wrapped in. Swizzle did not smile at the wheaten angels. He handed her the menu. Their eyes met. She blushed and looked away.

She was wearing the same claret-coloured dress. She suddenly smiled at him. Her teeth were strong and white. But her eyes, a pale blue, did not change. When she smiled, she looked almost pretty, and for a moment Gerald was reminded of the little girl riding a fat pony in an English field.

They ordered onion soup to start with. It was piping hot and very good.

They talked, as they drank their soup, in a desultory way of matters of little consequence.

"Do you often hear from Bob and Antonia?" he asked. "How are they?"

The woman took their soup bowls away and came back with plates of brochettes of lamb.

"I write to Mum fairly often," Swizzle said. "I spent my last holidays with them on the farm. It was nice to be back and have a rest. I'm lucky to have such a good job. But it's all go. Hard work, you know."

She jabbed a piece of meat with the end of the skewer.

"But don't you find it interesting?" he asked.

She looked down. Her smile was forced.

Gerald poured out more wine.

"They must be very proud, Bob and Antonia, of you."

Swizzle clamped her teeth on a piece of meat. Her lips were shut in a thin red line as she chewed. She could not conceal a smirk of self-satisfaction.

Gerald wondered where she got it from, this smugness, this primness. He wanted to prick it and make it burst like a balloon.

They were interrupted by the plump woman.

"It's come on," she said, "something fearful. It's a right blizzard outside."

Gerald got up and walked over to the door. There was no denying it. The snow was falling thick and fast outside. There was a wild wind blowing very hard.

"Shit!" he thought.

He went back to the table. The plump woman, who had been talking to Swizzle, looked up.

"As I said," she said, "there's no possibility of you going down the mountain tonight. And the workers haven't finished redecorating the rooms. We're having alterations made for the season. Everything is at sixes and sevens. I can only offer you my daughters' room. They're away. It's got twin beds. It's in perfect order. You're more than welcome."

"No possibility at all," said Gerald, "of leaving?"

"None whatsoever," said Swizzle.

"It would just be asking for it," said the woman. "But as I say, you're more than welcome."

Gerald lit a cigarette.

"It's very kind of you," he said to the woman. "What a nuisance for you, Swizzle."

"Not at all," she said.

"Coffee?"

"I'll get you both coffee," said the woman. "And hot mulled wine too. On the house."

She bustled away.

"It's quite an adventure, isn't it?" said Swizzle. She gave a little laugh.

The woman came back with coffee in little white cups patterned with edelweiss and mugs of steaming, spicy wine.

"Perhaps," he said, "we'd better make a move. We ought to try and make an early start. Work, you know."

"Weather permitting," said Swizzle.

Gerald noticed that Swizzle was slightly flushed. He put it down to the hot wine.

The woman led the way up the polished pine staircase. The room she showed them into smelled of mountain air and fly squirt. The walls were papered with patterns of cherries dangling from outsized stalks. Twin beds had already had their pink candlewick coverlets turned down. The pillows were edged with nylon frills and embroidered mottoes.

"But it's ever so nice," said Swizzle to the woman.

"I'll show you the bathroom," said the woman. "It's along the passage. You won't mind it being the family one? As I said, it's on account of the workmen."

They left the room together.

Gerald sat on the bed closest to the window. He kicked off his shoes. He swore aloud. He was still sitting on the edge of the bed when Swizzle came back into the room.

"Which bed would you like best?" asked Gerald.

He stood up.

"It doesn't matter. The other, since you seem to have chosen that."

He went to the bathroom.

When he got back into the bedroom, he found that Swizzle was already ensconced in her twin bed. She was not asleep. He saw at one glance that she was pretending to be. She had curled herself up in a position he thought that she thought was voluptuous. He stared at her. Her eyelashes flickered, betrayed her. He said nothing, but looked at the outline of her body between the sheets. She had peeled off the pink coverlet and folded it neatly at the foot of her bed. The very neatness put him off.

He switched out the light, undressed in the dark and got into bed.

Gerald dreamed of Catherine. He dreamed that they were picnicking together by the edge of a stream on a summer's afternoon. The picnic over, the afternoon warm, both of them drowsy with the effects of the heat and the wine, they began, very tenderly, to make love on the grass.

He woke up. It was still dark. He could not make out where he was. He felt his body being caressed. Swizzle was in his bed. He felt her hands run over him. For a moment, he pretended that he was still asleep. Then he turned over and fucked her. He fucked her very hard. She was not exciting, sexually. Halfway through, she began to mumble endearments to him. They meant nothing to him. He got out of the bed and into her empty one.

"I like to sleep alone," he lied. "The bed is very small."

When Gerald woke up in the morning, he saw that Swizzle's bed was empty. She was not in the room. He got out of bed. He crossed the room and pulled the curtains. The blizzard had died down. The gale had stopped. Great drifts of snow remained, but the sun was out, the sky was clear and the mounds of snow iridescent.

He wondered whether Swizzle had left him in the inn. He swore. He had a splitting headache, a hangover from the mulled wine.

The door opened. Swizzle came in. She was fully dressed. She had just had a bath. She looked very clean, capable and efficient. She smiled but did not look at him directly. She walked to the window.

"Lovely day," she said with her back to him.

"Yes," he said. "I'm glad it's cleared up."

"Breakfast," she said, "is ready. I spoke to the landlady on my way back from the bathroom. Why don't you have one, a bath? She says the roads are passable. See you downstairs."

She left the room.

Gerald lingered in his bath. There was a plastic shower attached to the taps. He hosed himself with cold water. It was glacial. He rubbed himself dry vigorously. He scrubbed his teeth three times over.

When he went downstairs, he found Swizzle sitting at the same table where they had had dinner the night before. She was eating breakfast and reading the local paper.

"It's hardly necessary, now, for me to mention why I wanted to see you," said Swizzle.

She looked at him over the rim of her tea cup.

"Why not forget it?" Gerald spoke kindly. "After all, it was probably the wine."

Swizzle went red. She put down her cup.

"I didn't mean that," she said. "If you want to know what I think . . ."

The woman came over towards them.

"I hope everything's all right?" she said. "But take care going down the mountain. It'll be as slippery as anything, I can tell you."

Gerald got up and went with her to the counter. He wanted to leave at once. He paid, leaving the woman a handsome tip.

Swizzle had finished her egg.

"Let's go," he said.

In the car, Swizzle strapped on her safety belt. She drove with skill and caution down the icy mountain.

"No," she said, turning a hairpin bend. "It seems I'll simply have to spell it out for you. I know all about you and Catherine carrying on.''

"I know you do," said Gerald.

"Aren't you ashamed of yourself?"

He laughed.

"Don't be ridiculous," he said.

"But what you don't know," said Swizzle, "is what she's really like. The kind of life she's led. She's raving. She's tried everything. You name it: drinks; drugs; the lot. She's even tried to destroy herself. She'll try and destroy you. You think she's like the heroine, Eleanor, in your book. That butter wouldn't melt in her mouth. But the real Catherine isn't like that. You can't say that I haven't warned you.''

"I'll bear it in mind," said Gerald. "But Swizzle, what business is it of yours?"

"I'm involved, don't forget," she said, "in her case. Anyway, it's highly irresponsible of you. You know perfectly well that she's a patient under care."

"Your care?"

Swizzle changed gear.

"I'm going to tell Professor Shubin," she said. "It's only my duty, after all. That'll put a stop to it."

Gerald fixed his eyes on the jagged horizon of white peaks cut out against the blue sky.

"In that case, I take it you'll tell him you got what you wanted last night as well?"

They were approaching the town.

"Do you think he needs telling about you? What everybody knows? That you're just a common lecher, utterly without scruples? Even my mother said so, once. That you're just a part of every young girl's education."

"Antonia said that?"

"Wouldn't any mother?"

He glanced at her chin which jutted out over her collar.

"I hope you enjoyed the final touch to your education, in that case.''

"Where would you like me to drop you?"

Her voice was icy.

"Oh, the Library, if that's not out of your way."

She stopped the car in front of the Library.

He leaned across her safety belt and kissed her savagely on the lips.

"That's what you'd like more of, isn't it?" he said. "What your mother warned you of. You can tell this precious Professor Shubin of yours what the hell you like. Supposing I don't give a fuck, after all?"

He got out. He was careful not to slam the door. He watched Swizzle reverse and drive off with a screech of brakes in the direction of the Clinic. He walked up the steps and went through the massive doors into the peace and quiet of the Library.

It was a late summer's evening. Midges flew over the shallows of the lake. Catherine was swimming naked in the deep water beyond the island. The evening was calm, idyllic. The water was warm. A dappled fish darted between her toes. The willows on the island dangled their branches into the lake. Turtle doves crooned in the blue of the evening.

Catherine turned on her back and floated. She lingered in the last of the light. She gazed at the deepening sky and at the covert of the varied shades of the broad-leafed trees which grew down to the edge of the lake on the opposite shore. She basked. Then a strong current of water broke over her body. Something violent stirred in the depths of the lake. Catherine turned. She saw a figure dressed in a black rubber frog suit swimming towards her.

The swimmer approached her steadily, relentlessly. A pair of powerful rubber-clad arms cleaved their way through the water and gained on her with every stroke. The dusk gathered. The sounds of evening faded.

Catherine struck out from where she had been idling in the deep water. She panicked. She scrabbled helplessly, treading water, unable to advance. The swimmer was upon her. It was Swizzle. The two girls struggled in the lake. Swizzle forced back Catherine's head and pressed her thumbs hard into Catherine's eyeballs. Darkness enveloped Catherine. A dreadful boom resounded in her head.

She woke up screaming.

"But you shouldn't eat tripe," said Poppy, "in these parts. It's well known. No wonder you had nightmares. But you are a sly boots, and no mistake. Don't let the grass grow under your feet, do you?"

Poppy was sitting up in bed. A tea tray laid for two remained on her bedside table. The tea had already been drunk and most of the cakes eaten. This afternoon, she wore a jacket made of yellow silk. The cut was distinctly Chinese. The collar and wrist bands were embroidered with green and scarlet dragons.

"I've had a visitor," she said. "Would you like a cake? There are some left. The green ones tasted the most interesting."

"I didn't know you had any friends here. No, I'll skip the cakes, thanks."

"Apparently, my niece Catherine is a lunatic. I'm told you've been philandering with her like nobody's business."

"Well, is it?"

"Anyone's business? All I can tell you is that people have made it so. I had a very nice, rather gangly man up here just now who has certainly made it his."

"Who the hell was he?"

"He said his name was Shubin. Perfectly charming. He's got exquisite manners and a very good taste in poetry."

"But Professor Shubin is Catherine's shrink."

"Exactly. Why they call them shrinks, I cannot think. Expanders would be more fitting, although I must admit it does suggest some piece of underwear, or possibly a patent bust developer. But shrinks, really they sound so like hunters in savage regions where they wear necklaces strung of human teeth and dangle shrivelled heads from loin cloths."

Gerald sat on the blue upholstered chair beside Poppy's bed.

"But you can't," he said, "just have talked about poetry."

Poppy gave him one of her teasing, malicious smiles. She rubbed the tips of her fingers together.

"I see," she said.

"I wish I did," said Gerald.

"But it's as clear as daylight, Gerald. You can't help it, can you, being fascinated?"

"By Catherine? Yes, I am. How can I not be?"

"Quite."

"But as for Catherine herself, apart from . . ."

"She can't be apart from, don't you see? She's part of."

"But that's only part of one aspect of the truth. She is also herself."

"And just who is she, when she's at home, I should like to know?" said Poppy. "Before you say another word, be an angel and get out some champagne. There's plenty in the fridge. Did you know that George Eliot was prescribed a pint a day towards the end of her life?"

He opened a bottle and poured out two glasses. He handed one to Poppy.

She held the glass at arm's length and admired it in the light.

"So pretty, isn't it? And thank God for the taste!"

A small, gold-encrusted travelling alarm clock ticked beside her bed. She looked beyond Gerald through the window. But she did not remark the view. Her mind's eye was otherwise engaged.

There was a knock at the door.

Gerald opened it. Four men in grey overalls stood outside. Beside them, on the floor, were a great many trees in plastic tubs.

"Delivery, sir," said one of the men, "of trees."

"My goodness!" Poppy exclaimed from her bed. "I thought they'd never come. Yes, do come in, all of you. With the trees. How delightful! They'll make all the difference, Gerald. You just wait and see."

Poppy had not exaggerated when she had said she had ordered a great quantity of them. The men staggered into the room, carrying tree after tree.

"I think we'll have the mimosas by the window," she said. "They can only benefit from the light. Besides, the reflections will be so enchanting. But then, what doesn't benefit from the light, apart from sloths and such? The palms, over there. The passion flowers by the sill. They will trail very nicely. Splendid! Splendid! You're doing very well. And you can drape the vine over my bed. This wretched bed with all its frames and things, like a four poster without curtains. It will sort of disguise it, don't you see?"

The delivery men appeared to take a peculiar pleasure in carrying out Poppy's instructions. One of them, the smallest, an agile little man, curled the dripping vine around the frame of Poppy's orthopaedic bed. He gave her a monkey-like smile.

"Where would you like the castor-oil plant?" he asked.

"Over there, behind the cupboard. Not particularly nice, is it?"

"And the lilies?"

"What do you think, Gerald? You see, from my point of view, I can only be here. And it's from here that I want to see them."

Gerald had been watching the enterprise with amused interest.

"I can't really tell from here," he said.

He was sitting in the blue armchair.

"No, I suppose not. For you are there and I am here. I can't get out of bed. You can't get in. But can't you help and turn things upside down, my dear, in your head?"

"It already looks like Manypeeplia Upsidownia," he said.

Poppy burst out laughing.

"Exactly! Oh, Gerald, you never fail! Because, of course, that is the point!"

Her laughter, as contagious as Catherine's had been, reminded Gerald of Tara. Her toffee-coloured eyes sparkled. He laughed too. The men, who had not understood the joke, enjoyed it too. The matter of the joke was of no consequence to them.

"Pour me out some more champagne, my dear," she said. "Don't think I've exceeded George Eliot's prescription yet. Do you think they would like some?"

She waved her hand towards the gang of workmen.

Gerald asked them.

"We wouldn't mind a beer," said the little man with the monkey smile.

"Beer?" said Poppy. "Well, I suppose they're both fizzy. But there isn't any. I'll ring down for some."

"How about over there," said the little man, "for the bamboos?"

"Wizard!" said Poppy.

There was a knock at the door.

"Their primrose path," said Poppy. "Must be the beer."

It was.

"Beer break!" she said. "But I don't think there are enough glasses to go round."

"Glasses!" said the monkey man. "We don't need glasses!"

He whipped out a cigarette lighter and levered the top of his beer bottle off with it.

"How fascinating!" said Poppy. "The tricks people get up to! I never would have thought of that. Might come in very handy. You never know. One lives and learns."

Sitting bolt upright in her bed, the bed now wreathed in vines and jasmine, she watched the workmen squatting on the carpet, swigging their beer. She was as unused to their antics as they were to hers.

"Not a bad performance," she said to Gerald, "as far as theatre goes. But as for what we were saying before the troupe came in. This Shubin seems to be not half a bad fellow."

Gerald took a sip of champagne.

"What's he like?"

"Oh, for God's sake! That's such a silly question! Like an Elgin marble playing balls. God knows what he's like. The question is what he is."

She put her hand to her forehead.

"I'm sorry, Gerald. I quite forgot to take my painkillers. Pain's so awfully bad for the temper. Forgive me for snapping."

The workmen had downed their beer. They were very neat and had made no mess. They restacked the empties into the crate. Then they got back to work, placing the jasmine and the agapanthus under the guidance of the monkey man's suggestions, with occasional directions from Poppy.

"I'm awfully sorry," said Gerald. "But I don't have a great deal of time to spare. There's a hideous amount of work I've left undone, got to catch up with. I must go before the Library closes."

Poppy shot him an inquisitive glance.

"How do you like that?" asked the monkey man.

He pointed to the final arrangement.

"You've done it quite beautifully," said Poppy. "How very kind of you. An admirable streak of imagination."

Gerald glanced at the lapis lazuli face of his wrist watch.

"He did say," said Poppy to Gerald, "that Catherine's state of mind isn't considered exactly reliable. But then, whose is? There's no such thing as an accurate yardstick for the wits, I wouldn't say. Nor does this gangly Shubin seem to think so, either. He says the poor child has the most dreadful pain. But in my opinion, it's because there has been repetition after repetition ad nauseam. It's time for a change."

The men had finished their work. They turned to Poppy.

"Well done!" she said. "And all the cleaning up, too."

They left.

"Would've thought," muttered one of the stoutest, "that they'd've put her where she belongs. Down with the others on Ward X."

"Don't know so much," said the monkey man. "Takes all sorts."
He whistled.

Gerald shut the door behind them. He leaned against the door.

Poppy clapped her hands.

"Do look!" she cried. "It's come on to snow. How glorious! Just
what I'd envisaged. A blizzard through the window and a jungle in
the room. I feel better already."

He walked down to the window where the passion flowers trailed
along the sill. He looked at the snow blowing over the mountains.

"What did you mean about repetition?" he asked.

"Repetition? Chains of events. The more frequently something
occurs, the more likely it is to happen again. And at some point, the
chain must be broken. The only way to do that is to find the starting
point. Then, the beginning can be the end and the end the start of
something else."

She looked away.

"You will put things in such rigmaroles," he said.

"I can't help that. Just consider what I've said. And consider
Catherine, too. As I say, Shubin is a sympathetic man. But you must
go now. It's one of my off days. Come and see me soon."

They kissed each other good-bye.

"Yes, I'll come and see you soon. I promise," he said.

After leaving the Library, Gerald walked slowly through the streets
of the old town back to his hotel. He was dissatisfied with his work.
He had not been able to concentrate. He had tried. But his mind had
wandered off the point. Even the notes he had made were
incompetent. He would have to do it all over again the next day.

He paced the room in his hotel. He lit cigarette after cigarette,
stubbing them out before they were half-smoked. He lay on the bed.
He got up. He took a shower. He looked in the fridge, took out a
bottle of champagne and then put it back again. He opened a book,
then discarded it. He lay on the bed again and stared at the ceiling, as
if the white space above him might make things plain to him.

He sat up and examined his toes. He went into the bathroom and
cut his toenails.

He came back and stood, in his dressing gown of black silk, and
stared through the window. An old woman with a shopping bag

crossed the street. She stumbled against the kerb. An apple rolled out of a paper bag in her basket into the gutter. She knelt in obviously arthritic pain and groped for the apple. Gerald watched her pick it up, examine its bruises with a thrifty regret and put it back into her basket. She went on her way. Gerald turned away from the window.

When his novel, *Da Capo*, had come out, it had been an instant bestseller. His agent had just negotiated an offer for the film rights. He saw the book wherever he went. He could not escape it. He wished that he had never written it. He thought of Catherine.

He reached for the telephone beside his bed. He asked the switchboard operator to put him through to the Clinic.

He waited for what seemed to be eternity.

"I'd like to make an appointment, please," he said, "with Professor Shubin. Yes. Important. Very. As soon as possible."

The appointment was made for the following morning.

Poppy had been right when she had described Professor Shubin as gangly. He was gangly. He sat behind a large wooden desk which was covered in books and papers. The walls of his room were a pleasant shade of blue. On one of them hung a beautiful pastel of a monkey by Simon Bussy. A jar of anemones stood on a small filing cabinet by the window.

Shubin was wearing headphones and did not look up immediately when Gerald was shown into the room.

Gerald waited.

Shubin waved towards a leather armchair placed at an angle to his desk.

Gerald sat.

Shubin took off his headphones. They were attached to a cassette machine. He handed the headphones to Gerald. Gerald was surprised. He had imagined Shubin to have been listening to a recording of one of the patients' conversations. But he was even more surprised when, having put the headphones over his ears, he found himself listening to a particularly good recording of *The Rite of Spring*. Gerald was entranced. He was extremely fond of the music. The recording came to an end.

He found that Shubin was smiling at him with an amused tolerance.

"You liked that, I hope?"

"Very much. Beautifully played. One of my favourites."

"I know."

"How could you possibly know that?"

Shubin laughed.

"You put it into your book. They listen to it by the water. Besides, it's one of Catherine's favourite pieces of music too. She tells me that Tara often played it to her."

Shubin stood up. He was very tall. He wore a tweed suit, a green and grey mixture. His hair was light and wavy. Gerald could not determine his age. He watched him walk over to the window. Shubin stood with his back to Gerald.

"Do you know why you have come?" asked Shubin.

He did not turn.

"Not exactly," said Gerald. "If I did, then perhaps I wouldn't have needed your help."

"My help." Shubin sighed. "Ah, yes. My help. But perhaps I need yours, too. I take it that you have come about Catherine?"

"Yes."

"I have read your writing," said Shubin. "Read most of it with considerable pleasure. But as to *Da Capo*, it has helped me immensely in this particular case."

"Because of what I wrote about the situation?"

"She has referred to you frequently."

"To me?"

"Yes."

"But she had never met me . . ."

"Nor had you when you wrote the book. It's tantamount to the same thing. And Poppy has filled me in with details."

"What details?"

"Details which I think one can consider irrelevant now."

Shubin turned.

"But what," he asked very gently, without taking his eyes off Gerald, "is it that you want to do?"

"I want," he said, "to take her away."

He described the island which he wanted to take Catherine to.

"Why?"

"Do you want her to stay," asked Gerald, "indefinitely? Isn't the point of her being here that she should leave?"

He crossed his legs.

Shubin returned to his desk.

"All cases are unique," he said. "At least they all have that in common."

He folded his arms and leaned them on the desk. He looked straight at Gerald. His eyes were dark grey. He smiled.

"Poppy talks a great deal about love," he said.

"She thinks falling in love is ridiculous," said Gerald.

"Well, you can work that one out for yourself," Shubin smiled. "She may never have been able to have fallen out."

"Yet she seems anxious as to whether I'm in love with Catherine or not."

"I dare say. Only you can tell. I wouldn't let that worry you. It's an idea, certainly. But have you considered Catherine?"

"I've scarcely considered anything else," said Gerald.

Shubin nodded.

"I may be of some repute in my field," he said.

"Swizzle certainly thinks so."

Shubin laughed.

"I'm glad to hear it. By the way, I've taken her off Catherine's case. But as I was going to say, your reputation is not undeserved either."

"My reputation?"

"As a writer. To permit Catherine to leave the Clinic in her present state would be considered highly unorthodox by most of my colleagues. But my methods frequently are. Unorthodox."

Gerald shifted in his chair.

"But I am not," said Shubin, "a prophet."

He looked sternly across the desk.

"And I make no claims to being one. If you take Catherine away, you will be stepping into the shoes of what one might call responsibility. I simply hope they will fit. A great deal will depend on you, you know."

"And not at all on her?"

Shubin sat back.

"She will depend on you," he said. "She will depend on you very much at first. She won't be aware to what extent. All things being equal, I hope you will turn out to depend on one another. But yes." He paused. "Not a bad thing to encourage her to write poetry," he added.

"Poetry?"

Shubin ignored Gerald's question.

"Yes," he said. "You may take her to your island, if that is what you really want. And if she accepts. I suppose it is, after all, your consideration, what you do really want?"

He hummed a few bars of a prelude by Chopin, not an easy thing for anyone to do. But the Professor hummed it with ease and as though he was alone. Gerald was sad when the humming came to an end.

"I can't help it," said Gerald. "Wanting."

"So much the better," said Shubin. "I'm glad. It's when people stop wanting that things go wrong."

He stood up. So did Gerald.

"But tread carefully," said Shubin, "in those shoes of which I spoke. And good luck."

They shook hands on parting.

Gerald and Catherine were laughing in Room 107.

"So I slid him the butter," she said, "across the table. He was so pleased, it was quite touching. He even smiled."

"Showed his fangs?"

"An inch or two. But then Christine came into breakfast late."

"Who's she?"

"Christine? Oh, she's just another lunatic, like the rest of us. But she has this terrible habit of slitting her wrists. Never very deep. She'd done it again last night. That was why she was late for breakfast. Usually, she eats toast and butter and jam. But when she came in this morning, she was feeling a bit stupid, I suppose, about her wrists. She said she was damned if she was going to eat any breakfast and chucked her butter at the werewolf. The butter is all wrapped up, you know, like it is on aeroplanes, in golden paper. I burst out laughing. I simply couldn't help it. And so did the werewolf. He showed all his fangs. We couldn't stop for ages. Nobody could think what the joke was about. But it's very sad, really."

"What is?"

"He's going home."

"Why should you mind so much?"

"It's not me, silly," said Catherine. "It's him. He doesn't want to go."

"Doesn't want to go? I'd have thought anyone in their senses would want to leave."

"But that's just it," she said. "He doesn't think he is. In his senses, I mean. He dreads the world. He can't bear talking to anyone. He begged to be allowed to stay, but they won't let him. He thinks they've given him up as a bad job. That he's incurable."

Gerald was silent. He stroked her wrist.

"But I said," said Catherine, "that one never knew. That things might change. He lives in the suburbs of a large town. His favourite thing to do, he told me, was to sit by a stream and stare at the water and at the sky. I asked him what the difference was, between the sky and the stream."

"What an odd question," said Gerald. "What did he say?"

"He said the sky was just the sky, but that when he looked into the stream, he could see the sky as well as the water."

"I'm glad they've taken away your drip," said Gerald.

"Yes, I did hate it. And that Swizzle's been replaced, too."

"Forget about her. Look, darling, if you could leave now, would you feel like the werewolf?"

"If I could leave?"

She looked at him.

The green exercise book which he had given her fell off her bed on to the floor. Gerald stooped and picked it up.

"You've been writing?" he said.

"Sort of. Scribbling."

"What? Can I see?"

She hesitated.

"I never show it to anyone," she said.

"Why on earth not?"

"It makes me nervous to think anyone can see I can make a mark on anything."

"Won't you show it to me?"

"Well, all right," she said. "But it's such rubbish."

"You'd be the last to know if it was rubbish or not. Simply because you wrote it."

He read what she had written. She lay back and closed her eyes while he read it silently.

"I like it very much," he said. "As far as it goes. But it doesn't go far enough. You ought to write much more. Every day. Like a pianist practising. But you haven't answered my question."

She sat up and looked at him.

"Your question?"

"Would you like to leave the Clinic?"

"But I told you before, it's out of the question."

"No, it's not. As you said to the werewolf, things change. Things have changed. Shubin says you may leave if you like, to come and stay with me."

"Leave?"

"Yes. I told you I wanted to take you to the island. It's up to you, now. Will you come with me, Catherine?"

She burst into tears.

"You really mean it?"

"Yes."

She held out her arms. They embraced.

"I'd go with you anywhere. Anywhere in the world. Let's go to your island."

"I never take coffee after lunch," he said.

She stirred the lump of sugar in her cup and ground it with her spoon.

He frowned.

She sipped. The coffee was hot.

"It's bad for the system. It makes one excitable."

She put down her cup.

"So do you," she said. "I want you to touch me now. Here. It's very important."

He looked at the waiter.

"Never mind him. I can come. Just by looking at you. Yes. Use your other hand to ask for the bill."

He watched her.

The waiter bowed.

He smiled at her. She kept her face still.

"Did you like it?" she said.

"Yes. Did you?"

"Thanks for the lunch," she said. "Now let's go and feed the ducks."

"No."

"But that's what you said."

"To hell with the ducks. Let's get out of here."

It was raining for the first time that year. In the city, the snow had lain grey on the pavements for months. As they drove towards the mountains, they saw lumps of old snow fall from the branches of the fir trees.

She wrapped her fur coat closer round her body. She turned to him.

"Darling, I'm afraid."

He stopped the car.

"Tell me."

"Spring is coming. It frightens me."

"You are being silly and wasting our time."

"No! You don't understand. I'm frightened that I may be stunted, blighted forever by this long winter."

"Get out!"

His face was white and blazing.

"Get out, damn you!"

She stumbled in the snow. Her thin, city shoes sank in the thick, white drifts. She bent down and unstrapped them and flung them far into the forest. Her feet were numb. She could not see. She fell.

He pulled open her coat and tore her dress. She could not scream. He hit her.

Later, they made love on the banks of snow. They clung to each other. He had thrown away her dress. But afterwards, he wrapped her up in her fur coat and lifted her back into the car.

"It's not here," he said. "It's not the place. It's not the season. These forests, this melting snow is not important for your spring. That will come. Did I hurt you?"

"Yes."

"Do you know why?"

"Tell me."

"I had to make my mark on you."

"Yes. You always will."

"Yes."

He drove very fast. They were already late.

When the nurse came in to remove the drip, she was worried because Catherine's pulse had dropped far below normal. Catherine opened her eyes and stared at the nurse blankly. Then she turned her face to the wall.

"Poppy's asked us to tea."

"I know," said Catherine. "The nurse gave me her invitation this morning."

"What's the matter?"

"I feel nervous. You'll think I'm silly if I tell you."

"Tell me."

"I've got nothing pretty to wear."

Gerald burst out laughing.

"I like that!" he said. "I've been coming to see you day in, day out for weeks and you've never seemed to mind wearing that hideous institutional nightdress in front of me. And now you want to doll yourself up for some old woman you haven't clapped eyes on since you were a baby!"

"I've got a dressing gown in the cupboard. But it's not much better than this nightie."

Gerald opened the cupboard.

"You're right," he said. "It's not."

He gave it to her and watched her put it on. She fumbled with the sash. Her fingers were trembling.

"Here, I'll do it for you."

He tied it round her waist.

They kissed.

"Come on," he said. "We're late."

When they went into Poppy's room, Catherine hung back and bit her lip. She was startled by her aunt, by her resemblance to Tara. Poppy was sitting up, looking very alert in her bed which was festooned with flowers. She wore her jacket trimmed with peacocks' feathers. Her eyes were brighter than usual.

Poppy kissed Gerald on the cheek. She invited Catherine to kiss her too.

"It's certainly a long time since we met," she said. "I believe you were only two."

"That," said Catherine, "is not my doing, exactly. After all, it's the first time I've ever been invited to meet you."

"Humph!" said Poppy.

Catherine smiled at her. She began to wander around the room, examining the jungle of trees in their tubs. She heard Gerald and Poppy talking. A leaf of eucalyptus fell on the carpet. She picked it up and sniffed it and crushed it between her fingers.

"You could always ask her," said Gerald. "She's never made it clear to me."

Catherine turned from where she had been leaning against a palm tree.

"I'm sorry," she said. "I didn't mean to be rude. I just wasn't listening. I was looking instead. After all, there is such an awful lot to look at."

Gerald smiled at her.

"Come and join us," said Poppy. "I invited you to tea because I wanted to get to know you after such a long gap. I don't quite see how we're going to make each other's acquaintance if all you do is gawp at my potted plants, although I'm glad to see you appreciate them."

"Oh, I do that all right. Appreciate them, I mean."

Gerald drew up a chair beside his own. Catherine sat down.

"But what did you want to ask me?" said Catherine.

A nurse came into the room carrying a trayful of tea things and a filigree silver cake stand piled high with small, elaborately decorated cakes in white frilly paper cases.

"Be an angel and pour out the tea, will you?" Poppy said to Catherine.

Catherine poured. Gerald handed round the cakes.

"One of the things I wanted to ask you," said Poppy, "was whether you wouldn't think it too infuriating to be told you looked like someone else?"

"That," said Catherine, "would depend on who it was."

"Would it?" said Poppy. "I should hate to think I was in the least bit like anybody but myself. But, since it seems you wouldn't mind, I'll tell you that I would have recognised you anywhere. At once. It's not that you haven't changed. Thank God you have! It would be an everlasting shame to be at one's best as a baby. But you do look uncommonly like Nellie. The spitten image!"

"I've been told that I resemble Pake as well," said Catherine.

Poppy eyed Catherine over the rim of her cup.

"It's not exactly unusual to take after one's uncle," said Poppy. "After all, they were as alike, to look at, as two peas in a pod."

Catherine laughed.

"Do you know," she said, "that the first thing I thought when I walked into the room was how much you reminded me of Tara?"

Poppy put down her cup and cackled.

"You certainly give as good as you get," she said. "That's one of the most rejuvenating things anybody's said to me in a long time. Do have another cake. They are most deceptive. The green ones taste of coconuts and the mauve ones of chocolate. I recommend the yellow. They are made of cherries."

Catherine bit into a yellow cake decorated with sugared violets.

"What was the other thing you wanted to know?" she said.

Gerald put his hand on Catherine's knee.

Poppy looked straight at her niece.

"You may think me an inquisitive old bird," she said. "But I can't help wondering what on earth you did with yourself after Malabay got blown up. I mean, what exactly happened to land you up in this bin?"

Catherine sipped her tea.

"Do you mind," she said, "if I have a cigarette?"

"Do," said Poppy.

For a moment, Catherine looked away through the window. She looked at the ravine, the frozen lake, the skiers on the slopes. She inhaled. She knew that she was being scrutinised. She turned her face to her aunt.

"It's not exactly easy," she said, "to explain. You see, after Tara's death and Malabay was blown to bits and Pake's death, I thought the world had come to an end. In a way, it had. My world, I mean. That was the only kind of existence I knew. The whole thing practically killed me; killed my spirit. But it didn't hit me until much later. Dreadful things don't really sink in at the time. In my case, it took years."

"But that," said Poppy, "isn't really an explanation of what you did."

"It wasn't so much what I did," said Catherine, "as what I didn't do."

Once more, Catherine looked out of the window. One of the skiers flying down the ravine nearly came a cropper. Catherine watched him teeter, almost lose his balance, then right himself and swoosh down the mountain. She drew her breath and looked at Poppy again.

"What do you mean, what you didn't do?" asked Poppy. "I don't think it's really possible to do nothing. It must be something, always, however unproductive."

"Well, that's just it," said Catherine. "After I left Malabay, I began to travel. I spent several years roaming about the world and I must admit I met some awfully odd people. But then, how was I to know? For I knew nothing. My life had been so isolated at Malabay; I knew nothing of the world. It'd take too long to go into all the details. Except I was so unhappy. I couldn't shake it off like a dog coming out of a river and I longed to. But all the drops of my misery clung to me. I didn't want to be anywhere. I didn't really want to exist. So I travelled all over the place, never staying anywhere for very long. I suppose you could say I became a voyeur."

Gerald put down his cup.

Poppy continued to look at Catherine.

"A voyeur?" she said. "A voyeur of what, exactly?"

"Everything," said Catherine. "Everything and nothing in particular. It all started when I met Pierre."

"Pierre?" Gerald's voice was distant. He did not look at Catherine.

"I was sitting on a bench in the Jardin des Plantes in Paris," said Catherine. "Out of perversity, really. It's one of the gloomiest gardens in Europe. And I was in a rather jaded state. I had a bad hangover and felt particularly measly after having looked at those animals cooped up in their wretched cages. There is a very mangy camel there. I was on this bench and an old man came up and sat next to me. That was Pierre. He was blind. He was extraordinarily ugly. He must have been about eighty-seven, I should think. He was so ugly that he sort of hypnotised me. He'd gone and got his collapsible white stick tangled up with the iron framework of the bench. I helped him to untangle it. That was how we got talking. He asked me pretty much the same thing, what I was watching things for. You see, he was dying to see. I described things to him. Described, oh, hardly anything, really. Blades of grass. The way the shadows fell. His face. He was fascinated. We used to meet almost every day, after that. Always on the same bench."

"But I don't see," said Poppy. "I don't see at all. I dare say this Pierre didn't either. How on earth could cheering up an old blind man have driven you round the bend?"

"The thing was," said Catherine, "that I began to lie. I moved in with him."

Gerald lit a cigarette.

"He lived," said Catherine, "in a really beastly apartment off the Rue de Buci. It was filthy. Dust everywhere. But of course, you see, one couldn't touch anything in case he stumbled. Nothing in it except for a bed, a sofa and a piano. No light bulbs."

"What did he do with the piano?" asked Poppy.

"Played it," said Catherine. "He had been, in his day, quite a famous pianist."

Gerald looked at Catherine.

"But what do you mean?" he asked. "This lying?"

"I mean, after a bit I got so fascinated by making things more interesting than they really were, I invented things that didn't exist. Only to amuse him, to start with. But then it all went to my head. I began to tell him the most grotesque stories."

"Like what?" Gerald tapped the ash off his cigarette.

"I'd rather not go into them."

"Oh, well," he said, "in that case . . ." He looked away.

"I will try to tell you, but you must try to understand," said Catherine. "It was really dreadful, leading poor blind Pierre up the garden, so to speak. I don't know if you've ever gone in for lying yourself. But I can tell you it leaves one with such a horrible feeling later. Lying, I think, must be the ultimate sin. It's treachery. And treachery is the worst thing of all."

Poppy hoiked herself up on her pillows.

Her treacle eyes gleamed at Catherine.

"Were your lies convincing?" Poppy asked.

"Yes," said Catherine. "That was the trouble. They were most fearfully. He swallowed everything. He used to, for example, ask me what I got up to when I went out. Actually, I never got up to anything much. I spent most of my time in the Bibliothèque Nationale. I was damned lucky to get a ticket for that."

"How did you wangle that?" asked Gerald.

"I simply said," said Catherine, "that I was a philosopher. That wasn't untrue, entirely. Almost everyone must philosophise to some extent."

"One could," said Poppy, "say that. But perhaps your methods wouldn't have been considered orthodox."

She reached for another cake.

Catherine laughed.

"Well, I didn't go into particulars," she said. "But I did love the Bibliothèque. It's such a sumptuous place. That ceiling. Those arches. The pillars. That skylight. No, I loved it. And I read a great deal. Everything from the wicked habits of the Borgias and the beastly Medici to the Anglo Saxon aptitude for assassination. But then, after that, I'd go and kind of transform all these things I'd read. I always made them more scandalous and set these fiendish happenings in modern times. I described, for example, acts of lechery in the Bois de Boulogne. I described perverts in the suburbs. I described sadists in bars."

"A born dramatist," Poppy mumbled into her pillow.

"And then?" Gerald looked at Catherine.

Catherine bowed her head.

"I was invited to a dinner party. One of the dullest I've ever been to. Except that I was introduced to an oculist. He told me he thought it might be possible for Pierre to partially recover his sight."

"But how wonderful!" said Gerald.

"Well, yes," said Catherine. "Wonderful for Pierre, but not for me. For then he would've seen how wild I'd been in my lies. I couldn't face it. I left. I just walked out. I did leave Pierre's name and address with the oculist and a cheque to cover the costs of the operation. I had, after all, this inheritance. Money was no object to me. But I never saw him again. It was only by chance that I read of his death in the paper some time later."

Poppy took another bite of her mauve cake. She finished her mouthful and looked at Catherine.

"I can't say you behaved very well," she said. "But I don't quite see how this business with Pierre sent you off your rocker."

Catherine rearranged a shell in a pot of amaryllis.

"It wasn't just that," she said. "It was the accumulation of events. Tara, Pake, Malabay. Everything. I don't think one ever knows why, exactly. If one did, then one would be all right. Things got worse and worse. I suppose reading of Pierre's death in the paper was just the last straw. I stopped going out in the daylight. I did nothing. Lay in bed and felt my spirit had died. Shubin calls this depression. I was in Italy. I'd got so used to watching things and inverting them to entertain Pierre, I developed a rather odd passion for watching the transvestites in the Boboli Gardens in Florence. I was sitting behind a bush gawping at a couple of them one evening, when it came over me that I was going to crack up completely. I knew suddenly that I was in desperate need of help. I came here. Shubin thought I should stay. So here I am."

"Well, all I can say," said Poppy, "is that no one can accuse you of lacking imagination. The only thing I suggest, is not to abuse it in future. Everyone has to be a little bit batty in order to keep sane at all. Otherwise we'd all be raving mad."

"Christ!" said Gerald.

He stubbed out his cigarette.

"Even if it's treachery by omission," he said, "I think it's bad enough. It's too simplistic to think that just because Catherine has a conscience it excuses her lies and actions, or, rather, lack of them. If anything, the fact that she has a conscience increases her guilt."

"I was afraid I'd upset you," said Catherine. "I suppose you thought I was just a poor little thing. A victim of circumstance."

"I can't say you're not," said Gerald. "But I think you're just as much a victim of yourself as anything that's happened to you. Why didn't you tell me all this before, when I first asked you why you were here?"

"I thought," she said, "you'd be put off."

She got up and went over to the window. She stared at the mountain. The skier was no longer there. She stood with her back to Gerald and Poppy. She did not want them to see the tears which she could not hold back and which were coursing down her cheeks.

"But at any rate," she managed to say, "at least you know now. About me, a bit more, I mean. There's nothing I can do to alter the past. Take it or leave it. I'm stuck with it. I can only be myself."

Gerald joined her by the window and gripped her by the shoulders. She was shaking.

"Turn round," he said. "Turn round and look at me."

She turned.

"Dry your eyes," he said. "After all, it's not as though you've gone and killed someone. What makes me cross is your self-destructiveness. Come on, here's another hankie. I don't think I've ever known a girl to cry as much as you do."

She wiped away her tears with the handkerchief Gerald gave her.

"That's because I was brought up in such a rainy place," she said. "Haven't you ever noticed how much people are affected by their environment, especially by the weather?"

He burst out laughing.

"You needn't, you know, stay stuck with it. Of course you can't undo it, but you can change your future. I don't mean it's you I want to change, exactly. Just I can't bear for you not to make the best of yourself."

"For you or for me?" she asked.

"For both of us," he said.

He put his arm round her and they walked towards Poppy and sat down again beside her bed.

The nurse came in to clear away the tea things. She had a pretty face. When Catherine handed her her cup, the nurse winked at her. After she had left, they could hear her laughing in the corridor outside.

Poppy smiled at Catherine.

"I do agree with you about one thing," she said, "and that is the importance of being oneself. I think people matter most in life, and much more as individuals than in collections. The larger the group, the less it has of any real consequence."

"But I'm afraid," said Catherine, "that the larger the group, the more consequence it actually has. Not as individuals. And I do agree, and I'm not in the least bit ashamed of it, that I'm only really interested in the individual."

"That depends on what you mean by reality," Poppy said.

Catherine laughed.

"If Pake were still alive," she said, "he would insist on determining the individual, since you can't have a group without one."

"He had his points," said Poppy. "Who, for instance, do you think you really are?"

"Any definition needs a point of comparison. You said you didn't care to be compared to other people. Why should I? But you are right, Poppy. I haven't got much idea."

Gerald lit a cigarette.

"Gerald must have," said Poppy.

"Must I?"

"Don't you have any idea of who Catherine is?"

Catherine looked appalled.

He laughed.

"She's just herself," he said. "But you'd be much more yourself, Catherine, more determined, if you like, if you determined yourself by getting on with something."

"Like what?"

"Old Shubin said it wouldn't be a bad idea if you got on with your poetry. I rather agree with him. I think all this shilly-shallying is a waste of time. Just get on with something and do it and that's it. The rest," he smiled, "is poppycock."

"Of course, Gerald is right," said Poppy. "To get caught up in it, to become part of this complicated web, that's the thing. And you're not. You're not at all, Catherine. I can tell, just by looking at you."

Catherine toyed with a dangling vine.

"Not caught up? No. I'm not caught up in your spidery web. But I'm fascinated by it. I like watching it."

"But that's not nearly greedy enough," said Poppy. "You must, you simply must, get caught up."

"Ensnared?"

"Involved."

Catherine stood up. Gerald watched her walk between the tubs of jungle plants. He noticed that Poppy was watching her too.

"It's another point of view," said Catherine.

She turned.

"You've no idea how refreshing it is to be up here," she said.

She looked with admiration at the eyes of the peacocks' feathers on Poppy's jacket.

"Yes, you look half starved," said Poppy.

"She is much too thin," said Gerald.

"That's not what I meant," said Poppy.

"No, I know," said Catherine. "That's not what you meant at all. It has made me feel quite drunk to be in a room with people and beautiful things and jokes and conversation."

She sat on the end of Poppy's bed and fondled Poppy's toes under the cover of the bedclothes.

"That's nice," said Poppy. "I had a grandmother who made me rub her legs with brimstone. She kept it in her sewing box. It does seem to me quite mad to think Catherine can get better without even a modicum, what you might call a splash, of civilisation. To lock her up in a broom cupboard in some bin can be no receipt."

She hauled herself up by an orthopaedic handle entwined with clematis.

"You ought to have some clothes," she said. "Proper clothes. It's ridiculous to think of a daughter of Nellie's going round in an institutional rag not fit to be a duster. She used to dress so well. It was a pleasure to see."

Catherine looked at Poppy and waited for her to go on.

"But that's all in the past," said Poppy.

She looked away.

Gerald, glancing from Poppy to Catherine, felt that they were sharing a common memory. He was right. They were both thinking of Malabay. Poppy remembered the night before the accident, the last time a dance had been held in the ballroom at Malabay. She remembered Nellie waltzing, a petal dropping from the flowers in her hair. Poppy's expression changed.

"All in the past," she repeated. "You know, I'm leaving the Clinic tomorrow."

"Of course. I'll take you to the airport," said Gerald. "No, I insist. And I want you to come and visit us on the island. It's quite civilised now, not nearly so Robinson Crusoe as it used to be. I think you'd like it, you know."

"We'll see," said Poppy. "I seldom make plans nowadays."

Catherine bent between the jasmine and the vines to kiss Poppy. Poppy held her hand.

"Yes," she said. "Go with Gerald to his island. Enjoy yourself. But don't forget your poetry. Gerald, after all, is not an easy man."

She laughed up at him, her black eyes full of affectionate teasing.

"No, you're not, Gerald. You're one of the most difficult men I've ever met in my life. And don't go and be a goat and think that you can do it all."

Gerald laughed.

Poppy turned to Catherine.

"So you see, my dear, you'll need something to fall back on for its own sake. Poetry will do very nicely."

She waved at them from her pillows. Catherine and Gerald left the room together.

ISLAND

They had left the jetty and were walking up the hill to the old tower and the house which Gerald had added to it. It was a cloudless day. The southern sun warmed them.

"But you never said!" said Catherine. "The smell! It's like honey! You never said how beautiful it is."

"No," said Gerald. "There was no point even trying to tell you in the Clinic."

The air was clear and sweet and scented with the wild mountain flowers that grew more profusely as they climbed the path from the sea. Catherine kept stopping to exclaim in delight at each new plant she saw: mountain cyclamen, wild hellebore, hebes and white myrtle.

"Stop," said Gerald. "I want you to see it from here."

The tower stood on a prominence overlooking the bay. The house was constructed on a series of terraces. The stone walls were overgrown with vines. Along the terraces Gerald had planted mulberries, peaches, quince and mimosa. The house stood in perfect proportion to the landscape.

"It's extraordinary," said Catherine. "You're a genius. It grows out of the ground. Even Poussin couldn't have done it better."

"There was no choice," said Gerald. "It was the only thing to do."

"It's the hanging garden of Babylon," said Catherine.

Gerald laughed.

"Well, my tower is not the tower of Babel, that's all," he said.

The house and tower were very close to the sea. Gerald was eager to get there. But they walked slowly. In spite of that, Catherine, who had been confined for so long inside the Clinic, was quite spent by the time they got there. He was worried by how tired she was, but he said nothing.

There was a great deal to be done on their arrival. Gerald made several journeys down to the boat to fetch up their luggage. He had brought a good many books and papers, the results of his research. After leaving the Clinic, Poppy had amused herself by ordering quantities of clothes to be sent to Catherine. They were exactly the clothes which Catherine would have chosen for herself — the right colours, the right fabrics. They were a perfect fit. Catherine had been amazed by such generosity. Gerald had said it was typical of Poppy. Together, they had examined them in delight. There were also crates of provisions and household goods to be carried up.

He carried his crates of books to the tower and unpacked and arranged his papers. Catherine unpacked her new clothes. She caressed the folds of the rich materials against her cheek and put them away. She unpacked for Gerald. She made the bed. Looking for the linen, she was impressed by how well-ordered things were. When she went downstairs, she looked about her. The main room was large; the bedroom to sleep in was a mezzanine above it. The fire was blazing in the huge fireplace. Everything was very clean and tidy. She went into the kitchen. That, too, was spotless and well-equipped. Gerald was still busy in the tower. She went out of the house and wandered down the terraces. She picked a handful of wild flowers, vetch and honeysuckle which grew between the fruit trees and the mimosa. She heard Gerald calling to her from the main terrace above. She went up to meet him.

"Let's have something to eat," he said. "Aren't you hungry?"

She had not noticed that she was.

"Yes," she said.

They went into the kitchen. Catherine put the flowers into a jar of water. They made a meal of smoked mountain ham and country bread and salt goat's cheese and they drank dark red wine. They ate on the terrace.

"It's delicious," said Catherine. "I haven't been so hungry for ages."

"You must eat lots," said Gerald. "I want you to get strong."
He cut another slice of ham. She ate it with relish.
"I love the house," said Catherine. "I don't know why, but I feel very much at home in it. It has a beautiful simplicity. In fact, it is incredibly well-organised. You must have spent a fearful amount of time working it out."
"Well, I did have builders," said Gerald. "But I did design it. I'm glad you like it. It wasn't like this to start with. But I've simplified it as I've gone along. It's only really to save time."
"I think you must be the most organised person I've ever met."
He laughed.
"I'm just the laziest," he said.
"That's too easy," she said.
"Let's go upstairs," he said.
They made love very tenderly. Afterwards, Catherine fell fast asleep in Gerald's arms. She slept for a very long time. When she woke, it was nearly dusk. She found that Gerald was kissing and caressing her most gently. She did not move. When he came, she opened her eyes. They smiled at each other in a moment of deep recognition. She opened her mouth to speak.
"Don't," said Gerald. "Don't say anything."
They lay entwined together, perfectly still. Then Catherine touched Gerald's mouth with her finger. He looked at her. She shook her head. She put her lips very close to his ear.
"Something," she whispered. "There's something in the room."
They listened.
"It's unearthly," said Gerald.
Something flew round them and encircled them. They held each other tight.
"It's a bird," he said.
"Thank God!" said Catherine.
"It's fabulous!" he said.
They watched it without moving as it swooped above them. It darted in between the wooden beams beneath the ceiling and once it hovered directly above them and shimmered in the fading light. Catherine held her breath.
"It wants to get out," said Gerald. "But it doesn't know how to."
The bird was becoming frantic.

"It's going to dash itself to pieces," said Catherine. "That will be frightful. What can we do?"

They gazed at the bird whose flight was growing wilder and wilder in its efforts to escape. Its feathers were a sheeny dark blue and white, its throat tinged with russet.

Gerald clapped his hands loudly.

The bird was startled by the noise. It swooped and dived downwards. Once it was down, it flew through the open door and out of the house.

"It thought it had to fly up in order to get out," said Gerald. "As though it was leaving its nest. The only thing to do was to make a noise and startle it into flying down instead. It was beautiful, wasn't it?"

"Magic," she said. "Pure magic."

She was radiant.

"It was a swallow," she said. "But it could have been anything. You know what it was."

Gerald was silent. He stroked the nape of Catherine's neck.

"You said it was fabulous," she said. "It was a kind of sign, I think."

"Do you really think that's possible?"

"Anything is possible."

Gerald lit a cigarette. He passed it to Catherine. She blew out smoke and watched it stream into a blue wisp above them.

"I couldn't put it into words," he said.

She handed back the cigarette.

"As you said," she said, "we don't have to say everything. Some things are better left unsaid. It was lovely, wasn't it, the bird, even in its mad flight? I'll tell you what. I'm famished."

He smiled and put out the cigarette.

"Let's go and eat an enormous dinner," he said.

It was early in the evening, just after the twilight had gathered. The sky was a gauzy blue which deepened by the minute. Across the bay, the mountains were obscured by shadow. The strand was a pale yellow. There was no one on the beach and the sea was empty. The stars were not yet out. The moon was just visible, pale in the mackerel skies.

Catherine walked along the sands in the direction of the tower. She walked slowly, gazing intently at the sea, the sky, the empty sands. Inland, amongst the dunes, grew thick grasses tangled with camomile, sea campion and maritime poppies. Their petals were furled. There was no wind. Catherine walked barefoot, her feet in the waves.

From the direction of the tower, Catherine saw someone walking towards her along the shore. She stopped. She did not recognise who it was, but she knew it was someone she knew very well. Then she made out the figure of a man. He was naked. He was very beautiful. He was Tara.

They walked towards each other, their steps slow and equally measured. She saw that he was smiling. They drew nearer. The distance between them was very close. It seemed to be very far.

Tara stopped just short of her. He looked straight at her. There was something shocking in his gaze. His eyes, which in life had been so vivacious, were now glassy and stark. They mirrored nothing but the sea.

As they drew together, Tara held out his hand. Catherine extended hers. The tips of their fingers brushed. For one moment, they held each other. But Tara was cold, icy cold. He smiled. With an unforgettable gesture of farewell, he left her. He walked into the sea and was engulfed by the waves.

When Catherine looked back along the strand towards the tower, she saw that he had left no footprints in the sand.

"Wake up, darling. What is it?"

He held her very close.

"Was it a bad dream?"

"No. But it was a dream."

"It's nearly morning, now. Can you hear the birds?"

They lay still and listened. They watched the light creeping up.

"Tell me about your dream."

She told him.

Later, he said: "Let's go and have a swim."

They walked down the path towards the sea. The birds were still singing. The wild flowers were not yet fully opened. Catherine wanted to leap and to dance down the path like a capricious goat. But Gerald noticed that she had great difficulty in walking and stumbled frequently over the stones on the path. Instead of continuing down the path to the jetty, Gerald turned off below the tower.

"Where are you taking me to?"

"To my private swimming pool." He laughed at her.

They reached the end of the wild grassland threaded with poppies and camomile and arrived at a great formation of curved, pale pink, grey and yellow lichen-covered rocks. At first glance, the rocks seemed to be impenetrable.

"You must tread very carefully," he said, "over the boulders. Don't lose your footing. Follow me."

"Good heavens!" said Catherine. "Your private swimming pool, indeed! Was it built?"

"Built? Of course not."

"But it looks so meant. I thought it might be an ancient temple."

The huge rock formation encircled and towered above a pool where the water was dark and very deep. Beyond, through a gap in the rocks, was the sea, much paler in colour and crested with white waves.

"But this is nothing," said Gerald. "Wait till you're in the water."

They stripped.

"This is the best rock to get in from," he said.

He dipped his foot into the water.

"It's very cold," he said. "It's still a bit early in the season. Just a short swim today."

In the water, they swam close together and then turned on their backs.

"You see what I mean?" said Gerald.

"It's an amphitheatre," said Catherine.

"Exactly. And this is the stage. The greatest luxury of all is that there's no audience."

They looked up at the great rocks which descended to the pool. Gerald hallooed. His voice echoed and rebounded back on the waves. Catherine suddenly plunged under the water. He could not see where she was in the dark pool. When her head bobbed up, she had swum to the far end of the pool near the gap in the rocks.

"Come back!" he called. "You're crazy!"

She did not hear him. She plunged and sported in the water as if she was a dolphin. She swirled over and over and blew the salt water out of her nostrils and gargled and laughed. He struck out and caught up with her. She did a duck dive and disappeared. He grabbed a foot. She came up and floated on the surface. She laughed. He thought he had never seen her look so alive. Her eyes matched the colour of the water. But he saw that her fingers were bloodless and white.

"Come out!" he said.

She laughed and splashed him.

"Come out!"

This time, she did as he said.

He got out before she did and held out his hand. But she stumbled against the rocks. She missed her footing. She grazed an ankle. Blood fell scarlet between the crevices of the grey rock and the yellow lichen. She caught his hand and pulled herself up. She had turned very white. He handed her a towel. She rubbed herself dry.

"Are you hurt?"

"It's nothing."

She was shivering.

"Get dressed," he said.

He led the way back to the house.

The sun was fully out by the time they got back, but Catherine was still blue with cold.

"Go and have a bath, Catherine," said Gerald. "Very hot. Then we'll have breakfast."

When she came down from her bath, Catherine found Gerald in the middle of making breakfast. She began to lay the table on the terrace. He was frying eggs in the kitchen. The door was open. She dropped a plate. It broke on the tiles of the terrace.

"What was that?"

"I'm terribly sorry. I broke a plate."

"It doesn't matter," he said.

They ate breakfast in silence. It was a miserable affair. A yellow butterfly came and perched for one second on the table and flew away into the blue sky.

"I said I was sorry about the plate," said Catherine.

"It's not the plate," said Gerald. "Why did you go mad swimming? I told you the water was cold. I said just a short dip. You looked like a ghost when you came out. I thought you were going to faint before we got back here."

"I don't know. It just came over me."

"You've only just come out of the Clinic. You get exhausted at the drop of a hat. You're not ready for that kind of thing."

"It was a bit crazy. I did it without thinking. But it was delicious."

"That's too easy. You must think. I can't think for you."

She stood up and began to clear away the breakfast things.

Gerald drove her in the small open car he kept, along a track to an inland lake high in the hills. The water was a deep brown and the lake curiously shaped.

"Like a Greek E," said Catherine.

Reeds grew down to the edge of the lake and birds skimmed over the surface. The water was warm and sweet.

"Makes a change from the sea, doesn't it?" he said.

She smiled and swam towards him where he floated by the reeds.

"Keep still! Tread water."

He had turned over and was peering below the surface. Catherine drew near cautiously. They saw a shoal of goldfish swimming in the shallow water near the shore of the lake. The fish, streaked with vermilion, blue and yellow, with silver fins and bellies, swam between them threading around their bodies. Then the fish formed into a collective pattern and streamed away.

Gerald and Catherine got out of the lake. There was mud between their toes. They sat on the bank and rinsed off the mud.

"I suppose they really were goldfish?"

"Definitely," said Gerald. "But it's the first time I've ever seen a goldfish in this lake and I've swum here countless times."

"I've only ever seen goldfish in glass bowls eating ants' eggs. Dentists seem very keen on them, goldfish in waiting rooms. I won one at a fair once at Ballingstown when I was a child. But never wild. Wild goldfish!"

She pulled her blue cotton dress over her head.

"They are carp, aren't they?" she said.

"Carp?"

"Yes. Monks keep them in ponds."

"Monks keep goldfish?"

"Another kind of carp you cook with eels."

Gerald lay on the grass. He chewed a stem thoughtfully. Catherine towelled her hair.

"I'm looking forward to getting back to work," Gerald said.

Catherine was silent. She looked across the lake and then at Gerald. His arms were crossed behind his head. His eyes were closed. She kissed him. He sat up.

"Aren't you?" he said.

"It's not the same for me," she said. "It's not getting back. It's getting started."

He stood up.

"It's time to go," he said.

During the drive back, Gerald was abstracted and Catherine thought he looked worried. She did not know what he was thinking about. He drove badly. The car bumped over stones and potholes in the track. Neither spoke. She was uneasy.

That night, after they had made love, they lay awake silently in the bed. After some time, Gerald put out his hand.

"I suppose you do have some idea?" he said.

"What are you talking about?"

"Have you any idea of what you're going to write?"

He stroked her back.

"I don't want to talk about it," she said. "Wait till I've done some. Then I'll show you."

"Good."

He kissed her and they fell asleep immediately.

Gerald was not there. Catherine turned over in her sleep. She opened her eyes and looked at the ceiling. Usually, they made love and were very sexy in the mornings. She heard the sound of running water. She went into the bathroom.

He was in the bath.

"Get in," he said. "I've been up for hours. I didn't want to wake you."

The bathroom was large and lined with Prussian blue and white tiles shaped like diamonds. The walls and the floor were tiled to match.

She climbed into the bath.

"What were you doing?"

"Catching up," he said. "I got up early and went to the tower. I started putting my notes in order so as to be able to get down to work."

"You've got a beautiful back," she said. "Your shoulder blades."

She soaped his shoulders.

"I thought," said Gerald, "we might take the boat out. There's an inlet beyond the bay I'd like to show you."

"Shall I make a picnic?"

He laughed and got out of the bath.

"No need," he said. "It's already there. All we need to take is a bottle of mineral water."

She floated in the bath and looked at him in surprise.

"Hurry up," he said. "You'll see what I mean when we get there."

He wrapped himself in a white towel and left the room to get dressed.

Catherine dried herself. She tied a green kimono over a blue bikini.

"I like the colour," Gerald said through the open bathroom door. "It suits you."

"Poppy chose it," she said.

They walked together down to the jetty. They climbed into an inflatable rubber boat with an outboard motor. They set off round the curve of the bay, past the promontory where the tower stood, towards a cove on the other side of the bay. Catherine sat on the stern. Her hair was tangled by the wind. They were splashed by spray flying into their faces. The boat whizzed along between the rocks close to the shore. It was very different to sailing long ago at Malabay. This boating with Gerald was of another kind altogether.

The cove was sheltered by outcrops of yellow rock which ran down into the sea. Above, the coast inclined gradually. The dark red soil was overgrown with glaucous green and grey scrub, juniper bushes, stunted wild cork and fig trees. The smell of the sea was mingled with the acrid smell of burnt earth and the sweetness of the vegetation.

They beached the dinghy. Gerald put the water to cool in a small rock pool.

"I'm famished," said Catherine. "I thought you said we were going to have a picnic."

"We are. I'm looking for spoons."

He stooped.

He handed her a small mother-of-pearl shell. It glittered, pink and silvery with veins of aquamarine and gold. It shone in the palm of her hand. She held it up so that she could see the sky and the green of the sea through the curved line of small holes that ran parallel to its rim. She smiled.

"Look," she said. "Here's another. But where's the picnic?"

"If you walk out to that flat rock where I put the mineral water, I think you'll find it."

Catherine crouched on the rock. She peered down into the shallow pool. The light danced; it was refracted in the transparent water. Between the rocks, she could see clusters of colonies of sea urchins. Some of their dark purple and blackish spines stuck out of the surface of the water. Their wet tips shone in the sun. She peered very close. Her eyelashes fringed the water. Small shells, pink, white and grey, lay scattered on the sand. A thin, silvery fish nosed its way out from a crevice in the rocks. It had grey hieroglyphic markings on its back, a forgotten alphabet impossible to decipher. It basked in the warm water. Catherine moved. The fish darted back into the crevice. She laughed and spat salt water. Gerald joined her. They gathered a mound of the purple sea urchins and heaped them between stones. Catherine cracked one open and washed away the particles of grit in the sea. She spooned out the coral with her shell and held it out for Gerald to eat as though it were the yolk of an egg. They ate a great many of them and shared the bottle of mineral water.

Gerald watched her spooning out another sea urchin. She sat on the rock with her feet in the sea. A gust of wind blew her hair across her face.

"I shall never be able to understand," he said, "how you manage to be so serene."

"Why shouldn't I be?"

She looked at him in surprise.

"If I were you," he said, "I should be terrified."

"But what on earth should I be frightened of?"

He sipped from the bottle of mineral water and handed it to Catherine.

"Time," he said.

"What are you talking about?"

"That's just it," said Gerald. "You don't seem to be aware of it at all."

"I don't understand."

"It's absolutely necessary," he said, "for you to write your poetry. It's become a condition."

"A condition? A condition of what?"

"You've got to do it. I don't even know if you can. In order for us to be together it's essential that you should write. You must do it now, have something finished before we leave. I would go to any lengths. I would even leave you if you don't."

Catherine looked at him. A gull flew overhead.

"But that," she said, "is blackmail."

"Yes. It is."

He ran the sand between his fingers.

"After all," he said, "what would you do in my shoes?"

"In your shoes? How can I tell? Exactly the same, I expect."

She got off the rock and stood in the sea. Her back was turned towards him.

"I'm going for a swim," she said.

He watched her walk away into deeper water before she struck out.

It was evening. Catherine had made the supper. She carried out the bread and put it on the table. From the terrace below, she could hear the sound of Gerald hosing the plants.

"Supper's ready!" she called.

"I shan't be long," he said. "I've just got to finish watering this terrace."

She went down the steps to join him.

He was watering a nectarine. The water had collected round the base of the trunk and was spilling over on to the terrace below.

"It takes an awfully long time," he said. "But it must be done."

Catherine looked up towards the house. Her eye was caught by the light of the setting sun shining on the roof and the gutter which ran down the wall. She laughed.

"Yes," she said. "But you like saving time, don't you? You're very miserly with it."

"You've got a wicked look in your eye," he said. "What's up your sleeve?"

"I'll show you later."

"I've got something to show you, too. It won't take a minute."

He had finished the watering.

"I'll turn the tap off when we get upstairs. The mulberry could do with an extra soak. I was wondering if you'd like to use this little garden room to work in. After all, I've got my writing room in the tower."

He opened the door of a small room that was half hidden by the overhanging vines. There was nothing in it except for a table, a chair and a camp bed folded away against the wall. The window looked out over the bay and the mountains beyond.

"It's quite perfect," she said. "You think of everything."

"Not quite," he said. "I can't think of what you're going to write."

"No." She walked towards the window. "But don't push me, Gerald. I can only do it in my time, not yours. I don't, after all, expect you to adapt yourself to my rhythm."

"How could I? You simply haven't got one."

"You're wrong. I have a very strong one. But it's just very different from yours. All I mean is, don't try and force me. It has a contrary effect on me. But the room is lovely."

"I'm trying to encourage, not force. I'm only giving you an opportunity. That's all the room is."

"I know," she said. "But I was thinking of what you said when we were eating the sea urchins."

"My blackmailing you? But I meant it, you know. Every word."

"I know you did," she said. "But it's a dangerous thing to do, you know. It puts us in jeopardy."

"Are you frightened?"

She turned from the window. He could not see her face against the light.

"Oh yes," she said. "It's a frightening proposition."

"But you haven't accepted it."

She laughed.

"I haven't refused it either. In any case, it's a perfectly splendid room to work in. Let's go and have supper."

They climbed the steps together, arm in arm. The light was beginning to fade. The first stars were out. Gerald lit the oil lamp on the table. The flame flickered. He turned it down and replaced the glass. The light steadied and shone out. A moth beat itself against the glass. Gerald cupped his hand and caught the moth. He let it fly away.

She passed a dish of ratatouille to Gerald and began to cut the bread.

"Do you want me to come shopping with you tomorrow? You said you needed to go to the port for the post and things."

"Not if you don't want to."

"I'd rather stay here," she said.

Gerald refilled their glasses. He smiled.

"So you've got an idea," he said.

She laughed.

"Yes," she said. "I'm not short of them. This one is a surprise."

It had grown dark by the time they had finished their meal. They lingered on the terrace for some time drinking coffee.

"Look at the stars," said Catherine.

"Let's go to bed."

He left the island early the next morning. Catherine stood on the terrace and watched the small grey dinghy move across the bay. She went to the outhouse at the bottom of the steps where the boat was stored in Gerald's absence and where sundry things and the tools were kept. It took her some time to find what she needed and several hours to accomplish what she wanted to do. When she had finished, she was tired and very dirty. She was delighted with what she had done. She took a long, hot bath, dressed, and then ate some bread and goat cheese and drank a glass of red wine before going down to the room which Gerald had given her to write in.

She had cleaned the room and put the table in front of the window. A large spider with spindly legs and a speckled body scampered from beneath the chair and ran across the floor. She took out the exercise book and the green fountain pen which Gerald had given her in the Clinic. She read through what she had written. She crossed most of it out. She made a number of notes. Then she fitted a blank sheet of paper into the typewriter. She began to work.

Gerald was away for much longer than Catherine had expected. It was late afternoon before she saw the boat return. She left the room and went down the hill to meet him. She found him lifting the shopping out of the boat.

He kicked the boat. They walked up the hill in silence, carrying the shopping. In the kitchen, Catherine began to put the things away. She lifted a carton on to the table. An orange rolled on to the floor.

"Christ!" said Gerald.

He was rather drunk.

"What happened?" said Catherine.

He poured out some wine and drank it.

"You wouldn't understand," he said. "I want to be alone. I need to be alone sometimes. Can you understand that?"

Catherine flinched at the tone of his voice.

"I'm going up to the tower," he said. "I've had enough for today."

He went out of the house. The door swung open behind him. She heard him running down the steps and later she heard the door of the tower bang. She picked the orange off the floor and poured herself some wine. The bottle was empty. Very slowly, she put the rest of the shopping away. She lit a cigarette and opened a new bottle of wine. She took it out on to the terrace and sat on the chaise longue. The light faded. One by one, she watched the stars come out. A bat flew out from under the eaves. She finished the bottle of wine and fell asleep.

Hours later, Gerald came out of his tower. He found Catherine lying fast asleep and very cold on the chaise longue. He picked her up and carried her up the stairs and put her into bed. He covered her up and then lay down beside her. He fell asleep at once.

They woke before it was light.

"How could you?"

"What was it all about?"

"It was awful."

"Perfectly awful."

"Hush."

He began to touch her.

"Listen!" she said.

His hands were between her legs and on her breast. He covered her mouth with his own.

"I have never known you so wild, making love," she said.

"No. You made me. You are such an odd mixture, Catherine. Very passionate and very logical. But sometimes you behave like a little child."

"I'm older than the hills in my soul," she said.

She laughed at him.

They were quiet.

"Listen," she whispered.

"What?"

"It's stopped."

"What has?"

"The rain. I woke once, much earlier and it was pelting down. I didn't want to wake you. And it's light now."

Her eyes were dancing with mischief and amusement.

"You look very wicked," he said. "What are you up to?"

"Come out on to the balcony and see," she said.

The light was already streaming in through the shutter. They got out of bed and stepped naked on to the balcony. The air was warm and hazy with the vapours of the evaporating rain. The scent of the garden was overpowering. The plants had shot up overnight. The clinging vines, the wistaria and the ivy growing against the wall were curled over the railings of the balcony. Each leaf was pointing upwards and still splattered with drops of the heavy rainfall.

"It's amazing!" said Gerald.

He leaned over the balcony and inhaled.

"But those hose pipes! What's that pipe doing there? Catherine what have you gone and done?"

"What you might call a spot of irrigation," she said. "I'll show you."

He followed her still naked down the steps to the main terrace. Catherine pointed to the roof.

"I did it when you went out yesterday. I just attached a pipe to the water butt where the water collects from the gutter on the roof," she said. "Look, do you see how all the water has been diverted to the roots of the first vine there?"

"You've dug a great hole round the roots."

"Yes, for the water to collect. And I ran a hose along the row and punctured it each time it comes to a plant until the end of the terrace, and then just let it drop like a snake on to the one below and went on until the bottom. It's very simple really. I thought it would save time."

"I'm staggered," he said.

She grinned and splashed her feet in a puddle.

"The only thing," he said, "is that it hardly ever rains at this time of the year."

She squelched the mud between her toes.

"I know. But the main tap for the garden is on the wall beside the water butt, so you can connect the pipe to that when it's dry. It just means you won't have to stand there all that time watering, every night."

She shook the rain off a branch of bedraggled jasmine.

"It smells so heady. I feel wild and jungly," she said.

"You look like a savage. Come and have a hot shower. Have you got a hangover?"

"No. I think I'm still a little drunk. But I'm starving. What happened when you were away?"

"I just had a fucking awful time," he said. "There was an absolutely maddening telegram from my agent at the post office. Then I bumped into some people I know. I really can't stand intrusions from the outside world when I'm here. I like to be as cut off as possible. But it was impossible to avoid them. We went to a bar and drank too much. That's all."

They ate fried eggs and mountain ham on the terrace. The earlier steaminess of the rain had dried out. The sun was warm on their backs. Gerald was unusually silent during breakfast. He poured out another bowl of coffee and lit a cigarette. Catherine was still eating bread and honey.

"How did you manage to work it out?" he said.

He stared at the gutter.

She licked the honey off her fingers.

"I didn't. It just came to me. It was when I was watching you watering the nectarine. I caught sight of the gutter. I think it was because the terrace reminded me of Babylon."

"Babylon?"

"Yes. You know, the hanging gardens. I thought of Queen Nitocris. She was very keen on irrigation, although for very different reasons."

"You mean that Nitocris in Herodotus?"

"She's the only one I know of."

"I would never have thought of that in a million years," he said. "What an extraordinary way of going about things. Or rather not going about them, but arriving at them."

"Does it matter? I thought you thought it was only the results which mattered."

Gerald did not answer. He stubbed out his cigarette.

Through the open window of her work room, Catherine could hear the uninterrupted clacking of Gerald's typewriter coming from the tower. She had got stuck. She stared at the page in the machine in front of her. She had not written a word for over twenty minutes. She left the room and went up to the top terrace and sprawled on the chaise longue. The sun was high overhead. She felt drowsy in the heat. She tried to let her mind float, to allow it to become receptive to whatever thread of thought it might choose to follow; to let it fish whatever image idled in some odd socket of her perception.

At the same time, she watched a green lizard bask vertically on the lichen-covered wall a few inches away from her, close to where the vines trailed. The lizard appeared to be as inert as she was. She gazed at it very intently. Its gills palpitated. It darted her a beady glance from the side of its head. A shadow fell over Catherine and the lizard. The lizard vanished into a crack in the wall.

Gerald stood behind the chaise longue.

"Sunbathing," he said, "is a curious way of writing. Of course, there are lots of people who write poetry in their heads. But I thought yours was going to be on paper."

His voice had an odd crack in it which Catherine had not heard before. She turned her head to look at him. He was wearing sunglasses. She could not see the expression in his eyes.

"I was thinking," she said.

"Can I get you anything? A drink perhaps?"

She recoiled from the sarcasm in his voice.

He lit a cigarette and leaned against the wall facing her.

"No two people," he said, "can exist together unless they can establish the same rhythm. It's very difficult for me to work when I see you behaving like a tourist on the terrace whenever I glance through my window, and when I know that you are supposed to be working too. It would be much easier if you didn't even pretend."

"I wasn't pretending."

"Then what the hell were you doing? You can't call lolling about working."

She sat up and lit a cigarette. She blew the smoke out very slowly through her nostrils.

"There's more than one way," she said, "of going about things. You have your way and I have mine. We are different people. We can't be expected to behave in the same way. Why should we?"

"The criterion is in the results," he said.

"That's all very well for you to say. You are what they call an established writer. I'm not. You must let me find my own way of going about things."

"It's precisely because I am that I can talk to you like this. I didn't become one by mucking about and deceiving myself, but by getting down to work and doing it."

Catherine smiled at him.

"I'm still not convinced," she said, "that there's only one approach. But it's true. I did get stuck. The emptiness was driving me mad."

He took off his sunglasses.

"I know," he said. "That is the most awful feeling of all."

They walked slowly down the steps together towards Catherine's work room.

"It happens to me a lot," he said. "I call it the blank page malady."

They went into the room. It seemed dark after the glare of the sunlight.

"I know," she said. "Tara told me. It was one of the first things I knew about you, that you suffered from this fearful disease. I thought it most sympathetic at the time."

"But if you keep going," he said, "then it's never as bad as you think."

"I don't know so much," said Catherine. "I think things are just as good or bad as one thinks. No more, no less."

She walked to the table and shuffled some pages together.

"Would you like me to have a look?" he said.

She hesitated.

He glanced beyond her through the window and saw the green, immature bunches of grapes dangling from the vine outside the frame. He let his hand fall to his side.

"No," he said. "On second thoughts I don't think I'd better read it until it's finished. Of course there is more than one way to write. That's not important. But the only thing, Catherine, that all writers have in common is sitting down and writing."

She bared her teeth and looked at him in mock derision and then flung her arms round him and kissed him.

"Oh, what sage advice from a well-established writer!" she said.

The days began to go by very quickly, each one strung into the other. Everywhere there was evidence of the time passing. The season changed imperceptibly from late spring into summer. The wild cyclamen, hellebore and broom which had been in flower on their arrival had now withered. Every day, the sun was hotter. Catherine developed an increasing panic. Every day, she sat in her room and tussled with her writing. She was often in despair. She became very jealous of Gerald's ceaseless bashing on his typewriter in the tower. Her own writing moved at a snail's pace. When she looked out of the window and saw the bay and the mountains, the blue of the sea and the sky, the beauty of it made her heart sink. At night, she often dreamed of the ugly streets and tenement blocks of a city in winter. She said nothing of this to Gerald.

Every day, they took time off to go to the beach. They were swimming in the bay. Gerald lay on his back. He turned his head and watched Catherine splashing in the water. The sea affected her like a drug. She would swim for as long as she could, plung- ing like a dolphin. He waved to her and she swam back to the shore. She joined him on the sand, tired and breathless, and lay beside him.

"You always stay in for too long," he said.

"But it's so exhilarating."

She fell asleep in the sun.

When she woke up, she did not open her eyes immediately. She watched the light and the tip of her nose through her eyelashes. She sat up. Gerald stood with his back to her, facing the tower. She could only see his silhouette against the light. He turned and walked towards her. She sprang up and ran to meet him. She flung her arms around him.

"Let's go back," she said. "Let's go back to the house now."

Generally they stayed for much longer basking in the sun on the beach. Gerald noticed that Catherine had gone pale under her tan. They climbed the hill back to the house. He led her up the stairs to bed and they spent a long time making love. Afterwards, Gerald stared at the heap of clothes on the floor: his shirt, half a bikini, a blue silk wrap.

"What happened on the beach?" he asked.

She did not answer.

He sighed.

"I wanted to go," she said, "to be alone with you."

He lit a cigarette.

"But we were alone," he said. "We are always alone. There is no one else."

"No, I know."

She took the cigarette from him.

"I thought you were Tara," she said, "just for a moment, on the beach. I didn't want him there with us."

"Do I often remind you of Tara?"

"You make me think of him."

"So do you," he said.

She shivered. Gerald covered her with the sheet. They held each other very close.

"He was much more dead before I met you," she said. "Before I read your book. Before I started to try and write."

"Are you writing about him?"

She hesitated.

"I thought I'd done that for you," he said.

"I have to do it for myself," said Catherine.

He tilted her chin towards him with his finger. He smiled. She stared back at him.

"Well," he said, "I think you'd better kill him off."

"That," said Catherine, "is the hardest part of all. You don't know about the power of the dead, really, do you?"

"You know, it isn't true any longer," Gerald said.

They were lying on the sand, their bodies stretched on the steep incline. The sea washed over their legs. Catherine peered at the grains of sand, the tiny pink shells, the white stones.

"What isn't true?" she asked.

"The thread that first bound us together. It's worn out."

"Do you mean Tara?"

"Yes. That common knowledge. I thought that that would always be our main bond, our main point of reference. Partly because you cannot undo someone's dying, the fearful damage it does to the living."

"No," she said, "that is the worst of it. The dead are dead forever. You can't even telephone."

"No. But there are other forms of communication."

She smiled.

The grains of sand, the tiny pink shells, the stones glittered. He put his brown hand over her upturned pink palm.

"I thought the same thing," she said. "I thought I was coiled up in that skein forever. But you've unwound it, untangled it."

"No," he said. "Not just me. Both of us."

They looked at each other.

"Whatever happens," he said, "don't forget that what binds us together now is of our own making."

"I shall never forget," she said, "whatever happens."

The moment was over.

They turned and swam the length of the beach towards the tower.

"But what are we quarrelling *about*?" said Catherine.

She put down her knife and fork.

For they had taken to quarrelling. They quarrelled violently and almost as regularly as they made love.

"First it was the vulgarity of Puccini which led us, I can't remember how, to the different ways of dressing a lettuce. Now it's the English Civil War. Why are we quarrelling?"

He did not answer.

"I'm bored with the Civil War. Why don't you pick the next subject, if you're going to pick a quarrel at all? Only make sure it's not whether Bacon wrote Shakespeare."

Gerald sipped his wine.

"You can be the most irritating person in the world," he said.

"I know. So can you. But why are we doing this? I can't bear it. And to tell you the truth, out of the quarrel, I'm not nearly as good at it as you are. You always win. I'd rather do it with pistols."

Gerald smiled.

"You wouldn't stand a chance," he said.

They both laughed. The quarrel had blown over. Catherine pulled her shawl more closely round her shoulders. They were having supper on the terrace. The wind came from across the bay.

She looked at Gerald.

"Do you know?" she asked.

"What?"

She hesitated.

"Why we quarrel?"

"Actually, I enjoy it. I'm a quarrelsome man. But I think it's because of the discrepancy between us. Your health is bad. When I'm not in the mood, the very idea of it infuriates me. I can dash about. I don't know. I expect you to be beside me and you're never there."

"But you don't seem to understand that it takes me as much effort to go one inch as it does for you to go a hundred yards."

"I do understand. But it doesn't alter the situation. Don't you see how impossible it is?"

Catherine picked up a crust of bread and crumbled it between her fingers. She watched her fingers move the crumbs into a deliberate pattern on the cloth. She went on moving the bits of bread. She could not stop. The pattern was complete. She glanced at it and then looked swiftly away. She had formed exactly the same pattern with her crumbs as she had seen Pake do every morning with bits of melba toast and crystals of salt at Malabay. She flicked the crumbs on to the floor.

"Yes," she said, "I do see. It's difficult for me to see clearly, because everything is distorted for me."

"What by?"

"Something very simple. Pain. I try to disguise it from you because I know that you can't bear it. It's as if, in order to glimpse anything at all, I have to draw back the heaviest black curtains, just to get a microscopic view. No, please let me explain. I am in the dark all the time with the most deafening din going on which is swamping me. I am a swimmer battling against the tide. Imagine swimming against a strong tide and having to tie up your shoelaces at the same time. I'm not even talking, you see, about the huge things in life. Just details. Even pleasant details, like having a conversation with you or looking at a flower or tasting a shrimp. I mean even the things you don't really notice doing."

"What things?"

"It doesn't really matter. Just things like the washing up. Things which you take for granted. How to unlock a door. Open a tin. Silly things. Pain is darkness and noise. The most excruciating noise. And it goes on all the time. It never lets up for one single moment. You are in the sunlight, Gerald, and I am in the dark. And for me to try and step towards you just to be in the shadow is a stupendous stride. You look over your shoulder and are cross because I am miles away. But I have come from thousands. You don't know what it's like, and I hope to God you never will."

"Don't," he said. "Don't tell me any more. It's too much. I can't bear it."

"No. Nor can I. But I wanted to try and explain what it is like."

Gerald got up and put an arm round her shoulder.

"I don't know what it's like," he said. "But I can imagine. When I see you do things which will only exacerbate your pain, I get angry."

"I do them partly to obliterate it. Sometimes, when I get drunk. Or when I get the giggles, which sounds odd because you don't associate laughter with pain. But it's a kind of exorcism, like a cathartic savage tribal dance."

"I want you to leap to the other side. I don't want you in a wild frenzy. I want you to leap, to soar above it."

"But I can't."

"You must, Catherine, you must. It's the only way."

She lifted her face.

"You're right," she said. "It is the only way."

"Come on," he said.

"I'll do it," she said. "But it'll have to be in my time. I can't do it in yours."

"But I'm not a patient man," he said.

"It's the only way," she said.

It was just after breakfast. Catherine was already installed in her work room. She was deeply immersed in her writing. A shadow fell across the page. She looked up. Gerald was leaning through the open window looking at her.

"What is it?" she said. "Have you been there long? I didn't notice."

"No, not long," he said. "You were so absorbed in your writing, you were quite oblivious to everything else and never noticed me. I'm sorry to interrupt you, but I wondered if you'd do me a favour?"

She smiled.

"I'd love to," she said, "if I can and depending on what it is. One would have to be nuts to promise you anything sight unseen."

Gerald laughed.

"I should never have taken you out of that blinking bin," he said. "But come outside, in any case."

She left the room and they strolled along the terrace in the shade of the trees, beneath the overhanging vine.

"What is it," she said, "that you want as a favour?"

"It's really just your advice. I was working on the filmscript of Da Capo up in the tower when I hit on an idea. The thing is I simply can't make up my mind if it's a brainwave, or really way off the mark."

"That's what I find," said Catherine. "That it's awfully difficult to tell about one's own stuff."

"Exactly. That's why I wanted your advice."

Catherine looked at him, surprised. She laughed.

"It's your turn for a visit to Shubin if it's my advice you're wanting," she said. "Still, spit it out. What's this brainwave of yours?"

"It suddenly struck me, to make the film a bit more dramatic, that it might be a terrific idea for the uncle to rape Eleanor. It would sort of spice things up a bit. What do you think?"

"For the uncle to rape Eleanor?"

"Yes. I say, are you all right? You look absolutely ghastly."

"I think I'm going to be sick," said Catherine. "Can you leave me alone? It's horrible when people watch one being sick. I'll join you up in the house."

"Call me if you need me," he said.

He left.

Catherine threw up.

Later, she sat on the ground and leaned against the trunk of the nisposa. She shook. It was with considerable effort that at length she stood up and climbed the steps to the upper terrace.

"I'm just going to brush my teeth," she said.

He looked after her as she went indoors and shook his head.

"Gerald," she said when she came back on to the terrace, "I think I'd like a drink."

"Yes, you look as though you could do with a stiff whisky. I'll get you one."

She sat down on the chaise longue and gazed out across the still waters of the bay to the mountains beyond. Gerald came out of the kitchen with two glasses of whisky in his hands. She took the glass he held out to her and sipped it.

"But what came over you?" he asked.

"Who knows?" she said. "I can't tell."

Gerald lit a cigarette.

"But this idea of yours," said Catherine, "that Eleanor should get raped by the uncle, I don't think it is a brainwave, after all. I think you should just stick to the facts."

"The facts?"

"Yes," she said. "I mean the facts already in your book. Obviously, I'm not talking about life. In your book, you make yourself and Tara lovers, which wasn't really true. For some odd reason that I haven't yet fathomed, people find fiction far easier to swallow than fact. And, in any case, it doesn't seem really credible, does it, for the uncle, who after all is really Pake, to go and rape Eleanor, who is really me?"

She gazed once more out to sea.

"Good Lord!" said Gerald. "I hadn't thought of it like that. No wonder you came over queer! You're right. I just thought it would make the film more interesting. I'm glad I asked you. It couldn't have been true."

"What?" asked Catherine.

She did not look at him, but continued to stare at the sea.

"Why, that Pake raped you?"

Catherine took a large gulp of whisky.

"What on earth put that into your head?" she asked.

Gerald smiled at her.

"Well, of course," he said, "it couldn't have been true. I was only teasing you. But it just followed on logically from what you were saying. I mean, if Pake had raped you, nobody would believe it, but they would if he hadn't. As for Hollywood, they would have baulked at it in any case."

Catherine did not move for one moment. Then she tossed her hair back and stood up. She looked directly at Gerald. Her face was against the sun and he could not see her expression clearly.

"I know that they say that fact is stranger than fiction," she said. "But as fiction has to be based on fact, or rather on an aspect of the truth you might call it, I don't really see that logic plays much part in it, leaving aside Alice, of course, and the whole pack of cards."

Gerald drained his glass. Catherine followed suit.

"I suppose we'd better get back to the grindstone," he said. "And thanks. How's your work going? You looked absolutely miles away when I was watching you."

"Oh, how can I tell about mine if you don't know about yours?" she said.

He put his arm round her and they climbed down the steps together.

Catherine waited for Gerald in the fishing port. She sat on a bollard. She had put most of the shopping in the boat. Gerald was in the post office. She watched an old man who sat on a kitchen chair in the shade against a wall. His hands were folded on a stick. He did not move. A half-starved cat slunk about between the nets hunting for an old fish head. A boy threw a stone. The cat turned tail.

Gerald came out of the post office. They finished loading the boat and headed back for the island.

"A telegram," he said, "from Poppy. She's coming for a couple of nights or so."

"When?"

"End of next week. On her way back from Alexandria."

The boat gathered speed. Catherine gazed at the swirl in their wake.

"Ignore me," said Poppy. "I'm dead. Dead to the world. I'm utterly exhausted."

She looked it. Tinier than ever and yellowed by the sun, Poppy was shrivelled. She had taken Gerald's arm walking up from the boat. They stood on the terrace.

"I'm sure it's quite beautiful," she said. "But I'll look at it later, when I've revived."

Gerald showed her straight to her room. He closed the shutters against the glare of the sun.

"Is there anything you'd like?" he asked.

"Sleep," she said. "Only sleep. If Catherine will bring me a cup of tea in the afternoon, I'll be perfectly all right."

He kissed her on the cheek and left her.

"Do you think she is?" asked Catherine. "All right, I mean."

"Poppy? Oh yes, she'll be perfectly all right if you take her some tea later on. You'll see."

It was the time they generally went to the beach. Gerald had got up very early to meet Poppy from the small airport on the mainland.

"I'm tired too," he said. "Let's skip the beach and take a long siesta."

Catherine watched Gerald sleeping. He flung out an arm across the pillow. He smiled in his sleep. She nestled beside him and dozed. When he stirred, she left the bed and came back with two cups of tea.

He sat up.

"Lemon," he said, "and honey. It's a luxury. Why do we never have tea?"

"I wasn't sure there was any," she said. "I found some in an old tin. I don't think it's stale, is it, like old hay?"

"It's delicious."

She sipped hers. She sat on the edge of the bed and stroked his foot.

"You look like a little girl," he said. "What's the matter?"

"Don't you think Poppy would like it better if you took her her tea?"

He looked at her.

"No," he said. "She specially asked you to. You mustn't be so shy. There's nothing to be shy of."

"One isn't shy because of things," she said, "just because of shyness."

"It's a bad habit," he said. "You should throw it away, like a paper handkerchief."

She laughed and put down her teacup. He leaned against the pillows and watched her dress. She put on a blue dress sprigged with cornflowers of a darker blue.

"I like your dress," he said. "I've never seen it before."

"It's the only dress I've got that Poppy didn't give me."

"Don't be an owl," he said.

From his tower window, Gerald watched them walking to and fro. Catherine was showing Poppy the garden. Poppy had changed into a grey dress printed with pale blue antelopes. She leaned on the handle of her green parasol and picked a leaf of verbena. She crumbled it between her fingers, then threw it away. She poked the earth with the spike of her parasol. They walked slowly, stopping to examine the plants and the trees. Catherine put her hands behind her back and began to speak to Poppy. Gerald could not hear what she said. Poppy nodded and laughed. She took Catherine's arm. They disappeared into Catherine's work room.

Later, he saw Poppy climbing the steps with a sheaf of paper under her arm. He was reminded of an African ant toiling away with a leaf. He watched her install herself in the chaise longue in the shade. She began to read. He heard her give an exclamation. She lit a cheroot. Once or twice, she laughed. She was evidently deeply absorbed. He turned back to his work.

"There's going to be a storm," said Gerald.

Poppy turned the glass in her hand.

"I must have brought the weather with me," she said, "although there wasn't any to speak of in Alexandria."

The wind had changed. It blew from the South. The waves were very high. They rose in a line of white breakers along the shore in the bay. They slapped against the rocks below the tower and curled back on themselves and slapped again. Poppy lay on the chaise longue. Gerald sat on the wall. The pages which Poppy had been reading rustled. She clutched them firmly together.

"What were you doing in Alexandria?"

Poppy's dark eyes glinted.

"I went to see an old colleague," she said. "Bedridden. Looked like an ancient lizard. He ate stuffed dates all morning. We spent most of the time playing chess and eating sticky cakes between conversations."

She wore sandals made of plaited cobra skin. Gerald glanced at them. She smiled and waved her ankle.

"They are nice, aren't they?" she said. "They were given to me by the sister of a snake charmer. I've had a wonderful afternoon, Gerald. I've been reading Catherine's play. She said she hadn't shown it to you. She's very nervous of your opinion. She shouldn't be. It's fascinating. I'm in the middle."

"I wish she'd get on to the end."

"Oh, the end is there all right," she said. "It's implicit in the beginning."

"If only she would finish it."

"But it is finished. Very."

Somewhere in the house, a door slammed.

Gerald stood up. He picked up the glasses.

"You had better come indoors," he said, "before the storm breaks. I must close the shutters. I think it's going to be a wild night. The sea is already very rough."

The light had deepened and the sky was streaked with grey and yellow. Great clouds had gathered overhead. The mountains on the opposite side of the bay were no longer visible. The sea was dark.

He led her indoors and lit the fire.

"Can I do anything?"

"Just stay comfortable while I shut up the house."

"Good. Then I can finish Catherine's play."

Poppy ensconced herself on the sofa by the fire and began to read. Gerald left the room. Time passed.

The rain came down. It beat heavily against the house. Gerald and Catherine came into the room together soaking wet.

In the bathroom, Catherine stood naked under the shower.

"You don't mind I showed it to Poppy?"

"Yes I do mind awfully. Awfully," he said.

She turned to him.

"Don't you trust me?" he said.

"More than anyone," she said. "But I was frightened."

She had never seen him look so unhappy. She flung her arms round him and pressed her naked body against his.

"I'm such a fool," she said. "I've hurt you and I wanted to make you the happiest person in the world. I only wrote it for you."

He held her close. His towel slipped to the floor.

"We're both idiots," he said. "But it makes it all right when we understand each other. But why didn't you tell me that you had finished it, that you were writing a play, not poetry?"

He sat on the edge of the bath.

"I couldn't. Do you remember on the beach, when you tried to blackmail me? I couldn't write a single line after that. And I didn't think it would matter. You just wanted some evidence, something tangible. So I wrote a play instead."

"And you couldn't tell me all this time?"

"I thought that if I did, the same thing would happen. That I'd just dry up again. I'm not like you. I can't write to order. It has to be in my time."

"My God! What fools we've been."

"No. I should have told you. I didn't have enough confidence in myself."

"I thought we were so close."

"It was to stop us getting any further apart. I had to do it alone. Do you understand?"

He held out his hand. She took it.

"I thought I'd feel so brilliant when it was finished," she said. "But I don't. I feel distinctly dreadful."

"Don't be silly."

"But I do. Will you read it, Gerald?"

"You're not frightened any more?"

"No," she said. "Not any more. Not of you."

"Get dressed, darling," he said. "Wear your green dress. I'm going to open some champagne. Of course I'll read it."

He kissed her.

"Don't be long," he said.

Catherine added another log to the fire. Poppy was still reading. She was wrapped in an azure silk shawl edged with purple tassels. Catherine laid the table. Occasionally, Poppy glanced up from her reading and watched Catherine as she moved about the room. They could hear the wind blowing harder against the house.

"I haven't seen a table laid like that in years," said Poppy. "It's the way you've put the spoons and forks head to tail. It was always done like that at Malabay."

"I always do it like that."

She sat down in the chair opposite Poppy.

"Do you ever think of Malabay?" she asked.

Poppy looked into the fire.

"I thought I'd put it out of my mind when I left," she said. "But you do bring it back so. I've finished your play."

She put the manuscript aside.

"It's very good," she said. "The only thing that baffles me is that it is so unlike Pake."

"You mean he doesn't come across?"

"Oh, no. He comes across all right. You've got him down to a T. Your play is evocative, very. I suppose it must have been the cook."

Catherine was bewildered.

"I'm starving!" Gerald called half way down the stairs.

The red mullet was delicious. Gerald had chosen the fish alive and flapping in the net in the port that morning. The mullet was followed by a dish of peas, salad, cheese, and a pudding that Catherine had concocted.

"What is it?" asked Poppy.

"I don't know that it's anything, really. I made it up. Almonds, mainly."

"But it's excellent. You cook very well. I never could. And I have such a sweet tooth."

Gerald laughed.

"What did you mean about the cook?" Catherine asked.

"That you must have learned the truth from her. From Nan. Pake would never have told you. Not in a million years. I simply don't believe it. It must have been her."

"What are you talking about?" said Gerald.

"Catherine's play, of course. It's very good. Highly indiscreet, but that seems all the rage nowadays. I'm sure it'll be a great success."

"I don't understand," said Gerald.

"Nor do I," said Catherine.

"But my dear girl, you must understand. After all, you wrote it."

"But I don't understand what you mean."

Poppy put down her fork.

"I expect she told you after the explosion," she said. "It would have been enough to unnerve anyone. After all, she was the only person left, apart from me, who knew."

Catherine stared at Poppy.

"Knew what?" Gerald said.

"The truth, of course. My dear, how can you be so blind?"

"The truth about what?"

"Why, Catherine's parents of course."

"You mean Nellie and Terence?"

"No. I don't. I mean Nellie and Pake. Catherine's put it all down in black and white as clear as daylight."

"But Nellie and Pake were brother and sister!"

"As I said, indiscretion is all the rage."

"But it's not true!" said Catherine. "Nobody ever told me a thing! Nan never told me at all. I just invented it, like the pudding. What do you mean, Poppy? That Pake was my father?"

Catherine was shaking. Gerald stood up. He put his arm round her.

Poppy looked at Catherine.

"I don't believe you did know, after all," she said. "To think that it was me, in the end, who let the cat out of the bag! I think you'd better give her some brandy, Gerald."

"I think we could all do with some," he said.

Catherine made a movement as if to leave.

"No, don't go," he said.

He handed her a glass.

They sat close to the fire. No one spoke. They listened to the storm outside. Gerald lit a cigarette.

"I would never have said a word," said Poppy. "Except I was convinced you must have known. You've put it all down, you see, exactly as it happened."

"How did it happen?" Gerald asked.

"You've only got to read the play," said Poppy.

"I want to know," said Catherine.

They both looked at her.

"But I want you to tell me," she said. "After all, I have a right to know."

"But you do know. Or at least you guessed."

"That is not the same," she said. "I didn't guess. It just came out of my head. I told you, I thought I was making it up. I need you to tell me."

"They were crazy about each other, Nellie and Pake. I knew they were very close. But I didn't know to what extent."

"How did you find out?" asked Gerald.

"It was pretty obvious when Nellie became pregnant with Catherine."

"But Terence?"

"Terence wasn't there."

"Wasn't there?"

"No. He'd been away for the duration. He didn't get demobbed until after Catherine was born."

"But why did she ever marry him?"

"She married him for money. For Malabay. I told you, they'd do anything for Malabay."

Catherine burst into tears.

"But half the world is illegitimate," said Poppy. "And incest is rife in every village, or used to be when I was young. And as far as I can make out, half the aristocracy and most of the intelligentsia are bastards. How can it change you one iota?"

"Of course it doesn't change me," said Catherine. "But don't you see, the knowledge of it does? Knowledge changes everything. Surely you can see that?"

She sat up and blew her nose.

"Yes. I do see," said Poppy. "But then, you see, I thought you knew."

Catherine wiped her tears away with her fist.

"I was thinking of Malabay," she said. "I've never been able to forget it. It's a memory that's in my blood."

She looked at Gerald. He was looking at the fire. Poppy looked at the floor. Catherine put her hand on Gerald's knee. He did not move. She withdrew her hand. He caught it and turned to face her. They exchanged slow smiles.

"Poor, darling Pake," she said.

Poppy jerked her chin.

"Why Pake?" she said.

"It must have been dreadful for him."

"But it wasn't easy for any of us," said Poppy. "It was dreadful for all of us, the situation. Not just Pake."

"Oh don't! They were dead. You had left."

"Of course I left. Neither of us wanted to stay together. Pake wouldn't see me for days after . . ."

"After the accident?"

"It wasn't an accident. It was Terence."

Poppy looked into the fire. Her rings flashed in the light of the flames.

Gerald leaned towards her.

"What do you mean, it wasn't an accident?" he asked.

"It was deliberate. Terence was an excellent sailor. So was Nellie, come to that. Terence capsized the boat. I don't think she ever knew. Pake thought it was both of them, but I still don't agree. Terence left a long letter, accusing us all, left right and centre. And with some reason. I found it later, in a drawer. Pake destroyed it. We had to say it was an accident. We simply had to."

"Just like Pake," said Catherine.

"Wasn't his death an accident in the bombing?"

"No. He ran back to the house. He knew he would get blown up."

They listened to the storm outside.

"What a nightmare!" said Gerald. "Pake did seem to me a bit unhinged. But then, the circumstances were pretty awful, to say the least."

"We were all unhinged," said Catherine. "Tara's accident, the only accident there ever was, was enough to unhinge anyone. But Pake hadn't always been like that."

"He was never exactly ordinary," said Poppy.

"That bloody cage," said Catherine.

"Yes. But he'd always been peculiar."

"I never understood why you had to leave then," said Catherine. "After Nellie and Terence were dead. I can see you must have hated Nellie."

"No, I didn't hate her. No one could really hate Nellie. In fact, I was very fond of her. But that didn't make things easier. Actually, it complicated them. Things, as it were, had already come to a head between Pake and me. It was more than I could bear. As I said, he wouldn't speak to me. You see, after Nellie's death, Pake became even more obsessed by her. It is not easy to give up the dead."

"No." Catherine stood up. "There was no choice," she said.

She went over to Poppy and kissed her.

"Goodnight," she said.

"I'll join you soon," said Gerald.

He sat in silence with Poppy after Catherine had left the room. Gerald sipped his brandy.

"But it was madness," said Gerald. "To have left Catherine there."

"No madder than anything else," said Poppy. "She was theirs, not mine. She belonged to Malabay as much as Malabay belonged to her."

"More brandy?"

"No, thank you. I must go to bed."

"Tara didn't know?"

"No. Tara never knew. I wrote to Pake. I thought he should be told. I thought they should both be told. But Pake wouldn't have it. He said the knowledge would destroy Catherine."

"He may have been right, then."

"And now?"

"It makes less difference now," said Gerald. "After all, it was she who thought of it."

Poppy gathered her shawl about her and stood up.

"I remember when I joined the Ministry," she said. "I said then that there were no such things as secrets."

"Goodnight," he said.

He kissed her cheek.

"She's extraordinarily like her mother," she said. "Goodnight, my dear."

Catherine lay naked, fast asleep on the bed. She had flung off the bedclothes. The balcony window had blown open. The rain came in. Gerald closed the window and covered her with a blanket. He went back downstairs and poured himself some more brandy. He added another log to the fire. He stayed awake late into the night, until he had finished reading what Catherine had written. Then he stumbled into bed.

"But it's absurd!" said Poppy. "Quite absurd. Of course you must go ahead. There's no question about it."

They were sitting on the rocks below the tower. Gerald lay on his stomach on the sand. The only trace which remained of the storm was the driftwood floating by the shore. The sea was calm. He dozed. He heard the voices of Poppy and Catherine drift in and out of the sound of the waves lapping against the rocks.

Catherine hugged her toes. She looked at Poppy.

"Do you really think so?" she said.

"It's my categorical opinion."

Poppy was dressed for a swim. She wore a trailing yellow negligée printed with peonies. Beside her, on the rock, was a pair of black flippers, swimming goggles and a green plastic rubber hat with spikes like chrysanthemum petals.

"It's not as though you hadn't invented it, after all," she said. "There's bound to be a grain of truth in anything you write. It's relative."

They laughed softly.

"No, go ahead," she said. "Publish and be damned. After all, wasn't that part of the bargain, didn't you say, with Gerald?"

"It wasn't exactly a bargain," said Catherine.

"Does it matter what you call it, so long as you both understand one another?"

"That's another matter. But you wouldn't mind if I did?"

"My dear girl, I'd be only too delighted. It's about time you did something. Go ahead! I'm going for a swim."

Poppy strolled towards the sea. Gerald opened one eye. He watched her sit down when she reached the water and fit on her flippers, adjust her goggles and clamp on her hat. She shot off at a terrific speed into the waves. He sat up. Catherine joined him. She was laughing quietly. He reached out his hand. Catherine took it. They looked at each other and smiled.

"Were you listening?"

"Not exactly. Couldn't help hearing. I've got a fiendish headache."

"Poor thing."

"But I think she's right."

"I feel pretty ropey too."

"Let's go and join Poppy."

"Join her? She's half way out to sea already like some flipping dolphin."

He looked at Poppy's green hat bobbing about in the waves. He laughed.

"Well, we'll meet her, then. We'll wash away the cobwebs."

"Some cobwebs!"

They walked into the sea together.

"If only it was as simple as that," said Gerald ten days later.

They were sitting in the same place by the rocks from where they had bathed with Poppy.

"Nothing ever is," said Catherine. "And hardly anything is what it seems or turns out to be."

"Do you mean in the end?"

She traced a pattern with her finger on the sand.

"That's always supposing such a thing exists," she smiled. "I'm not sure that it does. Things change, they're bound to. But I don't think they end, really. They just change into something else."

"I wish this could go on forever."

"I know."

She went on drawing in the sand. Gerald propped himself on one elbow and looked into her eyes.

"We're running out of time," he said. "But there will be other times. We've done what we came here to do. I've finished my novel. You know I've got to go when they start shooting *Da Capo*. You've written your play. Don't look like that, darling. You know I couldn't do without you now."

"We can't do without each other, but we can't do with each other either."

She obliterated her drawing in the sand.

"No. Not all the time," he said. "Could you?"

"Be with you all the time? It wouldn't work."

"No. It's the difference in our timing."

"You make us sound like a couple of eggs," she laughed. "It's always so intense," she said. "Either we quarrel or we are so close. And I'm so jealous. I'm not talking about other women."

He licked the tear off the end of her nose.

"No, I know you're not. You're just jealous of the things you can't do with me and the times we can't be together."

She burst into tears.

Gerald let her cry. He put his arms round her and waited till she was quiet. He ran his fingers through her hair.

"Don't cry," he said. "There's nothing to cry about."

"But I have no choice," she said.

"Nobody really has any choice. Not really. Your limits are just more circumscribed because you are not strong. Shubin was right."

"I can't go with you. It would drive me mad. I'd drive you mad. We'd end up in the bin together and drive Shubin mad too." She smiled.

"We'd be madder still not to be together when we can," said Gerald. "Just ditch the rest. By the way."

She laughed and showed her teeth.

"How do you expect me to tell you if you do that to me?"

"It'll keep," she said.

Later she said: "Tell me now."

"I didn't tell you I'd bought a cottage just before I met you."

"How very convenient." She looked up at him and laughed. "What's it like, this cottage of yours?"

"Utterly charming. There are lilacs, a garden, a pond. It's near Oxford."

"It sounds extremely suitable," she said, "considering how ill-suited we are."

He bit her ear.

"You are a fiend, Catherine!"

"I know."

"Are you tempted, fiend?"

"Yes, very."

"Then shall I find you there when I come back?"

"From all that shooting? No. After I've given my play to the agent, I shall go to Copenhagen. You can send me a telegram there the minute the shooting stops."

"Why there?"

"I like it and feel at home in it. I want to write something else now.

I'm going to adopt your method of staying in hotels. It seems fruitful."

They fell silent.

"I'll send the telegram there, then," he said.

They walked slowly back towards the house.

"Look back," he said.

The bay, the mountains and the tower were lit by the sun. The sea was alight. From the valley they could hear the croaking of frogs.

"Damn!" he said. "We're late!"

Gerald drove the hired car fast across the mountains on the mainland. She knew they had plenty of time.

"Will you light me a cigarette?" he said.

She passed him one and lit one for herself.

"You'll let me know?" he said.

"At once. As soon as I know. But they'll probably want me to re-write it from start to finish."

"That nearly always happens. Stick to your guns."

The road began to go downhill. Presently, they caught sight of the sea and the docks.

"The boat's already in," he said.

"Yes, but there's heaps of time," she said.

"You're mad! You'll only just make it by the skin of your teeth. Look at your watch."

"It's stopped. I forgot to wind it up."

"That," he said, "is the story of your life."

Catherine was silent.

He drew up alongside the boat. He took out her luggage. Neither of them could speak. He gave her ticket to an official. He would not look at her.

"Go on! Go on! Hurry up before you miss it."

The porter took her luggage.

She ran up the gangplank. She was only just in time. She leaned over the railing. She could see him on the other side. Tears started into her eyes. She could see tears in his. She knew that he could see her own. He made an elliptical gesture. She did not understand. His voice was drowned by the engine. The crane levered away the gangplank. The sailors shouted. The painter was slipped. A gull screamed. He repeated the gesture. Then she understood.

The harbour was very deep and narrow. In order for the boat to leave, it had to turn inside the harbour. As it began to veer round, Catherine walked deliberately away from Gerald and crossed the upper deck. By the time the boat had turned, she was facing him again. He lifted both his arms in the air and gave her the thumbs up signal. She waved and clapped. They gazed at each other, half blinded by their tears, across the widening gap of water until they were out of each other's sight.

Henrietta Garnett was born in Bloomsbury in 1945. Her father and great aunt were the writers David Garnett and Virginia Woolf. She has one daughter and one granddaughter and lives what she describes as "a nomadic life, between France, Italy and nowhere." She is currently at work on her second novel.

A NOTE ON THE TYPE

The text of this book was set in film in a type face called Griffo, a camera version of Bembo, the well-known monotype face. The original cutting of Bembo was made by Francesco Griffo of Bologna only a few years after Columbus discovered America. It was named for Pietro Bembo, the celebrated Renaissance writer and humanist scholar who was made a cardinal and served as secretary to Pope Leo X.

Sturdy, well-balanced, and finely proportioned, Bembo is a face of rare beauty. It is, at the same time, extremely legible in all of its sizes.

Composed in Great Britain

Printed and bound by Fairfield Graphics,
Fairfield, Pennsylvania